BADD
DADDY

A BADD BROTHERS NOVEL

Jasinda Wilder

BADD
DADDY

ONE

—✳—

Lucas

"*E*GGSHELL BLUE? THE FUCK KIND OF A COLOR IS THAT? Eggs ain't blue, y'dumbasses." I growled under my breath as I stood in the paint aisle at a home improvement warehouse in Ketchikan, sorting through sample books and color rings, trying to decide which color I should paint my apartment. I had my damned cane hooked over my arm while I stood half leaning against the shelf—the color samples were attached to the shelf via a length of chain, so in order to hold it and sort through it, I needed both hands. Which was damned tricky, as my leg was still weak from the accident. I couldn't stand on both feet for too long without needing to lean against something for support. 'Course, I should be going to therapy and strengthening it, but I'm too damn lazy and stubborn for that, so I hobble along with this stupid cane like some kinda damn geriatric fuck.

"*Periwinkle.* That's not too bad, so maybe." I was talking to myself, but I didn't give a shit if I sounded crazy. "*Electric Moonlight*? Who the hell comes up with this shit?"

A delicate, soft, musical laugh from the aisle on the other side of the shelf startled the hell out of me. "I'm actually rather partial to the *Electric Moonlight* shade." The voice was as musical as the laugh.

"Yeah, sure, it's a nice color," I mutter. "Name is stupider'n fuck, though."

I hear the click of heels coming around the end-cap, and I looked up to see a fuckin' angel—if angels came in the body of classy, svelte, sexy-ass women. This one in particular was dialed into her own brand of hotness: tall, standing five-ten or so, slender and sleek with just enough curve to her hips to make my dick stand up and take notice, breasts that looked plump and firm despite being on the smaller side; black hair cut short—angled downward from very short up in back to past her chin in front, covered with fringes and wisps and curls. On any other woman, it'd be a warning sign—an "I'd like to see the manager" haircut. On her? It just looked right. Dark eyes it looked like, but I was too far away to make out the exact shade—maybe *Midnight Moonlight*? She was dressed to kill, in a conservative way. Knee-length maroon skirt and a white button-down shirt with short sleeves—only the top two buttons were undone, allowing a tantalizing peek at the top of her tanned cleavage. On her feet were black flat-heeled slipper-shoe things, the kind of shoe you see chicks wearing all the time these days.

She had a clipboard in one hand, a pen in the other, but what really caught my attention were her amazing legs.

Not to mention a smile that made my weak leg go a little shaky.

She clicked and swayed over to me, and extended her hand. "Olivia Goode." Her smile brightened even more, and I swear it made me a little dizzy.

I gave her my best grin, the one that once upon a long ago time used to melt its fair share of panties. As far as I knew her undergarments were still in place, but I did notice she wasn't overly quick to let go of my hand, and her eyes searched mine for a bit longer than usual. She was looking up at me, which wasn't unusual since I was nearly six-five But even she, as tall as she was, had to look up.

"Lucas Badd," I answered, shaking her hand—I squeezed gently, and held on until she let go.

"A Goode *and* a Badd," she quipped, smirking.

"Whaddya know. Match made in heaven." I grinned back at her, lifting the color samples. "There are a lotta crazy names in here."

She laughed, another of those musical sounds she'd made on the other side of the aisle. "Well, there are a lot of different shades of blue, Lucas. You can't call them all just plain old blue, can you?" She indicated the various hues of blue with a sweep of a purple-painted fingernail. "These are all blue, but if you want your room to be eggshell, that's a much different feel than if you painted it *Electric Moonlight*."

I growled in annoyance. "I don't know what the hell I want. All I know is I'm painting my apartment and I was thinking blue. I come in here and find a billion and a half different colors of blue, and I got no clue what to do now."

"Well, what kind of general feel and aesthetic are you going for you in your space?" She tilted her head to one side and popped her hip out, twirling her pen around her finger and hugging her clipboard against her chest.

"My what?"

She gestured at the colors with her pen. "Like I said, different shades have different feels. They'll inspire a different overall emotional tone just from the light in the room. Eggshell is more uplifting and lighthearted, whereas *Electric Moonlight* is more inspiring and energetic." She gestured at another shade, darker than the others. "This one—well, it would be interesting as an accent wall, but I certainly wouldn't do a whole room in it."

I frowned. "Accent wall?"

She held back a smirk. "What does your place look like at the moment?"

I scratched my head with the handle of my cane. "Uh. I guess you might call it…spartan."

Yeah. Go with that. Heh.

She seemed to interpret this correctly, judging by the amusement on her beautiful face. "By which I assume you mean white walls, no pictures or paintings, and little if any furniture?"

I laughed. "Yeah, pretty much."

She looked at me for a moment, assessing. "Tell me a little about yourself."

"Uh. I dunno."

She rolled her eyes. "What kind of person are you?"

I snickered. "How the hell'm I s'posed to answer that? Jesus. What kind of person am I?" I smacked my cane down to the ground. "I'm a lonely, cranky, grumpy old fart from the ass-end of Oklahoma with no patience for silly girly colors on my walls."

She nodded. "I see. So you'll want something masculine, but still soothing." Her smile was gentle, but teasing. "Try to balance out all that crankiness and grumpiness."

"Good luck with that," I grumbled.

She laughed—and yet again, the pure musicality of the sound of her laugh sent some kind of electrifying jolt through me. "You really do have the grouch act down pat, don't you?"

I glared at her. "Who's acting?"

She smirked, and patted my shoulder; the electric jolt shivered south. "I think there's a soft old teddy bear in there somewhere."

I harrumphed. "Yeah, well, you got two words right at least—*old* and *bear*."

She only laughed all the more. "I could add a third word to that: silly. And then I could call you Pooh."

I took me a full thirty seconds to process the fact that she'd just compared me to Winnie the Pooh. "Number one, I wear fuckin' pants. Whoever decided cartoon animals should wear shirts and no pants, or pants and no shirt needs to get their damn head checked. Second, that stupid bear was a fat-ass moron. Gettin' stuck in the hole of his own damn house like some tubby bitch. Rookie move."

If I'd thought vulgarity would push her away, I was wrong.

She just laughed until she had to wipe tears from her eyes. "Oh my. Oh my! You're funny, Lucas. I've never thought of Winnie the Pooh that way." Her eyes narrowed a bit. "Funny that you know that much about Winnie the Pooh, though."

I waved a hand. "Got three grown boys. Triplets. I had like three movies when they were growin' up, and Winnie the Pooh was one of 'em . They wore the damn tape out."

Her eyebrows shot up. "Triplets, huh?" She sighed. "They must've kept you busy."

I guffawed, slapping my all-too-generous gut. "Olivia, you got *no* clue. Hellions don't even begin to describe 'em. Hellraisers. And truth be told, they still are."

"Are they here? In Ketchikan?"

I nodded, suppressing a growl. "Yep. They're the reason I'm here, actually. But that's a whole different story."

She seized on that, her eyes narrowing, one thin perfectly sculpted eyebrow arching. "And?"

I couldn't help a laugh. "Yeah. Let me just pile that awful mess on you within five damn minutes of meeting you. I don't think so, sweetheart."

She wiggled her hips saucily. "Oooh, you called me 'sweetheart.' I feel special." Even the sarcasm dripping from her voice couldn't douse the sparks that lit in me at that little hip wiggle.

"You are absolutely the only woman I've ever

called sweetheart," I said, holding up my index and middle finger. "Scout's honor."

She cackled. "That's not even the Scout symbol."

"Exactly."

She stuck out her lower lip. "So you mean I'm not special?"

Oh god—she was just playing along, but that lower lip. Damn. "Dammit woman, now you've gone too far."

She blinked at me in confusion. "What do you mean?"

I laughed. "That lower lip sticking out. Ain't fair."

She rolled her eyes. "I was just playing along, Lucas."

I shook my head and scoffed. "So was I, Olivia."

"My friends call me Liv," she said.

"Are we friends already?" I asked.

She shrugged. "Well sure." She smirked. "If you take me to your apartment."

I coughed, choking on my own shock. "Uh—what?"

She laughed, leaning into me, patting my shoulder, and then handing me a business card. "I'm an interior designer. I can help you decorate."

I frowned at her. "Out of the goodness of your heart, huh?"

She winked at me—and it came across as cute

and sarcastic and flirty, rather than sultry. Still hot, though. "Nope. I just need a design challenge."

I huffed. "Well. You'll have a challenge, that's for damn sure."

She tapped her notes on the clipboard with a fingernail. "I'm about done here. I just need to decide between two kinds of flooring for my client's kitchen."

"What are the two choices?"

She led the way to the flooring aisle, going right for the composite selection. Lifting a dark gray wood grain sample in one hand, and a pale tan bamboo replica material in the other, she glanced at me. "What do you think?"

I rolled a shoulder. "Guess it depends."

"Cabinets will be white, stainless steel pulls to match the appliances."

"I mean, I don't know shit about design. I just know the darker stuff," I tap the selection in question, "is more durable. Less likely to get damaged, and the waterproofing on it is better. Although, if it does get scratched or dinged hard enough to show, it's more noticeable."

She shot me a quizzical look. "I've asked three different employees here about this stuff and no one told me that."

I dug in my back pocket, pulled out the tag that identified me as an employee, and clipped it to my belt. "I get in trouble sometimes, because I tend to tell more of the truth than I should to sell the more expensive products. I just got no patience for bullshit."

"You work here?"

I nodded. "Yep. I usually work the open shifts, or I close the shop. I'm rarely here in the middle of the day."

She nodded, understanding dawning on her face. "Ah. That explains why I've never seen you here. I'm only here during the afternoons. I tend to look at my clients' spaces in the mornings, draw up designs right before lunch, and then shop for materials after lunch."

"And I'm always gone by lunch," I added, leaning heavily on my cane. "Old men need their naps."

She rolled her eyes at me. "You're not old."

I laughed. "I ain't pretending, Liv."

"Come on, now. You can't be more than forty-five."

I outright cackled in disgruntled amusement. "That's almost an insult."

She jotted down the item number of the gray composite flooring, and then glanced at me curiously. "How do you figure?"

I patted my generous belly, scratched the liberal gray in my shaggy, unkempt beard. "If I'm forty-five, I ain't aged well at *all*." I laughed again. "Shit, girl, I ain't aged well for sixty-two, which is my real age."

She stopped mid stride and stared at me. "You are not."

I shook my head. "Why are you trying to butter me up, buttercup?"

"Do you think you look old?" she pressed, the sweetness of her smile taking some of the sting of the deeply probing question away.

"Feel old, sometimes," I said, dodging.

She rolled her eyes. "That wasn't the question."

I waved my hand, hating this whole line of conversation for more reasons than I cared to think about. "Anyone ever tell you you're nosy?"

She snorted. "All the time." She sighed, a wistful, aching sound. "My husband used to tell me I was nosier than Pinocchio at a liar's convention."

I stumbled and had to catch myself heavily on my cane. "Goddamned cane. Goddamn gimpy-ass leg," I muttered under my breath. "You're married?"

She nodded. "Twenty-five years." She patted my shoulder when I hesitated—I refused to be the other man, no matter what, even if it was nothing but innocent talk. "He passed away three years ago."

I wiggled the rubber end of my cane against her linoleum floor sample, scratching at a nick in the wood grain with my thumbnail. "I...sorry to hear that."

We walked in silence up to the register. Bill

Hickham, behind the register, greeted Olivia by name, and she related her needs—several gallons of paint in a color to match a sample she handed him, thirty-six cabinet pulls to match the one she set on the counter, six boxes of flooring under the item number she read to him…the list went on for nearly two minutes.

I stared at her. "Interior designer, or general contractor?"

She laughed. "I choose and order the supplies to make sure it's exactly right. In my experience, if you tell a contractor exactly which product you want him to use, he'll get *almost* the right thing, and will usually either get the wrong thing by accident, or figure he knows better. So I order the quantity and specific items myself, see that it gets delivered on time and, that way, the project stays on target in terms of time and budget, and my client gets the exact look I designed."

I laughed. "Sounds like you don't have a lot of faith in contractors."

"I have faith in the ones I hire, because they trust me to choose and supply the best products for the job, and I trust them to build things properly, to code, and not cut corners." Her eyes went to my cane, which I'd hung off the counter while she was working with Bill to get everything ordered. "Bad knee?"

"Something like that," I mumbled.

Bill, at least twenty years older than me and yet somehow sprier, grinned at me. "Finally pick a paint for your place, Lucas?"

I growled. "No."

Bill guffawed, slapping the counter. "You never will, you indecisive old grouch." He glanced at Olivia, grinning. "He comes in every week on his day off, stares at the paint samples for twenty minutes or so, and then leaves without making a decision. Been going on for nearly two months now."

"It has not," I snapped. "And whaddayou know, anyway? You're so old, you remember when Alaska was still a territory."

He just laughed. "Territory? I was old when Alaska was owned by the Russians."

Olivia scoffed. "You two should be nice to each other."

Bill's laugh was caustic. "He ain't been nice a day in his life."

"Like you'd know," I murmured.

Bill arched a white eyebrow. "I knew your Pa. I helped him dig the trench to get you guys your electricity in that old place up off of Ward Creek."

I gave Bill a glare—hoping he would get the message. He oughta know better than to bring up the past.

Bill just cackled, knowing he'd pissed me off. He

just waved a hand at us. "Go on, kids. Get outta here. Liv, most of your order oughta be here by the end of next week." Then he turned to me. "If you ever decide on a paint, let me know. But knowin' you, you'll probably pick black, just to match your soul."

Before I could reply Olivia was ready with a response. "Don't worry, Bill, he's got me as his designer, now. I'll help him choose a nice color. Something to lighten him up a bit."

Bill looked impressed. "Good for you, Lucas. You've got the best designer in Ketchikan, our girl Liv." He made a face. "Didn't think you'd be able to afford her, not on what we make here."

I thought about whacking him upside the head with my cane, but thought better of it. "Bill, so help me, please, shut the fuck up."

"What kinda language is that to use around a lady?" Bill said with a cackle as he walked back to the storeroom.

Liv was laughing, though. "He is kinda funny."

"He's nosier than you are. Loudmouth motherfucker, too," I added.

Olivia's laugh was something a guy could get addicted to—it came easily, naturally, and beautifully. Her laugh made you feel like you were the funniest person on earth, and each note of it jolted through you like a thousand volts of pure electricity.

"You really are a fan of the colorful language, aren't you?" she said, not sounding offended, though.

"Ain't been anyone to care how I talk in... well..." A harsh sigh scraped out of me. "A long time."

Olivia's gaze was speculative as she led the way out of the store into the parking lot. "If I asked you what that meant by that, I'm guessing you'd dodge that question, too?"

I nodded. "Probably." A glance at her, a long glance in which I nearly lost track of myself in her open, questioning hazel-brown eyes. "You always make a habit of asking people about the hard-to-talk-about shit within ten minutes of meeting 'em?"

She shrugged. "Yes, actually, I do. My husband died of a heart attack, leaving me a widow at forty-three. One of the things I've learned is that life is far too short to waste it on small talk." Her smile was sad, but bright. "So, I ask about the things I want to know, when I want to know them. You don't have to answer, but I'm not going to feel bad about asking."

"Makes sense." I tap my bad leg with my cane. "Car accident." I tap my chest, over my heart. "Bad luck, bad choices, and bad people." I tilt my head to one side. "Although, I guess you could argue those are all one and the same."

She tucked her clipboard under her arm and rummaged in her purse, found her keys, unlocking a new red Canyon pickup. "So. Where do you live?"

I dig in the hip pocket of my jeans, pull out my keys, and pretended to blip an imaginary key—Olivia looked around, confused, and I laughed, pointing across the street with the key—which was just a regular old house key. "Over there."I gestured. "I live in that apartment building across the street."

She laughed, and my belly flipped and my skin tightened. "Let me put my stuff in my truck and I'll walk over with you." She hesitated. "Unless you'd rather a ride over? Save your leg?"

I waved a hand. "I need the exercise anyway. Both my leg and my…well, everything."

Truth was, I'd much rather have gotten a ride, but I was too stubborn and prideful to say so. Pretty women do that to a man. Make you do shit and say shit you got no call doing and saying. Like pretending you might be somebody you ain't.

But there's a sexy lady in the picture, so I'm pretending I'm a solid guy, and that my life hasn't been one colossal fuck-up.

Olivia sets her stuff in her truck, keeping her clipboard under one arm, and then she moves to stand next to me, smiling in anticipation. "Shall we head over?" Her voice was bright and eager and warm.

I extend my elbow to her, offering her my arm, acting as if I've been anything even close to resembling a chivalrous man. I barely have decent table manners, much less the gentlemanly bullshit you see on TV.

Yet, here I am pretending. How long can I keep this up? The better question might be, how long will she buy it?

She took my elbow, tucking her warm tiny palm against my thick burly arm. Well—an arm that used to be thick and burly, but was now as much flab as muscle. Still, as far as arms go, it ain't a small one, and her hand is warm and soft, curled against my bicep like it belonged there.

I do my best to keep my limp to a minimum as we cross the street, but I had to lean pretty heavily on the damn cane. The doc said the limp was temporary, and as long as I exercised it regularly and built the muscle back up, I would make a full recovery.

"So. Triplets." Olivia's sideways glance at me was inquisitive.

I nodded. "Yes ma'am. They're thirty—uhh, two? Thirty-two." I palmed the back of my neck in embarrassment. "Hard to remember, sometimes."

She squeezed my arm. "Don't feel bad. I have five daughters, and if someone asks how old they are, I have to stop and think about it."

I blinked at her. "Five daughters?"

She nods. "Five girls. Well…women, now. They are…" She laughs. "See? I have to think about it. Charlie is twenty-four, Cassie is twenty-two, Lexie is twenty-one, Torie is nineteen, and Poppy is eighteen."

I made a scoffing noise of amazed disbelief. "Damn, girl. Five kids, none of 'em multiples?"

She laughed. "Yeah. Darren and I were…busy."

I guffawed at that. "Yeah, clearly."

She blushed and bumped into me. "Not like that, you pervert."

I snickered. "I ain't the one with five girls in less than what, six years?"

"Are you trying to shame me?" she asked, but the smirk on her face told me she wasn't upset.

"Yep. You've had a lot of kids." I paused at the door to my building. "Charlie, Cassie, Lexie, Torie, and Poppy?"

"Charlotte, Cassandra, Alexandra, Victoria, and Poppy, which isn't short for anything—my husband's mother's favorite flower was a poppy. She had only months to live when I was pregnant with Poppy, and she made me promise to name the baby Poppy, if it was a girl." I held the door to the apartment building open for her and she stepped inside, turning back to wait for me to continue leading the way to my apartment. "Your boys' names?"

"Roman, Remington, and Ramsey." I rolled a shoulder. "I just thought they were cool sounding names."

"What did your wife think?"

I sighed. "No wife. Never married. Their mother…I think she was in too much shock about having triplets to care about names."

She frowned at me. "Shock I can understand, but not shock to the point that I wouldn't care what my newborn triplets were named."

I groaned. "You are sneaky, you know that?" I unlocked my apartment door and stepped in, closing the door behind us. "She wasn't a great person, and it wasn't a great situation. She wasn't interested in being a mom. She never really clicked into the role, you could say. She took off when the boys were seven. I haven't seen her since, and I'm not interested in doing so."

Olivia stood just inside my apartment, staring at me. "She left?"

I nodded. "Yep. I came home from work one day and she was gone. The boys got home from school before I got home from work, and when they walked in the place was empty. She had packed a suitcase, took the money we'd been saving in a coffee can, and vanished. No note, nothing. Just left. The boys didn't understand and, honestly, neither did I. Had no clue what I was s'posed to say to 'em. The bitter truth was their mama was nothin' but a bar slut I never intended to have kids with. But seven-year-old boys don't understand that shit."

"And you raised them alone after that?"

"Well…if you want the truth, I'd say *raised* might be a bit of an exaggeration. Getting them to adulthood without them starvin' or livin' under a bridge is about the best I can say for myself."

Olivia sighed. "I'm sure you're underestimating yourself."

I scratch my shaggy beard. "Possibly, but I doubt it." I waved at my apartment. "Anyway, here it is. I wasn't expecting company, least of all a beautiful woman, so I ain't cleaned up properly."

"I don't think you need to worry about that," she laughed, patting my shoulder. "There's nothing in here to clean."

I faked being offended. "I have an entire couch *and* a twenty-five-year-old fourth-hand television set, I'll have you know."

"And that's it," she said, snickering. "Literally. Not even an end table?"

I shrugged. "No point. Don't need one."

"What if you want to set a drink down? What about photos of your boys?"

I pawed at the back of my head. "Don't really set

my drinks down, now that I think on it. I drink 'em, finish 'em, and that's it." I frowned. "As for photos of my boys...? I guess I don't really have any."

She sighed. "Not even one?"

I shook my head. "Nope. Didn't have the money, or the time for that." I growled to myself. "Or at least, that's the excuse I've always made."

She moved into the middle of the living room, poked her head into the kitchen, then the bedroom and the bathroom. With a wave of a hand, she indicated my apartment. "So it's a totally blank slate right now. What do you want in here? What do you want it to feel like?"

I shrugged. "I ain't got a damn clue, Liv," I said, frustration tingeing my voice. "I guess all I can say is that I'd like it to feel like a home."

"This is an apartment, though. Will you be here for a while? Like, does it make sense for you to paint walls and such if you're just going to move in a year or so?"

I hang my cane on my forearm and sit heavily on the couch, massaging my throbbing leg. "I dunno. I'll be here awhile. My boys all have their own lives, serious girlfriends, and careers and all that shit. So I'm here because...well, that's another long story. But I'm here, and this is a nice spot. Close to all three of the boys. Close to a half-decent job. Grocery store. Video store. Library."

Olivia snorted. "Video store?"

I frowned, gesturing at the DVD player, which I got at the same thrift store as the TV and couch. "Yeah, the video store. How else'm I gonna find anything to watch?"

She stared at me as if trying to decide if I was kidding. "Uhhhh...Redbox? Netflix? Amazon Prime? Hulu? Apple TV? Roku?"

I blinked back at her. "Pumpkins. Rabbit. Sixty-two."

Her face twisted into a rictus of complete confusion. "Are you having a stroke or something?"

"Is that a joke about my age?"

"I just have no idea what you're talking about, or why you said those words."

I laughed. "Well, you spouted a bunch of gibberish, so I figured I would too."

She closed her eyes slowly and palmed her face as comprehension dawned. "Those are all alternatives to renting DVDs at a store, Lucas. Redbox is, well, a big red box from which you borrow DVDs. There's one close to here, actually. The other things I mentioned are all streaming services."

"Streaming services?"

Olivia shook her head. "Are you teasing me? I don't want to assume you're really this uninformed about current technology." She huffed a laugh. "I mean, you have three sons in their thirties. Surely they've tried to get you basic Internet, at least."

I snorted. "Sure, they've tried. Ain't interested."

"Lucas. Aren't you interested in trying things which may make your life easier and more pleasant?"

"I thought you were gonna help me spruce up my walls, not guilt me into getting a Wi-Fi gizmo or whateverthefuck." I snapped this with a bit more vitriol than I'd intended.

She frowned at me, this time not entirely playfully. "Well excuse me for wanting to improve more than just the color on your walls."

I leaned my head back against the couch and sighed. "I'm sorry. It's just an old argument. The boys are always nagging at me to try new shit, and I'm just a stubborn old grizzly—set in my ways doesn't begin to describe me."

She sat delicately and demurely on the edge of the couch a few inches from me. "Well, I'm not your boys in case you hadn't noticed. We could be friends—good friends, even. But you can't snap at me just because I suggest you stop living in the Stone Age and accept something as basic as the Internet into your life."

I scoffed. "Liv, take a look around. I been stuck in the Stone Age for forty years."

"Then it's high time to join the information age,

isn't it?" She set her clipboard on her knees and pulled a pen out from behind an ear. "So, you were thinking blue at the hardware store, but now that I'm here and I have had a chance to chat with you a bit, I think you may enjoy a green more than a blue. Because of the light in here, I would suggest something between pine needle and sea foam. I'll bring over a few little tins of sample colors and we'll see which strikes your interest. Part of the thing with those little color samples they have hanging off the racks is that it's hard to visualize what a color will look like on your wall. We can get a few ounces mixed up in a few different shades you like and put them on your actual wall. Then we can see which one feels right. Once you decide on the color, you prime the wall again and paint over it."

I nodded. "Never thought of that, but it makes sense."

"Pick a paint is the first and simplest step. You need a few more items of furniture, some pictures or paintings, some knickknacks to make it feel cozy and homey."

"Just don't make it look girly."

"You'll just have to trust me on this. If I didn't know how to reach a client's desired aesthetic, what kind of interior designer would I be?"

"I suppose that's a good point. So." I grinned at her. "Paint?"

She tapped her pen against her clipboard. "Let me do some thinking on the overall look. I'll come by tomorrow and we'll get started."

"I'm done working by eleven."

She jotted down a note, and her smile shifted from bright and professional to intimate and personal. "How about we start with lunch at twelve?"

I felt my heart thumping crazily in my chest—I'd already had a heart attack and knew the symptoms of that, but this wasn't that. This was just good old-fashioned nerves and anxiety.

"I. Um. Yeah. That sounds good." I tried to smile at her, but it ended up lopsided.

"Good. It's a date."

I choked. "Um. Okay. Yeah. Good."

Her smile was too much for me—as if I was somethin' worth her time. As if I had something to offer. As if I wasn't a fuck-up and a no-good lazy asshole. I didn't have the heart to tell her she was cozyin' up to an alcoholic with no car and no license, a dirty, sordid past, and a busted-up heart. 'Course, I doubted I'd have to tell her anything. She'd see the obvious soon enough.

Sadly for her, I was too damn selfish to try too hard to push her away.

I really liked Olivia Goode.

I liked the brightness and eagerness in her eyes. I

liked the sway of her slender hips. The quick delicacy of her hands. The intelligence in her features. There was a sadness to her, too, which I couldn't help but recognize; she was a widow, and yet despite her loss there was an optimism to her that drew me in like a moth to a bug zapper.

Goddammit.

I found myself wishing I knew how to be a better man. Wishing I could be the man she thought she saw when she looked at me. I'd known her less than an hour, but there was somethin' about the woman that just…

Well it made me feel, for the first time in forty years, that maybe there was hope for my busted-up heart after all.

'Course, I knew better than to put any faith in that kinda hope. It just left you more fucked up than you were when you started thinkin' shit could get better.

TWO

———⚜———

Liv

"I REALLY HATE IT HERE, MOM." POPPY, MY YOUNGEST daughter, wiped tear-tracks away from her eyes—the tracks were mascara-stained, smearing black across her cheeks. "I hate my professors, I hate my roommate, I hate my classes, I hate all the people in my classes. I hate the town, the bars, the keggers, the sorority bitches and the frat bastards. I hate the stupid restaurants and the stupid...gah. The boys are the stupidest of all."

I sighed and adjusted the iPad on my lap so I could see her better. "You loved Columbia last year, Pop."

"I know I did. But things have changed." She

pulled her massive sheaf of glossy black hair over her shoulder.

"Like Reed?" I suggested, my voice wary and gentle; Poppy was…defensive, shall we say, about her boyfriend.

She snarled wordlessly. "Fuck Reed O'Reilly."

"Poppy Estelle Goode, I raised you better than that, young lady."

"Sorry, Mom," Poppy muttered. "But he's a dick and I hate him most of all."

"I take it you broke up."

"If by broke up, you mean I broke his nose, then yes." She ducked her head so her hair fell in a shimmery raven-black curtain hiding her face from my glare.

"You did *not*." My glare is such that she was prudent to hide from it.

"He cheated on me, Mom! And not just with my best friend, but my roommate too—at the same time." She paused for effect. "IN MY BED."

I winced. "Oh. Wow." Don't say it, I told myself. Don't say it. *DO NOT SAY IT.*

Poppy tossed her hair away and glared back at me—I saw she was sitting in the common room in her dorm as students passed back and forth behind her, chattering and laughing, holding textbooks and Starbucks cups. "Go ahead and say it," she muttered. "You're about to burst."

"I'm not going to say it," I said, my voice crisp. "You know what I'm not saying, so I may as well not bother saying it."

She blew a raspberry at me. "But you'll get satisfaction from saying it. It's already as good as said, so you may as well say it."

"No."

"Mom."

"Poppy?"

"Say it."

I sighed. "Fine. I told you Reed was going to hurt you. I wanted to think otherwise, but I always got a bad feeling from him the few times I met him."

"You did not want to think otherwise. You disliked him from the start."

I arched an eyebrow at her. "Well, yes. Because I got a bad feeling from him. I didn't want you to get hurt, like you are now. I wouldn't be a good mother if I had a bad feeling about a guy and didn't say anything."

She takes a sip of an iced coffee—something with a bucket of sugar in it, probably. "Well, regardless. Reed being a colossal dickhole isn't the only reason I hate it here."

"Poppy, the language is unnecessary."

"Mom, quit acting like Captain America."

"What?"

"Never mind. I just hate it here, and Reed cheating on me isn't the only reason."

"You loved it at Columbia before this."

"I was wearing rose-colored glasses, Mom. I was obsessed with New York City my whole life and I was excited to be here. But now that I'm here and I've gotten used to it, I hate it. It's busy all the time. People are rude. It's expensive as hell. The classes here are unnecessarily hard, and I'm not learning anything to do with what I really want to do."

"It's your sophomore year, babe, you're still getting the prereqs out of the way."

"There shouldn't *be* prereqs, Mom! I know exactly what I want to do. I don't need history or math or chemistry to be an artist."

"Then why are you there?"

She huffed. "That's what I'm starting to wonder. Mom, I had this whole vision of getting an art history degree and doing all this amazing art, and living in New York, and becoming this amazing artist with a degree but, in reality, it just sucks. I just want to be in the studio all the time, and the homework sucks, the tests are stupid, the professors are arrogant snobs, my classmates are pretentious as fu—as heck, and I'm learning nothing worthwhile. I mean, I knew all the possible interpretations of *Starry Night* and all about the other paintings of his life by the time I was in eighth grade, and they're sitting here trying to tell me to write an essay about how Van Gogh's burgeoning madness informed the visual style of his most recognizable masterpiece. I mean, duh. That's elementary school bullshit, not undergrad art history material."

"Poppy—"

"And then when I *do* get into the studio, I have a pathetic wannabe who couldn't make it as an artist as my professor trying to tell me I need to find my voice. Like, shut the fuck up, old man! I *have* found my voice! If you would get out of my personal space and let me paint, I'd be able to find my voice a hell of a lot faster, because I wouldn't be dealing with *you*!"

"Poppy!" I shouted.

She huffed again. "What." Her voice is flat, bored.

"Did you call to rant at me, or do you want my input?" I asked.

"Honestly, I called you because I needed to vent."

"Well you're getting my input anyway." I glanced at the notepad on my clipboard, on which was doodled a cartoonish image of a bear. Can't imagine why I would be doodling bears all of a sudden. "You need to decide what you really want. You know I'm not in favor of spending four years and a hundred thousand dollars to get a degree just to have a degree. If you're pursuing a degree that will get you a job you couldn't otherwise get, then by all means, stay at Columbia. But, if you're pursuing a degree which you're increasingly doubting the value of, then I would spend some time seriously reconsidering your priorities. If your one real, true goal in life is to be a working artist, then you're wasting my money, your own money, your father's life insurance policy money, the government's money, and worst of all, your time. Which is the most precious commodity you'll ever have. Life is too short to waste it chasing a degree you don't want and won't ever use."

She eyed me through the screens. "You're telling me you think I should drop out."

I shook my head. "No. I'm telling you that you need to be certain of what you're chasing. A university degree is a great thing, when it has value to you. But it's a long hard road and you have to really want it, especially at the level you're in—Columbia is Ivy League, honey. The big time. It is not easy. So don't drop out just because it's hard and you don't love every second of it. But if you feel like all you really want to do, what will really bring you joy and value and meaning is to create art, then you may just be wasting your time. Only you can determine that for yourself, Poppy."

Poppy took another sip of her drink. "Mom, I just…I don't know. I need to think, I guess."

"Yes, you do." I frowned. "Does that have sugar in it?"

"Don't start," she warned.

"Poppy, you know how I feel about you consuming sugar."

"It's iced coffee, Mom. Chill."

"Iced coffee…with three pumps of mocha and whipped cream?"

She huffed yet again, this time with supreme annoyance. "No, Mom. Just coffee and half and half and ice. That's it. I promise."

"Fine. But if you're lying to me, I'll know."

"You're thirty-four hundred miles away, Mom. How are you going to know if I'm lying?"

"Mom powers." I squinted and frowned, touching my fingertips to my temples. "For example, I happen to know you spent a weekend in the Hamptons last month when you told me you were staying at the dorms studying for a test."

She groaned in irritation. "Fucking Cassandra. I swear I'm going to send her a glitter bomb. She's the most untrustworthy person I've ever met in my life."

I laughed. "Untrustworthy to you, maybe."

"Yeah! She's a snitch!"

"If you don't want her to snitch on you, don't do things she feels the need to snitch on you for."

"Or just don't tell her shit," Poppy muttered. "Never telling her anything again."

"And what is a glitter bomb?" I asked.

She cackled. "Exactly what it sounds like."

"Sounds messy is what it sounds like."

"It's awful. And she'll deserve it." Poppy sighed. "Anyway, it was me and Reed and Lucille and Tony. We stayed at Tony's grandparents' beach cottage and we studied."

"Studied what? Vodka tonic ratios?"

"Mom. Eew, no. Vodka is gross." She laughed nervously. "Not that I'd know anything about it."

I rolled my eyes at her. "I'm not stupid, sweetheart. You've been at university on your own since you were seventeen. You think I don't know you've spent a significant portion of your time drinking?"

She gave me a long, searching look. "Actually, less than you'd think. I don't really like it." Her eyes flicked away. "Not anymore at least. I got over that really fast."

"Anything I should know?"

She shrugged. "I'll tell you, someday. Not now. Nothing to worry about, though. Just a few bad experiences that made me realize it's not as fun as everyone seems to think." She twisted and glanced at someone over her shoulder, listening. "I have to go, Mom."

"Me too. I have a client meeting in twenty minutes."

She frowned at me. "So…this thing where you're living in Alaska now. You're seriously staying there? Like, forever?"

I laughed. "Honey, yes. I own a condo here. I have clients here, friends, a life. I live in Ketchikan, now, sweetheart. For real."

"I guess I was thinking it was a phase or something. Like you'd live there for a couple months and come back to the coast."

"I mean, technically, I am on the coast. Just…the other one. Sort of. It's not really on the coast itself, though. More, channels *near* the coast."

"Mom. Don't be obtuse."

I laughed. "Don't use my own phrases against me."

"Why, though?"

"Why what?"

She shrugged. "Why Ketchikan?"

"I love it here. It's quaint. Peaceful. Cute. Fun. There's lots to do, but it's not hectic. People are nice." I sighed. "Look, babe, this is a different conversation. You said you have to go, and so do I. If you want to talk about why I finally chose something for myself, call me when you have an hour or two to spare." I smiled at her. "I mean that, despite the sarcasm."

"You know, I just may do that." She blew me a kiss. "Love you. I'll call you later."

"Love you too, Pops. Bye." I closed the case on the iPad and leaned back against the chair.

Of all my kids, I worried the most about her.

Headstrong, independent, willful, talented, absurdly intelligent, and more than a little naive, Poppy was a tornado and a firestorm and a wild mustang all rolled into a tiny but explosive package. Her teachers had wanted her to skip grades as early as kindergarten, but I'd refused, wanting her to stay with her class-mates and friends. Year after year, she'd tested out of grades, and I'd refused to skip her ahead. Finally, by the time she got to her junior year of high school she was sick of being bored stiff at school and had gone behind my back, forging my signature to get herself sent to the local community college for advanced courses and college credit. I hadn't caught on until she was three semesters in, and realized I couldn't hold her back anymore. She'd graduated high school three weeks before her seventeenth birthday and had been accepted to not one, not two, but three Ivy League schools with partial rides. Now at eighteen, she was a sophomore at Columbia...and already over it, it seemed.

I had a feeling I'd have company here in Ketchikan before long.

I had to laugh at how indignant she'd been about Cassie telling me about the Hamptons trip. Fact was, I hadn't needed Cassie's information—Poppy had used her credit card, and I'd gotten alerts about it. She didn't think about things like that. When I'd given her the card for sundry expenses and emergencies, I got notifications every time she used it. She had the mind of an artist—big picture, head in the clouds, full of passion and zeal and always onto the next thing, but never thinking about things like detail or logic or sense. Or, sometimes, basic responsibility.

Despite all that, Poppy could take care of herself, despite last-minute scrambling, sudden realizations, and a lot of reminders from me and her sisters.

Letting her live alone in New York was the scariest thing I'd ever done, and I still wasn't sure it had been the right thing to do. It was what she wanted, though, and I knew if I'd refused to let her go, she'd have run away or done something silly like that. I thought it was better to send her in a way I could keep tabs on her rather than have her go off on her own with no checks and balances.

I sighed. I had a feeling I'd be getting an angry call from Cassie soon—when Poppy threatened to send a glitter bomb, she wasn't kidding; that was the kind of thing she'd actually do. Crazy child.

Setting the iPad aside, I tugged my clipboard in front of me and perused my notes about what to do with Lucas's apartment. I'd decided on something just a few shades lighter than pine green for the walls, and we'd go to a resale shop—different than a thrift store, in terms of the quality of items—for an easy chair, a love seat, a coffee table, and some end tables. I'd find some macho, masculine artwork for the walls—sailboats or pirate ships, animals, landscapes, things like that. I assumed he had little to nothing in the way of dishes or kitchen utensils, so we would need to get that organized, as well.

Sigh. Men. Totally helpless without a woman around. Darren had been the same way—if I left him alone for a weekend, laundry would pile up to the ceilings, dishes would go crusty and moldy, and he'd eat nothing but pizza, frozen chicken nuggets, and carryout.

I set those thoughts aside—specifically Darren and his dietary choices, and the results thereof.

Lucas, though—I knew I needed to stay away from him beyond friendship, simply because he bore the hallmarks of everything that had led to me being a widow in the first place... and then some. He was clearly carrying a few extra pounds, and he knew it. And there were signs of other issues in his life.

But there was an intensity to his gaze, a power in his bearing that even the extra weight couldn't hide. He was funny, if a little vulgar. Self-deprecating, but there was an air of confidence, too. Or maybe not confidence, necessarily, but a sense that he knew he'd survived the worst life could throw at him and was still on his feet. He knew there was nothing in this world that could take him down—except himself.

Why was I doing this? He couldn't pay me, and I didn't need the money. I don't think he even really wanted the makeover I was planning for his apartment. But he needed it, and I knew that. I didn't work pro bono—that was for lawyers, not interior designers. Especially not one with my credentials: before Darren had passed away and I'd been faced with the biggest upheaval of my entire life, I'd boasted senators and congressmen and even a former president as my clientele, not to mention high-powered attorneys, investors, and Wall Street bigwigs. If there was a high-end home on the East Coast, and you wanted it to look magazine-worthy, you called Olivia Goode.

Now here I am in tiny, cute, quaint little Ketchikan, where those credentials mean nothing to most everyone. I work for cheap, just to stay busy, and I take clients who think the height of design is a wall full of dead animals.

Nothing wrong with that—I'm not antihunter or vegan or anything, I just eschew taxidermy as a design aesthetic.

Again, I find myself questioning why I'm doing this. Why I'm gathering my keys and heading to Lucas's apartment, clipboard in hand, fully intending to do a job for free that could've cost a couple thousand at a minimum.

For me, it was those big, deep, sad puppy dog eyes, and the story he hadn't told, but had hinted at.

And dammit, I was lonely. I told Poppy I had friends, which was true enough—there was a group of local women who I went hiking and stand-up paddle boarding and horseback riding with, had coffee with, or the occasional brunch. But nothing...deep. Nothing meaningful.

Did I think I'd get it with Lucas? He was shuttered and wary. Hard-hearted. But there was a hint of a softie in there, under that big gruff bearish demeanor.

There was something about him I was attracted to, and I saw no reason, as yet, to pretend otherwise. We could be friends. Just friends.

Being friends didn't have to mean anything. And if I had the occasional dream about huge, strong arms and rough, powerful hands and deep, chocolate, ursine eyes, so what? He didn't need to know, and it didn't have to mean anything.

I parked outside his building and turned off my truck, but didn't get out right away. Instead, I checked my makeup in the rearview mirror—since moving here I'd stopped wearing much at all, opting instead for a little color on my lips, some contouring on my cheekbones, and maybe a little mascara. Before, I'd been an avid practitioner of what Darren called "false face", or the elaborate mask of makeup designed to make one look perfect and ageless. I'd had the smoky eyes and the heavily contoured cheeks and sculpted lips, and my body had been hot yoga trim and my clothes flawlessly understated and elegant.

That was the old me. The East Coast me.

Here, in Ketchikan? I found someone else in her place.

Someone who didn't like wearing makeup at all most days, who was as comfortable in jeans and flannel and heavy boots as I was pencil skirts and silk blouses and three-inch heels. There had always been a part of me that had loved being outdoors and being active, and Darren had shared that with me, but this was something beyond that.

I wasn't sure who she was, this new Liv, but I think I liked her.

So why was I fixing my makeup? Something told me Lucas wouldn't care.

In fact, I had a feeling if I was wearing a lot of makeup, he may even find me less attractive.

I wanted him to like me, though. I wanted to make him laugh. I wanted to get him out of that crusty, coarse, gruff shell of his, and see if I could bring out the man I saw lurking beneath it.

I was wearing my most comfortable skinny

jeans, colorful sneakers, and a pale blue, half-zip, pull-over fleece. My hair was pulled back from my face by a thin headband, and I'd switched my stuff from my favorite Louis Vuitton purse to a Patagonia crossbody. Casual and sporty rather than the more professional business look I'd sported yesterday—which I'd worn because I'd had a meeting to provide a quote for a client who wanted to update their summer cottage. In other words, wealthy clients who hired me based on my credentials had certain expectations.

Today, my time was my own. No clients, and no work to do.

Sigh. So why was I worried about my makeup?

On impulse, I reached into the console of my truck and fished a makeup remover wipe from the package I kept in there, and used it to scrub my face clean. For minimal makeup, it was weird that I needed two of them to do the job. What had I been thinking when I got ready this morning?

Oh, that's right—I'd been thinking about Lucas.

But now that I was about to actually see him, I realized I didn't want to be wearing all that makeup.

Weird.

I'm still me, with or without it.

But I wanted him to see the Ketchikan version of me.

I exited my truck and buzzed his apartment.

THREE

Lucas

I WASN'T EXACTLY EXPECTING OLIVA TO SHOW UP. I HOPED she would, but I wasn't banking on it. Nonetheless, I took a shower after work, changed into the cleanest, newest pair of jeans I had, and the only collared polo shirt I owned. I even combed my hair and brushed my beard, although it didn't get the trim it needed. One step at a time. If she showed up and this turned into some kind of a real friendship, I'd think about cleaning up a bit. So far, though, I'm assuming it ain't nothing. A passing interest, at best.

So, when my buzzer went off, I was pleasantly surprised. I buzzed her in, and opened my door for her. I heard her coming up the steps, and felt my heart thumping in a way it hadn't in years and which, considering the heart attack I had a couple of years ago, may not be so great.

She sashayed down to the hall to my door, and my mouth went dry. Dark blue jeans tight enough to hug her slender but strong legs. Mmm, those legs. Her smile was bright and eager, and possibly even a bit nervous.

"Something different about you today, Liv," I said, as I let her in.

She shrugged. "I'm not all dressed up today. I had a client meeting yesterday."

I held a straight face. "So I ain't a client? Meanin' I don't rate the fancy clothes?"

She snorted. "You're a friend, meaning you *do* rate the comfy clothes." She swept a hand at herself. "This is the real me."

"I was teasin'. I like the real you. 'Course, I like the fancy you, too. Both are damned beautiful." I stared at her, trying to figure out what was different from yesterday. It hit me, but I wasn't sure how to put it. "You ain't wearin' makeup. That's what's different."

She smiled, but it was hesitant and nervous. "True. I…I don't know." Her chin dropped, eyes flicking down and away from me.

I touched her chin, lifting her gaze to mine. "I like you better this way." I frowned, hesitated. "Not that what I like should make a difference. I'm just sayin'. Liv, you are goddamned gorgeous, and you don't need a lick of makeup to be that way."

Her smile returned, brightened. "Thank you, Lucas. That…it means a lot to hear you say that."

"So. Lunch?"

She nodded. "I know a place close by. I thought we could take my truck."

"Sure." I hated feeling like less of man for not being able to pick her up.

I snagged my cane, stuffed my wallet and keys into my pockets, and gestured for her to precede me out of the apartment. We climbed into her truck, and she drove us to a cafe a couple of miles away—farther than I'd be able to walk, and not somewhere I'd been, yet.

We took a booth in a back corner, perused the menu in a companionable silence and then, after we'd ordered, we eyed each other, each waiting for the other to speak first.

"Tell me something about yourself that no one knows," Olivia said.

I fiddled with a sugar packet. "Um. Only folks livin' who know a damn thing about me are my boys, and I ain't told 'em much about myself, so honestly, that ain't too hard." I winced. "Well, finding somethin' nobody knows is the easy part. Sharin' it? Not as easy."

"No? Why not?"

I shrugged. "I mean, 'cause most of it ain't pleasant." I set the sugar packet aside. "My life ain't been… well it ain't been a storybook tale. Put it that way."

"I'm not afraid of unpleasant things, Lucas. There's some of that in my own story."

"Of course there is. None of us get out of life unscathed. Some shit is worse than others, though."

She nodded. "Try something easy, then. Doesn't have to be a deep, dark secret."

I spent a moment thinking—and then our food came and I kept thinking on it while we dug in—her into a salad with chicken, avocado, berries, and shredded cheese, and me into a fat, juicy bacon cheeseburger, with fries.

She didn't say anything to me, but I caught an odd look on her face when she glanced at my food. I arched an eyebrow. "Okay, so let's trade. I'll tell you something nobody knows about me, and you tell me what that look was for."

She winced. "I'm sorry. That's my issue, not yours."

"I'm still interested in knowing what it was about and why."

She rolled a shoulder and nodded. "Okay. So… what's your fact?"

"My twin brother, God rest him, was always the

good one. I was the troublemaker, if you could believe it." I laughed, and smeared a fry in ketchup. "We were, oh…sixteen? Seventeen? Identical, too. Even our folks couldn't tell us apart if we were dressed the same. So, one day, Liam wrecked our truck. Wouldn't have been anything else to the story except he wasn't supposed to be out, because it was well past midnight, and he'd been drinking with…Lena. His… girlfriend—sort of. Anyway, they were out late, past curfew, drinking, and he wrecked the truck. I took the blame, said it was me, by myself, and Dad never knew Lena was involved at all."

She frowned in confusion. "Why would you do that? Take the blame like that?"

I shrugged. "Complicated."

Her eyes searching mine were sharp and penetrating. "Does it have to do with the way you hesitated over Lena's name?"

I scoffed. "You are a damn sight too smart, Liv."

She just smirked. "I think you think you're harder to read than you are." She hesitated. "So, you took the blame more for Lena than your brother."

I nodded. "Yeah. 'Course, I got somethin' out of it from Liam, you can bet. He had to do my chores for a week."

"What kind of chores did you guys have to do? Where did you grow up?"

"Grew up on a spread out near Ward Creek, not far from Ward Lake. Due north of here a ways."

"Oh. So you grew up in Alaska? Bill mentioned he knew your dad, didn't he? I'd forgotten."

"Yep, born and raised on that spread. It wasn't more'n a little log cabin in the woods, built by my great-grandpa. Dad was born there, Liam and I were born there." I paused to demolish half of my burger in a few bites. "Chores were chopping wood, checking the traplines, hunting, bringing in water from the creek. Things like that."

"Bill mentioned bringing you electricity?"

I nodded. "Yep. That'd be, oh...late fifties. Bill woulda been just a young fella, his dad and our dad helping Gramps. They had to run a trench, since there was no way to get posts into the ground through the brush. I don't even know how far they ran it, to be honest, I just know it was a hell of a job, but it got us lights and a radio."

"Did you have plumbing?"

"Hell nah," I said. "Outhouse and a well, babe. Old school."

"And...traplines?"

"We trapped for rabbits, foxes, coyotes, martens, otter, things like that. Fur and meat. We'd eat the meat and sell the fur down in town." I anticipated her next question. "Hunting was for subsistence, too. If we didn't bag a deer, we'd go hungry."

She tilted her head to one side, thinking. "Why did you live up here, off the grid like that?"

I shrugged. "Hell if I know. Gramps was in the Great War, Pops was in World War Two, and Liam and I only missed going to Vietnam because we lived way the fuck out in the boonies like we did, without a mailing address or birth certificates or nothing, so Uncle Sam didn't even know we existed to be able to draft us." I glance at the ceiling. "I know Great-Gramps had Gramps late in life. I think Great-Gramps fought in the Civil War."

She blinked. "Really?"

I nodded. "Yep. I mean, I was born in fifty-seven, and Pops was thirty-two when he had us—late as hell for that period of time. So Pops woulda been born in twenty-five. Figure Gramps was, what—twenty-two?—when he had Pops, and that would have meant Gramps had been born in 1898, or thereabouts? So Great-Gramps coulda fought in the Civil War and had a kid late in life. I know he lived to be over a hundred—he died in…oh god—fifty-five? Fifty-three? A couple years before I was born." I pause again, finishing the burger. "I think after the war ended, Great-Gramps was sorta just through with folks, wanted to be left alone. Then Gramps fought in the Great

War, and he had a similar feeling. Like, people suck, you know? You seen the worst humanity can do to itself, you just kinda wanna get shut of pretty much everyone. Pops, too. He was a grumpy, surly, mean old cuss, my pops. Teetotaler, and just plain ol' mean. Came back from fighting in Belgium with a heart full of hurt and anger and just...cold-bloodedness. So he didn't want to be around nobody neither. Which means Liam and I grew up half feral in the Alaskan wilderness—Mom passed on from some kinda cancer or somethin' when Liam and I were just little tykes, leavin' Pops and Gramps to raise us alone. I was huntin' squirrels when I was barely big enough to carry my own BB gun, and I could pop 'em through the eyeball from fifty yards with a .22 by the time I was six, and so could Liam. We ran through the woods wearing shit-all but boots and old shorts, giggin' frogs, bagging squirrels and deer."

She shakes her head. "I can't imagine that life."

"No?"

She shakes her head again, stabbing at her salad with her fork. "Not at all. I'm from the East Coast originally. Grew up in Connecticut, upper middle class as a kid, and then firmly upper class after Darren and I got married."

I looked her over again. "Rich kid, huh?"

She frowned. "I don't like that label. Yes, growing

up we had money, but I didn't get driven around in limousines or anything like that."

I laughed. "So just rich, instead'a super-rich?"

She frowned. "I can't tell if you're teasing me, or if you're serious and just being a jerk."

I huffed. "Eh, probably a little bit of both. Didn't mean to hurt your feelin's."

She rolled a shoulder as she chased the last few bits of salad around the plate. "You didn't hurt my feelings, more just…annoyed me. I mean, I literally just said I don't like being pigeonholed as a rich girl, and you went and did it again, just differently."

I winced. "Hey, now. I wasn't pigeonholing you as anything. People fit in boxes, Liv—loosely, at least. We ain't always the person in the box we fit in. I mean, sure, I'm a country redneck through and through. I'm more comfortable in a trailer in a holler than I am in an apartment in the city. I don't know shit about crap like Wi-Fi and computers and all that nonsense. I know woods and huntin', and trucks and I've eaten roadkill."

She squinted at me. "You have not."

I laughed. "Sure as hell have."

She made a grossed-out face. "You ate roadkill?"

I nodded—I had a feeling she was envisioning something a bit different than the truth, and decided to play with her a bit. "Yep. We was down to the last of our vittles, see. Nothin' in the pantry 'cept a couple cans of beans and some Spam. So, when Pa ran over a big ol' coon, he pulled over, tossed it in the back of the truck, and we took it home and threw it on the grill. Li'l bit of barbecue sauce? Tastes just like chicken, only mebbe a mite gamier."

She stared at me for a long moment. "You're pulling my leg."

I held a straight face. "Nope. Grilled up coon is actually pretty good."

She tilted her head to the side, glaring. "Lucas. Please, tell me you're kidding."

I couldn't hold back the laughter any longer. "Yeah, I'm just playing you." I arched an eyebrow. "Sort of."

"Sort of?" she asked, and then sipped at her iced tea.

"Well, it was when the triplets were just, oh god…nine? Ten? I was still comin' to grips with the fact that their mom wasn't coming back, and keeping food on the table was…challenging." Mostly that had been because I'd been spending most of my income on Evan Williams, but I wasn't quite ready to say that to Liv. "So, I was drivin' 'em home from the store. Sorta late, like just past sundown. A big ol' doe jumped out right in front of my truck. Smashed the hell out of my front end, too. Well, I went to check on her, see if she was dead. I mean, I ain't gonna leave a poor thing lyin' on the road suffering, you know? Turned out, she'd taken the worst of the impact to her head, smashed her brains to goo."

Liv shuddered, gagged. "Really? I hardly think graphic details are necessary."

I chuckled. "Sorry. Anyway, point is, it was only her head that got wrecked, rest of her was fine. So, I tossed her in the truck bed, took her home, cleaned her up, and we ate nice fresh venison for weeks." I grinned at her.

She rolled her eyes at me. "Well, that's not what I imagined when you said you've eaten roadkill."

I laughed again. "I know. I had a feeling you were imagining me scraping flattened squirrels off the road."

She laughed. "I was, I admit it."

"I've been desperate, but not that desperate. Close, a few times."

"Really?"

I nodded. "Yep. When I took off and left Alaska, I had twenty-six bucks to my name and half a tank of gas in a truck I didn't even really own myself. No food, and just the clothes on my back. I drove till I ran out of gas, found a fella a few miles down the road who needed some chores done, and got a fill-up out of it. Worked my way south that way—doin' chores and odd jobs in exchange for gas and maybe a bite to eat, or sometimes just cash. Things got real thin a few times. If it was a choice between putting miles between me and Alaska and eating, I'd often pick the miles. So, yeah. I've been hungry enough that I've thought of going back to grab roadkill to cook and eat."

Her gaze was speculative, interested. "I can honestly say I've never been that hungry."

I shrugged. "Lucky you. It ain't fun." I waved the topic away with a swipe of my hand. "Anyway. I think I've told you a bunch of stuff nobody knows. Your turn."

She sighed. "My turn."

"Yep. You gave me a look when I started eatin', and I'd like to know what it meant."

"I didn't mean it as a judgment on you, Lucas."

I tilted my head and squinted. "Liv, I may be country, but I ain't stupid. Tell the whole honest damn truth, at least."

She winced, rubbed her cheek. "Lucas…"

I arched an eyebrow. "Liv?"

A long sigh. "Fine. I told you my husband died of a heart attack." She paused, thinking. "It was avoidable. His doctor warned him he was at risk, and that he had to adjust his diet, but Darren wouldn't listen."

"So *this*—" I slapped my belly, "is a sore spot for you."

She nodded. "Yes. He…" She licked her lips, stared off to the side instead of at me. "We were active. We hiked, we did yoga, we rode horses, we took long walks around the neighborhood. I suppose he assumed—or, really, I know he assumed, as he said as much—that he was active and healthy, and he was going to enjoy his food."

"Only he wasn't as healthy as he thought."

She shook her head. "No. Clearly not." Her eyes were downcast, her shoulders hunched. "I did everything I could think of to get him to eat more healthily. Tried to sneak veggies into things, didn't buy certain things, bribed him, begged him. But he just had a weakness for certain kinds of food."

"Cheeseburgers?"

"Potato chips, too. Those were his real drug. He could eat a whole bag in one sitting, and not even think twice. It wasn't just one thing, though. It was a lifetime of consistently bad nutritional choices, along with a genetic predisposition. And staying fairly active just wasn't enough." Her eyes went to mine. "So seeing you eat something which I know contributed to Darren's death is just…hard. And yes, I gave you a look of disapproval, and it was judgmental, and I'm sorry."

I pushed my plate to one side, wrestling with unease—with truth. "Liv, the honest answer here is that you're right. You're right to look at me that way." I growled, tilted my head back to look at the ceiling. "I did have a heart attack, actually. Only barely survived it. I...well—I ain't a healthy man, Liv. That much is obvious. And I know I need to change things if I want to stay alive, but...honestly, there've been times lately when I just didn't necessarily see the point."

She reared back. "Lucas—"

I smiled at her. "I'm startin' to see the error of my ways, though." I winked. "Gorgeous women have a way of doin' that."

She blushed even as she rolled her eyes at me. "You just met me."

"Minds can change in a heartbeat, babe." I paid the check, and we headed out to Liv's truck. I settled into the passenger seat, and then continued when she was behind the wheel. "In all seriousness, though, I need to get healthy because I want to be around for my boys. And I got a whole pile of nephews to get to know, too."

"A pile of nephews?"

I nodded. "My brother had eight sons."

"Had? Past tense?"

I growled under my breath, and then sighed. "Long story."

"Seems like you have a lot of long stories."

"Like I said, my life ain't always been...pleasant,

or easy." I noticed, then, that we weren't heading back to my apartment. "Where are we going?"

"We're picking up the paint for your apartment, and supplies to start painting."

I blinked at that. "We are, huh?"

"Yep." She smiled. "I've got a great shade picked out."

I blinked again. Did I particularly want to paint? Not really. Did I want to spend more time Liv? Absolutely.

"Sounds good," I said.

FOUR

〜╬〜

Liv

LUCAS WAS... NOT GREAT AT PAINTING. I HAD PUT DOWN drop cloths, taped off around the windows and light switches and such, and had even borrowed painter's coveralls for both of us from a contractor friend of mine—mine were enormous on me, pooling around my ankles and wrists even after being rolled half a dozen times; his were too small by at least a full size, straining around his belly and those colossal shoulders of his.

He had paint on his cheeks, in his beard, on his nose, in his hair, all over his hands...very little was even getting on the walls. He was grumbling a non-stop stream of curses under his breath the entire time as he held a tray of paint in one hand, wielding a trimming paintbrush in the other. He was supposed to be doing around the painter's tape while I did the broad sections with the roller. Really, our jobs should be reversed, but it was just funny to watch him struggling with it, cursing and grumbling with such comical irritation.

"Piece o' shit fuckin' paint brush…goddamn stupid drippy-ass paint," he muttered, glopping way too much paint on the end of the brush, cursing again as it dripped down the brush and onto his wrist, and then onto his boots and the drop cloth.

He touched the brush to the wall beside the taped-off light switch, only to have the paint drip and roll down the wall.

"Motherfucker," he snarled.

I couldn't help it, at that point—I burst out laughing. "Oh my god, Lucas."

He glared at me. "Glad somebody's getting some enjoyment outta this shit," he snarled.

"You know, I'm not even going to apologize for laughing," I said. "You're just so darned funny. Such a grump."

"It's stupid, and I hate it. It's gettin' fuckin' everywhere 'cept where I want it to fuckin' go."

I set my roller aside and moved beside him. "Oh, Lucas."

I took the brush from him, and found myself standing perhaps just a tad closer than was strictly necessary; I could feel the broad warm sweep of his bicep against my arm, his hip bumping mine.

"Look, try it like this." I dipped the end of the paintbrush in the paint tray in his hand, dabbed the excess off, and carefully traced a line of paint around the outside of the light switch.

He frowned at me. "You make that look easier than it is."

"You just need a lighter touch."

"I don't have that."

I laughed. "Clearly." I watched as Lucas eyed the roller, with something like longing in his eyes. I held out as long as I could, and then I laughed again, enjoying his cranky discomfiture. "You are so easy to bait, you know that?"

He glared, but I could see a hint of humor wanting to creep out from under the grouchy exterior. "Whaddya mean?"

I gestured at the roller. "I meant for you to do the rolling, because I've always been better at the fine-tune sort of details, but you just grabbed the brush and started…painting, we'll call it. So I just let you go with it."

He looked at the wall where he'd been painting, and then at the area I'd done, and huffed a laugh. "Yeah,

you better do that trimming stuff. Gimme that roller."
He limped toward the roller where I'd set it on the floor,
rolled it through the tray, and then began applying the
pale green paint to the wall, taking up where I'd left off.

His limp seemed to come and go, which confused
me. I wanted to know more, but I knew I'd already
pushed him into talking during lunch, and wasn't sure
how much farther I could go.

He was just such a puzzle. By turns insightful and
obtuse, articulate and nearly incomprehensible, con-
fident nearly to the point of arrogant yet self-effacing.
He was simply an enormous human, standing at least
six feet four inches tall and weighing well over three
hundred pounds—yes, a certain portion of it was carried in his belly, but it was also breathtakingly clear
he was a massively powerful man. Or, at least, he had
been, and could be again.

He just needed to find the motivation to become
a little healthier.

I focused on painting, but mentally I was berat-
ing myself for getting sucked into this. I did not have
the emotional wherewithal to be his motivation. We
barely knew each other. I was a widow still trying to
make sense of my life without my husband. I had five
daughters who needed me—or at least, I liked to tell
myself they needed me, even if they didn't need me
on a daily basis like they once did.

Ugh.

I just couldn't afford to get hooked into things with Lucas—he was unhealthy, and by his own admission had suffered one nearly fatal heart attack, and yet seemed to show no signs of feeling the need to change anything.

More worrisome yet was his almost throwaway statement that for a long time he hadn't seen the point in trying to get healthy…meaning, he hadn't seen the point in trying to stay alive.

"I can almost hear you stewing, over there." Lucas spoke without pausing in his rhythmic application of roller to wall—he was tireless at this job, methodically covering far more of the wall in less time that I'd been able to. "You got shit on your mind, you may as well spit it out."

"You know, I don't know if I've heard you make a single statement in the entire time I've known you without at least one curse word included," I said, eyeing him sideways.

"I grew up surrounded by gruff old soldiers and woodsmen. I learned to swear when I learned to talk and walk and hunt and spit." He dipped, rolled. "Gettin' me to eat more salad and less cheeseburgers is one thing. Gettin' me to quit cursing? You got a better chance of puttin' me in a frilly pink tutu and dancin' ballet, and you can imagine how likely *that* shit is."

"Pick my battles, then, is what you're saying," I asked, grinning at him.

He snorted. "Yeah. Somethin' like that. 'Course, you ain't gotta pick nothin', if you know what I mean." He paused, letting the roller rest in the tray, eyeing me with interest. "So. What's on your mind, princess?"

"Princess?" I asked, with a wrinkle of my nose.

"No?"

I scoffed. "No."

"Darlin'?"

I nodded and lifted a shoulder. "I can live with that, if you must use such overly precious language."

"First I curse too much, now I use…whatever the hell you just said. Startin' to think maybe you don't like me for me, Liv."

I frowned at him, pausing with my brush at the edge of the tray. "Hey, now. I don't think that's quite fair. I can like you for you and not like every single element of your personality."

He tilted his head to one side. "I guess that makes sense." He went back to paint rolling. "So? What are you thinking about?"

"How likely I am to get you to tell me how you hurt your leg."

He didn't answer right away. "Told you, car accident."

I snorted. "Yeah, but I can't help thinking there's more to the story."

"Ain't there always?" he asked. "Nothing worth talking about."

I looked at him for a moment, and then nodded. "If you say so."

He was focused on the wall, on the paint, on anything but me. "It's really not a very interesting story. Pullin' a trailer behind my truck. Lost control, rolled it into a ditch. Totaled the truck, the trailer, and damn near myself. Broke my left leg and right arm—arm healed fine, leg hasn't."

I still sensed there was something he wasn't saying. But I could tell by his stiff posture and the way he avoided my eyes that whatever it was he wasn't saying, I wasn't getting it out of him just yet.

And really, how much did I want to know? Why did I feel such a strange, powerful compulsion to know more about him? He was bad news. Bluff, coarse, and unhealthy. Everything I didn't want or need in my life.

Yet here I am, in his house, helping him paint. Unable to stop thinking about him, or wondering what he is hiding.

"Eight nephews, huh?" I asked instead.

He sighed. "You are a curious woman, ain'tcha?"

I laughed. "I sure am."

"Yeah. Eight nephews. I was estranged from my

brother. We, uh…well, we had a falling out and he died before we could patch things. He and his wife had eight boys—Sebastian, Zane, Brock, Baxter, Canaan and Corin, identical twins, Lucian, and Xavier."

I blinked, frowning. "Those names sound familiar, for some reason."

He chuckled. "I imagine so. They've become what you might call local celebrities. They own a bar here in town, and co-own another with one of my boys, Roman. My other son has a tattoo parlor he runs with his fiancée and her cousin."

"And the third triplet? What does he do?"

"He's a wilderness guide. Runs hikes, hunts, fishing expeditions, shit like that, except he guides people interested in going way out where you gotta really know your wilderness survival to get in and out. The kinds of hunts where you get flown by seaplane into a remote lake, hike out into the forest, pitch a tent, and hike out to hunt, and then hike back to camp with your kill."

"Wow." I made a surprised face. "That's…very manly."

He cackled. "Yeah, my boys don't exactly lack in testosterone, that's for sure."

I paused in my painting. "What's that mean?"

He gestured at himself. "Picture me, thirty years younger, without the decades of bad food and…other stuff, and a serious dedication to fitness and weight lifting and such, plus just plain ol' good genetics. Their ma was a fine-lookin' woman, just didn't have a fuckin' soul to go with it. And, believe it or not, I didn't use to be s'damn soft and fat myself. You've had the misfortune of meetin' me well past my prime, you might say."

I snorted. "You need to be nicer to yourself, Lucas." I went back to painting, focusing now on going around the baseboard molding. "Your sons sound impressive."

"They are. Spent over ten years fighting wildfires, first as forest service regulars, then as Hotshots, and then as Smokejumpers. Then they…retired, and moved up here to try their hands at other stuff."

"From what I hear, those wildfire fighters have to be in peak physical condition all the time."

"Absolutely. My boys could hike eighty-pound backpacks up a mountain at damn near a run, get into their gear, fight a fire, and hike back out. Then they became Smokejumpers, which means they jumped out of an airplane as close to a wildfire as they could get, hike into it, and fight it without any hope of backup, using only the equipment they jumped in with."

"Sounds frightening."

"They like livin' on the edge." He sighed. "Comes from the way they grew up, though."

"And how's that?"

"Sorta the way I grew up—half wild. Or, maybe more wild than not. Their mom left and I didn't have a single damn clue what the fuck to do with three maniac boys, and I don't think I did a very good job of what I did do. They spent more time running wild than they did at home or in school. They were the terrors of the county, I'll tell you. They weren't bullies as far as I know, just…hellions. Trouble with a big ol' capital T." He sighed. "I think they joined the forest service to get away from me and from Oklahoma, if you want the truth."

"I think you're being too hard on yourself. All children seem desperate to get away from their parents, I think. They feel the drive to figure life out for themselves, do things their way, on their own."

He was silent a long time. "Yeah, you may be right."

"You don't sound convinced."

He shrugged, and then set the roller down to stand in the middle of the living room, examining our handiwork: we'd managed to get his whole living room and kitchen done. "I like it."

I smiled. "You do?"

He turned in a slow circle, pivoting on his good leg. "Yeah, I do. It's peaceful. Quieting." He glanced at me with a grin. "But not girly."

I grinned back. "Well, good. I'm glad to know I haven't lost my touch."

His gaze sharpened, grin going wolfish. "No risk of that, I don't think."

I blushed, hearing the sly innuendo in his tone and the look on his face. "Lucas."

He chuckled. "What? I'm saying you've got a good eye for color."

I snorted. "Yeah, that's exactly what you were saying."

"If you heard somethin' else, well…that's on you—your interpretation of it."

Ohhh, is that how it was going to be? Two could play at that game.

I pretended to feel an ache in my back, setting my brush and tray down, intentionally facing away from him as I bent over. Then, slowly, luxuriously, I stretched, bringing my arms over my head, palms up in a basic yoga stretch, leaning backward and then forward again, this time bending at the waist.

I heard Lucas cough, then I straightened and turned to see him suddenly and busily rolling the excess paint off the roller.

"What?" I asked. "Something wrong? Tickle in your throat?" I had to fight back a grin at the discomfited expression on his face.

He glared at me. "You did that on purpose."

"Did what on purpose?"

"That business." He waved a paint-splattered hand at me. "You know what I mean."

I endeavored to look clueless. "I do not."

He snorted, dropped the handle of the paint roller. And then bent over at the waist to retrieve it, sticking his butt out. "Ohh, well, excuse me," he said in a high-pitched, breathy voice. "I just…dropped this. Let me just pick it up."

I couldn't help cackling at him. "I have never in my life said or done anything even remotely like that. Nor do I sound like that."

"You're tellin' me that's just how you stretch."

"Yes."

"Bullshit."

"It is not!" I protested, lying through my teeth. "I was just innocently stretching the…*kinks*…out of my back. If you saw something else, that's on you."

His turn to laugh, then. "Oh, I see. Payback, is it?"

I put on an arch, haughty expression. "I have no idea what you mean."

He had the paint tray in his hands and was crouched, somewhat stiffly and awkwardly, prying the lid off the paint can. With only the briefest pause, he glanced up at me, smirked, and then dipped his fingers in the paint and flicked them at me. Since I was standing only a few feet away, I got splattered all over the face with paint.

"Lucas Badd! I do *not* think so!" I snapped, irate since I now had paint in my hair.

"Oops." He grinned at me, taunting me to retaliate.

I still had my paintbrush in hand—I whipped it in his direction, sending paint splattering him. He roared a laugh, staggering to his feet as I chased him, flicking paint at him until he was even more splattered with droplets and gobs of pale green than I was. Abruptly, he stopped trying to get away from me, pivoted, and his mammoth hand closed around my small, delicate wrist—and just like that I was face to face with all those inches of brawny, bearish brute strength, his deep brown eyes piercing, his scent enveloping me. His hand was warm and rough and implacable around mine, unbreakable and brutally strong, yet still gentle. He firmly and easily plucked the paintbrush from me, and with a hot slow grin, dabbed me on the nose with it. The bristles were rough and ticklish and wet, the paint cold and sticky.

I grabbed his hand and tried to stop him, but it was like trying to stop a hydraulic machine. "Lucas, do *not* get so much as another speck of paint on me, I swear—"

He just grinned, and brought the brush straight

down my chin, my throat, and my breastbone to where the coveralls zipped up. "Oops."

"Oops?" I wrenched free of him—meaning, he let me. I stomped over to the paint tray, which I hadn't yet emptied back into the paint can, and before he could stop me, upended it over his head. "Oops."

Pale green paint glopped thick into his hair, dribbled down his ears and the back of his neck and onto his shoulders.

He just stood for a moment, staring at me in disbelief. "Wow. You really go from zero to a hundred in nothin' flat, don't you?"

"I *told* you not to," I said, my voice prim and arch.

The paint had glopped down his chest and arms and all over his torso, and when another mischievous grin slid across his paint-coated face, I backed away from him.

"Oh no you don't!" I snapped. "Lucas, do not—"

He did.

He grabbed me, wrapped me up in his long arms like iron bands, hauled me inexorably toward himself and, ignoring my breathless pleas, smeared pale green paint all over me—rubbing his cheek against mine, his forehead against mine, until I was almost as paint-smeared as he was.

I gasped in shocked disbelief…and something else fluttered low in my belly, indicating that I didn't at all mind his proximity, or the way his arms enveloped me and his heat pressed against me. I didn't mind at all. Despite being covered in paint, I was grinning, laughing breathlessly. I dragged a fingertip through the paint coating his cheekbone.

"I think we better call a truce," I whispered.

"Yeah?" His voice was a deep, quiet rumble that shivered through me. "Not sure who won."

"Me neither."

He let me go and backed away, scraping paint away from his eyes. "You oughta rinse off here. I imagine your place is a mite nicer than mine, so getting paint in my bathroom ain't no big deal."

I thought of trying to clean off enough to even get into my truck without ruining the upholstery, much less tracking a mess through my nice clean condo with the teak-stained bamboo floors and exposed brick walls. I winced at the very thought.

"I think I agree." I tried to clean paint away from my eyes and mouth, but really only succeeded in smearing it even worse. "If you don't mind."

He harrumphed. "Wouldn't'a offered if I minded."

I narrowed my eyes at him. "You're not going to make this a…a *thing*, are you?"

He arched an eyebrow, although it was hard to tell that's what he was doing through the thick layer of green paint. "I do declare, Miss Goode," he said in a thick, syrupy exaggeration of his southern accent, making "declare" sound like *dih-clayah*, "I haven't the slightest notion what you might mean by that statement."

I laughed. "Of course you don't, Mr. Badd. You are the very picture of gentlemanly innocence."

"In all seriousness, Liv, go ahead and rinse off. I'll stay right here and clean up this mess."

I felt my heart thumping like a snare drum. "I'll be quick."

He waved a hand. "Don't worry about it. I got nowhere else to be and nothing else to do, so take your time."

"But you'll need to rinse off too, so I don't want to use all the hot water."

His eyes fixed on mine. "Don't worry about that, Liv." Under his breath, then: "I might just need a cold shower anyway."

I almost didn't hear him say it. And combined with the way his eyes fixed on mine, then flicked down and back up…

I was covered in paint and wearing baggy coveralls, and he couldn't take his eyes off me.

It felt good.

Too good.

I shouldn't enjoy the way he looked at me—I

didn't have the heart space for a man larger than life like Lucas Badd.

I smiled at him once more, a little shyly, a little hesitantly, trying to keep my thoughts off my face, and then headed for his bathroom. I closed and locked the door, and then stripped out of my coveralls, turning them inside out as I took them off, to keep the paint on them rather than anywhere else, and then washed the worst of the paint off my hands.

I felt oddly reticent to strip the rest of the way— this wasn't my bathroom, and Lucas was right outside—I could hear him moving around, humming gruffly under his breath. I knew he couldn't see me, and that he wouldn't do anything anyway. But still.

Being naked in the same apartment as him made me feel…odd. Not quite uncomfortable, but…

Gahhh, I don't know how it made me feel.

A lot of different things.

I swallowed the nerves and stripped out of my clothes, carefully removing my shirt so I didn't get paint on it.

Eventually, I had my clothing set aside and the water running hot—it took quite a few rounds of scrubbing and rinsing with soap and washcloth, but I got the paint off my skin—getting it out of my hair took a bit more work, and without my organic, hand-crafted shampoo and conditioner my hair felt like straw, but at least it was clean.

Problem was, I couldn't abide dressing in a steam-clouded bathroom—my clothes would stick to my skin and be all damp and gross. God, no.

Which meant wrapping around myself in the too-small, threadbare towel that was all he had clean under the vanity, opening the bathroom door, and carrying my clothes out of the bathroom.

And enduring both his gaze and my own crazily pounding heart as I paused in the hallway, clad in nothing but a towel.

God, what was this life I'm suddenly living?

And why, oh why was it so damned impossible to stop myself from liking this complicated mess of a man?

FIVE

Lucas

HOLY FUCKING SHIT ON A CRACKER.

  I wasn't sure my ol' ticker could take the sight of Olivia Goode in nothing but a damn towel. Her raven's wing black hair was wet and slicked back away from her beautiful, angular face, leaving her wide dark eyes to pierce and mesmerize me.

  The only towel I had clean was a tiny little old thing I couldn't even get around my waist—on her, it just barely wrapped around her torso under her armpits, and only just barely hung to mid-thigh. Even then, there were teasing, tantalizing gaps between the edges of the towel. She, smartly, had wrapped it around herself so those gaps were at her side rather than in front. But god, lord, help me Jesus—she was so fuckin' gorgeous. Long, strong, tanned legs, shapely and curvy and toned and damn near endless. Just the teeniest hint of cleavage under the top edge of the towel. Just enough to make me look twice and wish I could see more, and then curse myself for an asshole for wishing it.

She was my friend, and she was helping me. She was a widow, and fairly recently, too. This wasn't a thing. I wasn't gettin' nothing outta this except some company…and a nicely decorated condo—I kept calling it an apartment, but it was actually a condo; I had purchased it once I'd decided I really did have no choice but to move back to Ketchikan after all these years, and my retirement from the manufacturing plant in Oklahoma where I'd worked for forty years was paying for it. The job at the hardware store was just for extra spending cash, to stretch the retirement package out a bit further.

I couldn't stop looking at Liv, and she seemed frozen, rooted to the floor in the middle of the hallway, her eyes on me. I couldn't read her expression.

"Don't look at me like that, Lucas," she murmured.

"Like what, Liv?"

"Like…" She swallowed hard. "Like I'm something you…"

"Like I can't take my eyes off you?" I suggested.

She nodded. "Like you're thinking things I'm not sure I should know about."

My feet carried me across the living room, into the hallway. I stared down at her, meeting her large, expressive eyes—this close, I could see flecks of gold and streaks and gray and even hints of forest green. She wiped her palms on the front of the towel, licked her lips.

"Sweetheart, you're standin' in my hallway, wearing nothin' but a tiny little towel, dripping wet, lookin' like temptation on two sexy legs." I felt a streak of boldness rifle through my veins, and my hand lifted, seemingly by itself, to brush a thick lock of inky black hair behind her ear. "If you can't imagine what I might be thinkin', then I ain't quite sure how you managed to have five kids."

She bit her lip, tensing all over. "Lucas, I…"

"You what, babe?"

She lifted a shoulder in a tiny, demure, unsure gesture. "I said *shouldn't*, not…*can't.*"

"Why shouldn't you?"

I saw her swallow. "Lots of reasons."

I wasn't sure why I was pressing this, but I couldn't stop. "Like what? List one or two."

She stared up at me, eyes wide and unreadable, chest swelling with slow, deep breaths. "I…" She shook her head, and turned away. "I'm going to dress in your room, okay?

I nodded. "Sure thing."

I watched her go into my bedroom and toss her pile of clothes onto my bed—which was unmade as usual. She glanced at me through the still-open door, and then smiled small and quick before closing it.

I turned away, rubbing the back of my neck, wondering how I was going to dry off, seeing as Liv had my only clean towel. I had one I'd used for my last shower in the hamper in my room, I remembered, and turned back to my bedroom door, intending to ask if I could grab it before she started dressing.

I'd forgotten one small detail: my bedroom door didn't latch quite properly unless you pushed on it, and it had a tendency to slip open a few inches on quiet hinges.

When I turned to the door, it had swung open a few inches. And, in that moment, I caught an accidental, forbidden glimpse of Heaven.

Liv, caught in the act of having just dropped the towel, facing the cracked-open door. The towel was still settling on the floor, and her eyes flew open. It was a split second only, but it was enough. She gasped, one hand moving to cover her sex, the other arm crossing over her chest.

An instant, a split-second. I didn't hesitate, didn't

take a moment to appreciate what I was seeing—I ain't that much of a bastard. I turned around, saw her through the crack, and turned right back around.

"Shit, shit, shit," I snapped. "Sorry—I'm sorry. Forgot to tell you that you have to push to get the door to latch. I live alone and don't usually bother, so I forgot."

I heard the door click closed, latching. "It's fine," she said, her voice oddly flat. "It was an accident."

"Liv, I only—"

She cut in. "Don't, Lucas. We both know you got an eyeful."

I wasn't sure what to say. "It wasn't on purpose, Liv. I hope you know that."

"I know."

My brain was spinning, the image of her as I'd seen her emblazoned onto my mind. I went into the bathroom, closed the door, stripped out of my paint-covered coveralls and the clothing beneath it, and got into the shower.

I did my best to make quick work of getting clean, and to keep my thoughts away from Liv, but it was a losing battle.

God, she was fit. So sleek, slender. Like a gazelle, all long slender limbs, and a tiny torso. Her breasts were, as I'd surmised when I first saw her, small but plump, firm and round and perky despite being nearly fifty and having had five children.

"Goddammit," I growled, trying desperately to keep that vision of her out of my head—to keep my libido from taking over.

It was difficult enough telling myself we were just friends, were never going to be anything but just friends—the last thing I needed was to let my stupid lonely horny male brain sexualize a perfectly good friendship.

I'd scrubbed my hair, face, and beard as clean as they could get and got out before I gave in to the temptation to fix my situation myself.

The only towel left in the bathroom was a hand towel, so that's what I used to dry myself as well as possible, and then peeked my head out the door. "Liv?"

She was dressed and wandering around, using the towel to rub her hair dry. "Yeah?"

"Gotta run across to my room," I said.

She gestured with the towel in her hand. "Was this your only towel?"

I grinned at her, just my head sticking out of the door. "Only one clean, yeah. Ain't done laundry yet."

She grimaced. "So you don't have a towel.

"Well, I dried off with the hand towel." I laughed. "Hell of a lot of real estate for that little thing, but it worked all right. I just need to pop across to my room and get some clothes on." I couldn't help teasing her, just to try to lighten the tension I felt between us. "Unless you're interested in trading a peek for a peek."

She blushed furiously, mouth opening and closing as if trying to come up with a response to that, and couldn't. After a moment, she just turned away and headed into the kitchen, still dabbing and squeezing sections of hair in the towel.

Once she was out of sight, I bolted across the hallway and into my room—and remembered to make sure the door latched. Dressed, I reemerged from my room and found Liv at my kitchen table, reading something on her smartphone, a pinched expression on her face.

"What's up?" I asked. "You look like you bit into a lemon."

She lifted her phone in gesture. "Email from my youngest daughter, Poppy."

"Not a good one?"

She tipped her head side to side. "Well, it's tricky with her. She's not sure what she wants, or that she's happy where she is, but she's not sure what to do about it."

I sighed. "That is tricky. I never had to worry about that—my boys were laser-focused on graduating high school and getting to California to work for the forest service. I think they wanted to get out of Oklahoma so bad that it actually kept 'em out of any real trouble."

She set the phone down and glanced up at me. "Lucas, I…"

I held up a hand. "I'm sorry, Liv. It was an accident. I forgot that door doesn't latch. I should'a told you. I may not be the most chivalrous or sophisticated fella in the world, but I'd never do anything like that on purpose." I shrugged. "If a woman wants me to see her naked, I won't have to manufacture an accident."

She smiled faintly. "That is true."

I tried to stop the next words from tumbling out of my mouth, but couldn't. "It was an accident, but I ain't gonna pretend I didn't see nothin'…and that I didn't appreciate what I saw."

Her blush deepened, and she shifted in her chair. "Lucas, I…I honestly don't know how to respond to that."

"Don't need to."

Her eyes flicked up to mine, taking me in as if for the first time. "Do you happen to have a brush? Or even a comb?"

I nodded. "I think I have a comb somewhere. No brush, though."

She smiled—that sweet, innocent, unassuming

smile that shot straight to my gut every single time. "I just need to get the worst of the tangles out of my hair." Her smile turned teasing. "You could probably stand to use it yourself."

When I went into the steamy bathroom to get the comb, I glanced in the mirror and chuckled—my hair was a wild mess, sticking up in every direction, shaggy and unkempt at best, and my beard wasn't any better. In fact, this was one of the few times I've even looked at myself in the mirror in recent memory, I realized I didn't like what I saw…at all.

Probably why I avoided the mirror, because I knew I wouldn't, but now, with Liv out there, I suddenly gave a shit about how I appeared…and I knew I was long, long past having let myself go.

I ran the comb through my hair and beard, slicking back the bushy mess of thick gray-brown as well as was possible. Didn't make much difference, though—I was still a fat, unkempt, gimp-legged old alcoholic with a bad heart and a worse past.

I growled to myself and hobbled out of the bathroom, bringing the comb to Liv. She drew the comb slowly through her glossy, short black hair—not a trace of gray anywhere; she did so absentmindedly, rereading the email from her daughter.

"What would you do, Lucas?" she asked.

I scoffed. "You're askin' *me*?" I shook my head

slowly. "I sure as hell ain't one to be givin' no parenting advice, Olivia. The fact that none of my sons are drug addicts, criminals, in jail, or dead don't have a single goddamn thing to do with me. They made good in spite of me, not because of me."

Her expression reflected sadness. "You are far too hard on yourself."

I snarled. "Ain't hard enough, babe. You don't know the half of it."

"Did you beat them?" she asked, her gaze frank, her tone unapologetic.

"No. God, no." I paused. "They got brought into this world and then were abandoned by their mother. Even at my worst, I knew they didn't deserve the life they had…" I swallowed hard. "I didn't do right by them, I neglected 'em, didn't know how to…how to love 'em, how to show 'em I loved 'em. But I never hit 'em. Not once."

"Then you can't—"

"Being able to say I didn't beat my boys ain't exactly an absolution for my sins as a father, Liv. It just means I wasn't a total monster."

"You're not a monster, Lucas," she whispered.

I gazed at her levelly. "I just wish I was the man you seem to think you see when you look at me."

"How do you know what I see when I look at you?"

I shrugged. "I don't. But the fact that you can look at me at all tells me it's probably best I ain't shared some of the shit I done."

"We are all flawed, Lucas. I am far, far from perfect—as a wife, as a mother, as a woman."

I laughed. "Good thing I ain't about to tell you about the worst moments of our lives. You'd run screaming for the hills, sweetheart, and that's a fact."

"You don't know what would send me running," she said, lifting her chin. "Perhaps I'm neither as weak-minded nor judgmental as you seem to think."

"Now hold on a goddamn second. I don't think you're either of those."

"Then quit trying to hide your past from me."

"Why? You really want to know?"

"Answer me a couple questions, and then we'll see."

I shrugged. "Okay, shoot."

"Have you ever killed anyone?"

I sighed, sort of laughing but not quite. "No. Thinkin' back on some of the bar fights I was in back in my younger days, it's a wonder I can say that. But no."

"Have you ever raped a woman, or done anything without express consent?" Her gaze was razor sharp, watching for the least sign of evasion or untruth.

"*Fuck* no. I want a woman to want me her own

self. I sure as fuck ain't some knight in shining armor, but I can say I taught my sons the value of a woman. Mainly 'cause they never had one in their lives that was worth a damn, but I did teach 'em to get the yes instead'a taking what they want."

"You already said you never beat them," she continued. "So that answers the big questions."

I cackled bitterly. "Liv, if your standards are so low that having never killed anyone, raped anyone, or beaten children is all it takes, then you need new fuckin' standards."

"That's *not* what I meant," she snapped. "Those aren't my standards—not in the way you mean. I only asked that much because if you were able to say yes to any of them, I would say perhaps we shouldn't be friends. You seem to think the worst of yourself, which is an odd juxtaposition for a man with as much bluster and brawn as you have." Her eyes and her voice both softened. "But I think you're not giving yourself enough credit." Her phone buzzed, and she glanced at it. "I have to go. My daughter wants to talk."

"Listen, I appreciate you helpin' me paint." I glanced around the room, now brightened and softened, soothing yet still somehow masculine. "I really did have a good time today."

"You never answered my question."

"Which one?"

"What would you do? About Poppy."

"I don't know the situation."

"Well, the short version is that she is an artist, living in New York attending Columbia, studying for a degree in art history. But she's coming to realize she hates the city, hates the degree she's studying for, but she's too stubborn to give up. She got an amazing scholarship to one of the best universities in the world, and she's spent over a year working toward the degree. But she says her circle of friends are...well, not very good friends, and she has no time to do the one thing she really loves, which is make art. And she wants me to tell her what to do so she doesn't have to make the decision, but...as her mother, I'm just torn. If I tell her what to do, I'm worried she won't learn anything from the experience and will rely on me, or maybe even blame me if she ends up doing the wrong thing. But I don't want her to suffer or to waste precious time chasing something she doesn't want and won't use in life." She sighed, rubbing her cheeks with both hands. "Plus, I'm worried if she leaves Columbia, she'll move back in with me and never leave. Not that I don't love my daughter and want to spend as much time with her as possible, but...she has to make it on her own. And I'm just torn." Her eyes searched my face. "So. What would you do?"

I mulled it over a moment or two. "I'd tell her a

degree, even from someplace like Columbia, is only worth what you make it worth. If you're doin' somethin' you hate, that degree ain't nothin' but toilet paper, and you may as well wipe your ass with it. If she decides to leave, and needs to get back on her feet, give her a few months to figure her shit out. I'd let her come home, but only temporarily. Don't let her get too comfortable. You're her mama, not her best friend, so in the end you gotta give her the straight hard truth—that sometimes, you gotta waste time in order to realize that's what you're doin', that there's somethin' else you want more. And then you gotta want it bad enough to do what it takes to go get it."

"Wise words." She smiled at me. "Thank you."

I waved a hand. "You'd have done that regardless. You love your girl, and you're a good mama."

"I feel like a bad mama for thinking how I just really hope she doesn't end up living with me again. I mean, if she needs to, I'll let her, but after twenty-odd years of raising the five of them and taking care of my husband and all that, I must say, it has been rather nice only having myself to care for." Her expression darkened. "I don't mean that."

"Hey, it's okay to mean it."

"They weren't a burden, and that's how I made it sound."

"No, you didn't. You dedicated your life to

caring for your family. Now you have yourself to take care of. Don't mean you didn't care about them, love them, and do what you did happily."

"You can see the best in me, but not yourself."

I wasn't falling for that bait. "Just listen to her, Liv. She'll come to the right conclusion eventually. She may fuck up along the way, but that's life, and she's gotta learn that one way or another."

"I can't protect her from getting hurt or screwing up, is what you're saying."

I nodded. "Basically. And that you ain't gonna do her any favors by trying, even though it may seem like it."

She stood up, fiddling with her phone before stuffing it into her purse, which she slung over a shoulder. "I enjoyed today." She smiled up at me. "Tomorrow, we go furniture shopping."

"For what?" I asked. "I got a couch to sit on, a bed to sleep in, and a table to eat at. What else do I need?"

She laughed, that merry tinkle of amusement sounded so much like a bell, like music. "Spoken like a man."

I snorted. "Well, I am one, so…"

She smirked, her eyes raking over me almost as if she liked what she saw. "I've noticed. Believe me."

She seemed to falter, leaning forward as if to

embrace me and then thinking better of it. "I…well. Tomorrow?"

I wanted to hug her, hold her. See if her skin was as soft as it looked, if she smelled as sweet as I thought, if she would fit in my arms as neatly as I imagined.

"Yeah," I said, shoving my hands into my pockets. "Tomorrow. Furniture I don't need."

She hesitated, eyes flicking back and forth as she gazed into mine, looking for…something. I wasn't sure what. And then, perhaps seeing whatever she was looking for, she did lean forward. Into me. Her hands flattened against the backs of my shoulders, her arms stretching to reach around me. Her head fit under my chin, her small but taut frame pressing against mine; my hands splayed over her shoulders, and my hands had never felt so big, so unwieldy.

She was that soft—that sweet smelling. More. I was dizzy, holding her like this. Smelling her, inhaling her scent. Her breasts were hard round bumps pressed against my chest, and I fought the erection I felt growing. This was not that—this was a hug between friends, and nothing else.

She didn't want that—not with me. She couldn't, and shouldn't.

She was the first to back away, and I dropped my hands to my sides—I suddenly didn't know what to do with them.

"Bye," she whispered.

"See you tomorrow." I watched her walk out the door of my condo, then went to the front window and watched her get into her truck. She slid behind the wheel, started the engine, settled her phone into a holder thing, and backed out; I saw her mouth moving as she reversed, and I knew she was talking to Poppy, her youngest daughter.

I wondered if she would mention me, and then wondered why I should care if she did.

Once she was gone, I made a spur of the moment decision, and my first action was to call Roman. I had to dig the ancient flip phone I kept around for emergencies out of the drawer in the kitchen, powered it on, and dialed Roman.

"Hello? Dad, that you?"

"Yep."

"I didn't know you had a phone."

"It's the oldest damn thing you ever saw, and I only use it for emergencies."

"You have an emergency?" I heard his voice go wary, worried.

"Nothing like that, Rome. I'm fine, everything is fine. I just…I need your help."

"With what?" Still wary.

I sighed. "It's a long story. Come get me. I hate talking on this fuckin' thing."

Roman laughed. "Me too. That's why we text, Pops."

"Text? What kind of text?"

He laughed again, harder. "Text messages, Dad."

"Heard of 'em, don't know what the hell they are, though."

"You really are a fuckin' dinosaur, aren't you?" Roman laughed. "We gotta get you a real phone, teach you to text."

"One thing at a time, kiddo."

"What's that mean?" he asked.

I growled. "Just get your ass over here, okay?"

"All right, all right," he grumbled. "Don't get your rumples in a stiltskin."

"The fuck is that supposed to mean?"

"Nothin'. Just means keep your shirt on. I'll be there in ten."

True to his word, Roman was stomping down the hall to my apartment in ten minutes. He let himself into my apartment and stopped dead in his tracks.

"Holy fuck, Dad, you actually painted." He stared around at the green walls, the drop cloth still on the floor, my meager furniture—couch, TV, third-hand TV stand—clustered in the middle of the room. "Green?"

I shrugged. "It's a nice shade. It's called like palm frond verbena or some shit."

He stared hard at me. "You drinkin' again, old man?"

I was tempted to whip something at his thick skull, but I didn't. It was a fair question, after all. "No," I groused.

He blinked at me. "You combed your hair and your beard. You painted. And you're walking around without that cane you hate." A slow, shit-eating grin spread across his face. "You got a girlfriend."

"Roman, do *not* fuck with me on this, okay?" I gave him as close to a pleading look as I was capable of bestowing. "Please?"

"But there is a woman."

"You know anything else on this fuckin' planet that could make me ask my own son for fuckin' help?"

He grinned. "Nope." The grin faded, and he eyed me carefully. "So. What's up, Dad? No more jokes, I promise."

I sighed. "I just...I..." I growled, raked my hand through my hair. "I'm a fuckin' mess, Rome."

Roman wrinkled his nose. "You gotta crack a window, Pops. The paint fumes are making me dizzy." He gestured at the door. "Let's go grab a coffee and talk, all right?"

I nodded, hobbling across the room to crack open a window, and then followed Roman out to his truck.

"I hate not being able to drive," I grumbled. "Fuckin' sucks."

Roman clearly wanted to say something, but figured anything he would say would end up sounding snarky, so he just shrugged. "I bet it does," he said eventually.

I rubbed my jaw. "You don't have to tiptoe around my feelings, Rome. Say what you mean. I figure I've earned it."

He glanced at me side eye. "She's got you in a twist, don't she?"

I tilted my head backward and snarled. "Yes, she fuckin' does."

He chuckled. "Women."

I huffed. "Women," I agreed.

We pulled into a parking spot on the street and went into a small coffee shop—I sat down at Rome's insistence, and he brought two huge white porcelain mugs full of black coffee.

"So," he said. "What d'you need help with?"

"This," I said, patting my bad leg. "And this," I said, patting my stomach.

Roman grinned. "I can do that."

"I know you can. That's why I asked, dumbass," I said with a grin, making my insult affectionate.

"So, before we work on your gut, we gotta get your leg back to full strength." He hesitated. "You probably also oughta think about making some changes to the way you eat." He said this warily, because he knew, in ages past, that I'd have snapped like a wounded bear if he had brought up the idea of dieting. "I know you don't like to—"

"Rome, don't." I sipped my coffee, and took a moment to think before I spoke. "Being in Ketchikan is fuckin' hard, okay? Seeing you and your brothers here is hard, because the three of you are spitting images of me when I was in my prime, except you three are blond like your bitch of a mother…" I trailed off with a sigh. "Another thing I probably oughta address, is letting go of my hatred of that woman. Anyway. Being here is sorta forcing me to…face things. Like how bad I've let myself get. And then this friendship with Liv? Man, nothing'll force you to take a long hard look at the man in the mirror like a good woman."

"Is she?" Roman asked. "Good?"

I nodded. "Too good." I cackled. "Too Goode."

Roman frowned. "What's so funny?"

"Her name is Goode," I answered. "With an 'E' on the end. Olivia Goode."

"She painted your apartment for you, huh?" Roman surmised.

"Nah, we both did it."

His eyebrows lifted. "Oh *really*?" he drawled. "Painting rooms together already?"

I glared. "I told you not to fuck with me and I meant it, punk."

Roman held up both hands. "Okay, okay, I'm sorry." He tilted his head, staring at me hard. "You said 'friendship.'"

I nodded. "Yep. That's what it is. A friendship."

Roman's eyes narrowed. "Friendship, huh? With a woman?"

I shrugged. "I know. But there it is."

"In my experience, if there's a woman in your life you consider a friend, you're thinking of something else. At least a little bit, even if you're trying not to." Roman lifted a hand palm up. "But what do I know?"

I growled. "She's classy, beautiful—upper-class East Coast transplant. Fashionable, smart, successful. A good parent, and a good person."

Roman saw through me. "And you don't think you're in the same league as her."

I shifted uncomfortably. "This is a weird conversation to have with my son."

He leaned forward across the table. "You know, we don't have to be just father and son, Dad. We can be friends."

I cleared my throat gruffly, coughed, growled. "I weren't no—I wasn't any good as a father when you guys were growing up. Maybe…maybe I could do better as a friend, now that you're grown."

Roman sat back, grinning broadly. "I haven't met her yet, but I think I already like this Olivia of yours."

I arched an eyebrow. "You don't know how to quit, do you?"

He just laughed. "Nope. Learned that from the best."

I couldn't help laughing at that. "Can't deny that."

Roman slugged back his coffee. "So. Step one, strengthen that knee of yours. You've been favoring it and hobbling around for long enough. Step two, eat better—no sugar, no refined carbs, and no more than one cheeseburger a week." He was well acquainted with my weakness for burgers—I nearly burned down the trailer more than once in his childhood, trying to fry burgers on the stove while sauced out of my mind. "Step three, start lifting."

I frowned at him. "I just want to get rid of the gut, not bulk up."

Roman waved my protest away. "Best way to cut fat is to lift heavy. You could run around for fuckin' days without stopping and you'd never really make much progress. Lift heavy, keep the rest times short, and eat right. You'll be back in peak shape in no time."

"You make it sound easy."

He laughed. "Easy, no. Simple, yes." He jutted his chin at my coffee. "Drink up, old man. We start now. I'm taking you grocery shopping."

"If you fill my fridge with lettuce, I'm disowning you."

Roman just cackled. "Do I look like a fuckin' bunny rabbit to you, Dad?" He gestured at the massive, impressively muscled shoulders and arms. "You don't get a body like this eating lettuce. Although, more salad is a good idea. But, no, not all salad. Just… better food. Real food. Lean meat like turkey and chicken, brown rice, salmon, sweet potatoes, stuff like that. Cut out the chips, fries, doughnuts, soda, all that garbage."

I nodded. "I mean, that's simple enough. Like you said, maybe not *easy*, 'cause you know damn well I love that shit."

He nodded. "Oh, I know. I run a bar, Dad—I serve bacon cheeseburgers and chili fries and tater tots and Shepherd's Pie and shit like that all day long. You think it's easy staying on the healthy nutrition wagon when I serve up all that delicious crap all day long? I love that shit as much as you do. But my desire to stay shredded like a motherfuckin' Adonis is stronger, so I keep my diet clean." He glanced at me. "You may think about getting cleaned up. Haircut, beard trim. Make you look less like a hobo and more like… well, me, " he said with a wink at me.

I rolled my eyes at him. "Humble, you ain't."

He just grinned, a wicked, shit-eating grin he

learned from me. "No kidding, Pops. But look who my role model is."

I narrowed my eyes at him. "The fuck you say. I ain't nobody's role model."

Roman groaned, rubbing his face with both hands. "Dad, can you just get over yourself, already? Yeah, you were a drunk ass piece of shit for most of my life. Yeah, I spent a few years being pissed at you. But you know what? I'm here. I'm strong. I'm healthy, I'm happy, I've got a place I love, a woman I love, and work I enjoy, and my brothers are around me. And so are you. And you've been sober—what, a year, now?"

I dug into my pocket, hauled out my wallet, and removed a bronze coin about the size of a poker chip; I set it spinning on the table, and Roman snatched it, examined it.

"One year, one month, two weeks, and three days," I said.

Roman flipped the coin over a finger, his expression difficult to read. "I'm really proud of you, Dad."

I choked. "Hearing my fuckin' son tell me he's proud of me is…" I blinked hard, cleared my throat with a gruff growl. "Bittersweet." I stood up, slammed the last of my coffee, burning my tongue and throat in the process. "Let's go shopping for rabbit food."

SIX

Liv

"CHARLIE—LISTEN, NO—HOLD ON, PLEASE, LISTEN—"Charlie was on a tirade the likes of which I'd never heard from my eldest daughter.

"—And he told me, can you believe this? He told me it was *my* fault! My fault! I've spent five years with the bastard, paying the lion's share of our rent, buying most of the food, doing his laundry and my own, going to school full-time and then interning full-time and now working full-time, and all I ever asked of him was fidelity and affection. And did I get either one? NO! He was boinking my boss! You wanna know the funniest part of all this? My boss is fifty-five, she's married with grandchildren, and hasn't seen the underside of two hundred pounds since the nineties, and that's being generous, considering she's barely five feet tall." She was silent a while. "I don't know what to do, Mom."

"I'm sorry you're going through this, Charlie," I said. "What are your options?"

She hummed a musing sound. "Well, I could stay here in Boston and continue working at Denoyer and Whitcomb. I'd need a new apartment because we're both on the lease and I'll be damned if I'm going to let him stick me with a four thousand dollar a month lease. I've loved working at the firm, but Vera Denoyer is now public enemy number one and I'll be damned and double damned if I'll work for her for another minute, the dirty old cuckolding slut."

"Charlie!" I snapped.

"Mom, you know what—"

I cut in. "Be very careful how you finish that, Charlotte Grace." I kept my voice quiet and calm, but my tone was one she knew very well meant business.

She restarted. "I don't take it back. She's a dirty old cuckolding slut. But I will apologize for my language." Another huff. "Anyway, staying at the firm would mean requesting that I work for Isaac Whitcomb and, from what I know and what I've heard, he's pretty aggressively handsy, but he's old money and basically untouchable, and one of the most in-demand real estate attorneys on the entire East Coast."

"You wouldn't last five minutes working for him, Charlie. He'd get handsy one time, you'd slap him so hard his dentures would fly out, and then you'd be fired *and* jailed for assault."

She sighed. "Exactly. So then my option becomes finding a new job and a new apartment. But I only moved to this city because this is where Glen wanted to be. I had great offers in DC and L.A. I only took the job in Boston because Glen wanted to get involved with the DNC here."

"Charlie, I don't want to say it, but…"

She groaned. "I know, I know, you warned me about taking a job because of Glen." A heavy pause. "You warned me, and you were right."

"I didn't want to be."

"Does it ever get annoying, always being right?"

I laughed. "Yes, it does. People don't want to believe me when I say I'm nearly always right about certain things, and then they resent me when it turns out I was right. It's very annoying, as a matter of fact."

"So what do I do?"

I laughed through a sigh. "Charlie, I can't tell you that. Only you can decide what's best for you."

"You were right then, and I didn't listen. I'm ready to listen, now."

"I wish it worked that way, sweetheart." I sighed. "You're in a place in life where you need to figure this out for yourself. I'll be here, and I'll do whatever I can to help, but I can't tell you what you should do."

"But I don't *know* what to do."

I switched the phone to my other ear. "You should talk to Poppy."

"Why?" Her voice was skeptical. "What's she got to do with this?"

"She's going through similar circumstances. Maybe if you two spend some time together talking things over, you'll help each other come to some decisions."

"We will end up trying to kill each other within five seconds, Mom."

"Perhaps now is the time to resolve that. Try talking to her as a sister and friend instead of being the big sister."

"Gahhh, Mom! Getting a straight answer out of you is like talking to Yoda!"

I chuckled. "Small and green I am not," I said, in a terrible attempt at a Yoda voice.

"Oh god, Mom. Don't ever do that again."

"Talk to Poppy. Listen to her. Be her sister and her friend. You both need that, and who better to get advice from than your sister?"

"She's vague and irresponsible and naive."

"And you're bossy and overbearing to an almost comical degree."

"Overbearing?"

I laughed. "Yes, Charlie. You can be overbearing at times. And I'm your mother."

She groaned again. "Why Poppy?"

"Why not? She's your sister."

"We've just never gotten along."

"I know. To my great chagrin, I know. But you're both going through very similar situations, and I think you really could both benefit from leaning on each other."

"You do know Boston and New York aren't *that* close, right? Like, I can't just pop down to New York for a quick cup of coffee with Poppy."

"Your life is up in the air, and so is hers. Maybe you should both throw caution to the wind and just… spend time together, figuring things out."

"What, like a road trip?"

I smiled to myself. "Something. I think you both need to get away from your current situations—get space in terms of time and distance from everything you're trying to figure out. Answers have a way of cropping up when you stop trying to force it."

"Great. So when you finally do give me a straight piece of advice, it's something I'd rather eat glass than do."

I frowned. "Charlotte, now really. What is your issue with Poppy?"

"I don't know, Mom."

"Well, this is your chance to find out and fix it. You can do whatever you want, but you wanted my advice and, well, this is it. Spend time with Poppy."

"Why not Cassie, or Lexie, or Torie?"

"Because as far as I know, things are copacetic for them. So far." I sighed. "God, now I've probably jinxed myself." I laughed. "Point is, I know Poppy is going through something like you are because I just talked to her the other day—it was a very similar conversation, actually."

She's silent another moment or two. "I'll think about it. I certainly could use some time away from Boston."

"And she could use time away from New York," I said.

"Fine, fine. I'll call her."

I smiled to myself. "Good. I really don't think you'll regret it—you're just going to have to learn to give Poppy space to be…Poppy."

"You make that sound easy."

"No harder than it will be for her to give you space to be you," I chided.

Another long pause. "You know, I've been talking about me this whole time. What's going on with you, Mom?"

I was tempted to ask her how she'd feel if I was

dating someone, but bit the words back. What I had with Lucas wasn't that, and couldn't be. And it was none of Charlie's business, at this point at least.

"Mom?"

I held back a sigh. "Oh, you know. One day at a time."

"That is the most vague and evasive answer I've ever heard in my life, Mother. Now I know where Poppy gets it from. Usually when I ask you that, you're off a mile a minute like Cassie or Poppy, telling me all about what your neighbor said and who's having an affair with whom in your paddle boarding group…"

"Well, maybe right now there's just…" I trailed off, unsure what else to say.

"Something going on you're not ready to talk about," Charlie guessed. I remained silent, and Charlie correctly interpreted my silence. "What's his name?"

I laughed. "Whose?"

"Whoever it is that's the reason you're not telling me what's going on."

I wiggled my toes into the thick shag pile of the rug under my bed. "I need some time before I'm ready to do that. But for now…yes, I've made a friend."

"A friend, huh?"

"Charlie," I warned. "Don't."

"Don't what?" She sounded amused. "I thought you didn't want to talk about it?"

I snorted. "I have to go. I have a lunch meeting."

"Eee-*va*-ding!" Charlie said in a sing-song.

"You're pushing it!" I sang back.

"I have to go too," she answered. "My train is here." I heard the sounds of a PA system announcing an incoming train, and the ambient noise on the other end increased until it was hard to hear her.

"Call Poppy!" I said. "I love you!"

"I will," she said. "Love you, too."

I tossed the cell phone onto my bed beside me and considered Charlie's and Poppy's plights. I wondered if Charlie would actually call her youngest sister, and if they'd be able to overcome their differences long enough to help each other through their hardships.

Time would tell.

For now, though, I needed to get ready. I had a lunch meeting with a client to discuss design ideas for a condo renovation. I'd already sketched out my concept after viewing the space, so the meeting should be short—I also had samples of the various materials I was suggesting in my work satchel.

Two hours later the meeting was over. It had been short and sweet as the client loved my ideas, approved the materials, and told me she'd contact my recommended contractor.

Meeting concluded, I sat in my truck with the window open, listening to "Country Roads" on the radio, trying to tell myself I should go back home and finish the three other design concepts sitting on my desk. The problem was, it was one of those rare, perfect Alaskan afternoons: warm but not hot, a gleaming, brilliant sun in a clear blue sky, and just enough of a breeze to ruffle the hair…

I didn't want to work anymore. I wanted to change my clothes and head for a hiking trail.

But I needed to get this work done. One client's home was still in the beginning stages, nothing but photographs of the current space and some color palette preferences; the second was further along, some sketches, some proposed structural changes with a definite modern industrial motif; the third design concept was nearly finished, with the sketches needing only finishing touches and a list of materials to obtain samples for.

Gah. The sunlight bathed me in golden warmth, and the thought of being in my office behind walls and under a roof, sketching and designing? No. I just couldn't do it.

I had a go-bag on my backseat, a backpack with a change of hiking clothes, a spare pair of hiking boots, a couple bottles of water, some imperishable food, and a few other hiking necessities. I took the change of clothes back into the restaurant, changed in the bathroom, and returned to my truck.

When I put the truck in gear and pulled out onto the road, I found myself heading not for the highway and the nearest trailhead, but in the opposite direction.

"What am I doing?" I asked myself out loud. "God, I'm an idiot. He won't go hiking with you, Olivia."

I didn't listen to myself, of course. I ended up at his apartment and lucky for me someone let me in the front door. I headed upstairs to Lucas's apartment, knocking and waiting. He answered the door clad in nothing but a pair of baggy, ripped, khaki cargo shorts, a pair of kitchen scissors in one hand, his beard looking…unevenly trimmed at best; he was clearly frustrated.

I bit my lip, trying to hold back a laugh. "Lucas…"

He narrowed his eyes at me. "Liv. I'm, uh…"

I snorted, snickered. "You need help."

He closed his eyes and sighed, and his shoulders slumped after a moment. "Yeah. I need fuckin' help. Story of my life, lately."

I waited, but he didn't move, or invite me in. I arched an eyebrow at him. "That was me offering to help you even out your trim, Lucas."

"Oh. You, uh…you'd do that? You can do that?"

I snorted a laugh. "Was that two different questions, or one?" I patted his shoulder; his skin was so warm to the touch it was almost hot, the muscle firm. "Yes, I will, and yes, I can. I cut Darren's hair every single month during our entire marriage." I pushed away memories of Darren's hair between my fingers, his familiar scent in my nostrils.

"Well, come on in, then." Lucas stepped aside and let me in.

I looked around. "The green looks great now that it's dried."

"I like it." He grinned at me.

"Now you just need some better furniture."

He waved a hand. "Nah, I got what I need."

"What you need from a utilitarian standpoint is not the same as what will make this feel like a proper home," I said. He led the way to the bathroom, which is where he had been trimming his hair—or attempting to. I stopped before entering the bathroom, though. "You know, it would be easier if you sat on a chair in the kitchen."

"Oh. Right."

In another moment, he was sitting on a chair in the middle of the kitchen, hands fidgeting restlessly. I stood behind him, feathering my fingers through his hair, fighting a powerful wave of memory mixed with a surge of attraction.

I blinked, and for a moment it was Darren sitting there; he'd crack a joke about me giving him a bowl cut like his mom used to—the same joke every time. I blinked again, and it was Lucas, his broad shoulders like mountains, his hair shaggy and uneven, his skin bronze and freckled and hairy.

I continued to toy with his hair, now trying to decide what I was going to do with it. Before going into interior design, I'd gone through beauty school, so I was actually trained in cutting hair, but I'd realized I didn't like it enough to want to do it every single day.

"Do you know what you want it to look like?" I asked.

He snorted. "Shorter. Neater. Beyond that, I got no fucking clue. Last haircut I got was from a meth addict who lived in a trailer next to the bar I used to drink at, down in Oklahoma. She gave me haircuts for enough cash for her next fix." He sighed. "She was terrible at cutting hair, but she'd do it for five bucks and it was right there."

I wasn't at all sure how to respond to that. "Um. Wow. Okay."

He laughed, a bitter sound. "Glamorous, ain't it?"

I fingered the ends of his hair, it was very uneven, even before he'd attempted to trim it himself, but it was thick and healthy. "Why don't you just go to a barber shop?"

He shrugged. "Too far to go right now."

"Insurance wouldn't pay for a new truck? Or even towards a replacement?" I asked, as I started cutting.

He didn't answer for a long time. "It's… complicated."

I trimmed the back of his neck until you could see his actual hairline, and then began working up around his ears. "Do you have clippers, by the way?"

"Nope. One of my boys may, though." He dug in the pocket of his cargo shorts and pulled out a flip phone that looked like it had been old ten years ago; he found the number he was looking for and held it to his ear. "Hey, Rem. Uh, you happen to have clippers? Yes, for, like, hair, you dumbass. What's it matter who's clipping it for me? Can you run 'em over? Thanks, Rem. See you in a minute."

"I get to meet one of your sons, then?" I asked, my stomach doing flips.

He paused before answering, as if he hadn't considered that fact. "Yeah, I guess so. Remington. The tattoo artist." He sat silently as I continued cutting, working my way around his forehead, trimming the shaggy hair until you could see his face more clearly. "Your girl figure things out?"

I chuckled. "No, I don't think so. But my oldest daughter discovered herself in a very similar situation, so I sort of pawned the problem off on her. Or, rather, pawned them off on each other."

"Yikes. Two girls both having crises, huh?"

I paused, teasing the hair out, examining the ends and the lines. "Yes, it seems so. I'm just praying my other three stay out of crisis mode. I'd really love to not have to put out five fires all at once."

"What's your oldest's issue?"

I hesitated. "Um?"

He waved a hand at my hesitation. "None of my business, I guess. Sorry."

"Her boyfriend of five years cheated on her with her boss, so now her entire life is up in the air. New job, new apartment...I'm thinking she'll end up moving, it's just a matter of where."

"What does she do?"

"She works at a law firm in Boston."

"Lawyer, huh?"

"Well, working toward that. She's working there while studying for the bar."

"So moving her entire life ain't exactly a simple thing."

"No, it's not. It means transferring to a different law school, but she has a really good job that provides direct experience in her field with people at the top of her field. But now? I really don't know what she's going to do."

"And she wanted you to tell her what to do?"

"As the easy way out, yes. Which is unlike her, as

she's usually fiercely, almost violently independent and strong-willed."

He grinned up at me as I moved in front of him to scrutinize my handiwork. "Imagine that," he muttered.

I clicked the scissors at him. "Hey, bub, watch it," I said with a smirk.

At that moment, his door opened, and I turned just in time to see a breathtakingly enormous, heavily muscled, chisel-jawed, blond young god swagger through the door. His forearms were covered in tattoos, and more crawled up his chest out from under the V of his tight black t-shirt, and more yet wandered down his legs—he had a set of keys on his index finger, which explained how he'd gotten in without needing to be buzzed.

I felt my jaw fall open, and heard Lucas chuckle. "Yeah, they get that a lot. And, yeah, all three are identical."

I glanced down at him, clearing my throat and blinking hard. "Wow. Okay."

He just grinned. "Don't worry—they're all spoken for. Good women, too."

"Why would I worry?"

He rolled a heavy shoulder. "You got five daughters, and I know I've mentioned my boys being troublemakers. Most moms take one look at my sons and hide their daughters as far away as possible."

The blond Adonis laughed. "They *try* to hide 'em. Usually the daughters just escape and come looking for us."

"Humility is a family trait, I see," I said.

He grinned broadly at me, and even as a woman old enough to be his mother, and a woman attracted to his father, I felt a little dizzy and weak-kneed. "Remington Badd, at your service." He took my hand and shook it, firmly but not painfully.

"Olivia Goode," I replied.

Remington eyed me with intense scrutiny, and then turned his gaze to his father, sitting shirtless in the middle of the kitchen. "Clippers," he muttered, handing over a pair of professional grade clippers in a bag with a full set of guards. "I'll need 'em back though, Dad."

Lucas took the clippers, and then handed them to me. "Thanks, Rem. How's business?"

Remington shrugged. "It's the busy season. Ink is thinking of opening another location closer to where the cruise ships dock, which would work for Juneau and me. She'd like to be closer to the wharf anyway, and that works just fine for me."

"Would all three of you work at the new location?" Lucas asked.

Remington shrugged. "Dunno. Probably not. Ink's regular clientele won't want to go near the tourists and, honestly, neither will Ink. Juneau and I are better suited to a busy tourist shop anyway. Plus, I think the three of us are a lot of personality in one shop."

"You hear from Ram lately?" Lucas asked, his voice a deep rumble.

Remington snorted. "He's way the fuck up near Coldfoot, guiding a group of big game hunters on a month-long hunt. Won't be back for, like, two and a half weeks. Poor Izzy is going loony, too. Shoulda taken her with him, if you ask me."

"Surprised she didn't make him take her along."

Remington cackled. "She likes hiking and camping with him, but a full month away from toilets and Wi-Fi is a bit much, even for her."

"You ever think of going on one of those long hunts with him?" Lucas asked.

I continued fine-tuning the haircut with the scissors while Lucas spoke with his son, but I was ready to start using the clippers to blend and trim the beard.

"Nah. I don't mind a week or even two out in the wilderness, but where he's at? Man, that is the *real* wild. Plus, Juneau says that's how she grew up, and she fought like hell to get away from it, so why would she go back to it voluntarily? And if she ain't going, I ain't going. Not for a full month. But Ram and Izzy have their own way of doing things. They like a little time apart, I guess. June and I, not so much."

"So what's Izzy doing while Ram is gone for a whole month?"

Remington shrugged. "Annoying the shit out of me, that's what. Over at our place all the damn time." He huffed and waved a hand. "I don't mind, for the most part. But it's becoming a bit much. I get that she's bored and lonely, but it's putting a serious crimp in my A-game, if you know what I mean."

Lucas glared at his son. "Remington."

I snorted, pulling the scissors away and covering my mouth. "If you think I've never heard my daughters speaking that way, boy, do I have news for you." I brushed hair off of Lucas's shoulders, laughing to myself. "Lexie, my middle daughter, once told me her college town only really offered two forms of entertainment: parties, and…boys." I hesitated. "Although, she didn't use the word boys. She used a much dirtier word which I won't repeat. I cut the limit on her credit card down to a thousand dollars for two months for that one."

Remington laughed. "Hit 'em where it hurts, huh? The pocketbook."

"Yes, exactly," I said. "Those cards are only supposed to be for emergencies, but they have a way of thinking everything is an emergency solvable by Mom's credit line."

Remington laughed again. "I had a credit card once. For emergencies only, I told myself. But then I ran up a huge bill on things that seemed like emergencies at the time, and I ended up cutting that fucker up into a million pieces."

"Probably smart," I said. "But with the five of them being scattered to the four corners of the country, and me up here, I sleep better at night knowing they have something to fall back on in case of a real emergency, and I keep the limits low enough that they can't get into any real financial trouble. And they do all have at least part-time jobs to help pay down the minimums."

Remington slugged his father in the shoulder. "I gotta get back to work. See ya 'round, old man."

"See ya, Rem. Thanks for bringing the clippers."

Remington eyed me again, clearly wondering about my relationship with his father, but not asking any questions. "Yep. Nice to meet you, Olivia."

"You too, Remington."

He shot me another of those grins. "Hey, any friend of my dad's is a friend of mine. Especially such a pretty friend." He winked at me. "Call me Rem."

"Turn the charm off, Rem. Don't be a hound dog," Lucas growled.

I just laughed. "Charm is harmless, Lucas."

Lucas chortled with wry amusement. "Not with my boys it ain't."

I laughed and waved at Remington as he left, and then set to work with the clippers, blending the sides and back of Lucas's hair before clipping his beard down and reshaping it into a neat oval.

Finished, I brushed the excess hair off his shoulders and stepped back, nodding. "Not bad for kitchen scissors," I said. "Next time, I'll use my actual grooming set and it'll look even better."

He lumbered to his feet and headed for the bathroom—I noticed his limp was more obvious. He peered at his reflection, turning his head this way and that.

"Damn, girl. I ain't had a haircut this good in my whole damn life!" He stroked his beard, ran his hands through his hair. "Don't look like a bear just coming out of hibernation."

"You look at least ten years younger," I said. "And easily twice as handsome."

He glanced at me in the mirror. "Twice as handsome, huh?" He grinned.

I blushed, dusting the hair off of my forearms and hands. "You may want to rinse off, now, or you'll be itchy."

He turned to face me—I was standing just inside the doorway, leaning against the frame.

"Thank you, Olivia. I was making a damn mess of it."

I shrugged. "You're very welcome. I'm glad to help." I couldn't help meeting his eyes. "Do you have plans for the rest of today?"

He took a towel from the ring and used it to dust his shoulders off, and then shook his head. "Nah. I did my hours at the hardware store this mornin'."

I hesitated. "I, um. I was headed up to the Deer Mountain trail. It's a beautiful day out, and I wondered if you'd like to…you know, come with me."

Lucas huffed, rubbing the back of his neck with his palm. "A hike, huh?"

I resisted the urge to overexplain. "Yes. Not a long or difficult one. Just a nice walk in the woods."

He let out a long breath. "I dunno. I did some work with Roman yesterday, tryin' to get this bum leg of mine back up to normal."

I nodded. "Okay, that's fine."

He eyed me, his expression unreadable. "It's not that I don't want to."

I shrugged, lifted a palm. "I know. Strengthening your leg after an injury is important."

He growled. "It should be back to normal already, though, dammit. The wreck was a fuckin' year ago."

I frowned. "Oh. It must have been a pretty bad wreck, then."

"Yeah, it wasn't pretty. Messed up the leg pretty bad. Didn't need any hardware in there, but it was a touch and go thing. Doc wanted to put screws in, but I was hopeful it'd heal." He leaned a palm on the counter, letting out a harsh breath. "Problem is, I ain't been workin' it like I should. Babyin' it, limpin' around with the damn cane like a man twenty years older than I really am."

I had a million questions. "What really happened, Lucas?"

He shook his head. "Old news and a bad story. Nothin' you need to darken your life with."

"So…is that a no, then? For the hike?" I asked, hating how let down I felt.

"I just dunno, Liv. I really like spending time with you. I just don't know that I'm ready for a hike in the woods."

I nodded, ignoring the hollow, cold pit in my stomach. "Sure. I understand. Maybe another time." I pushed away from the doorframe. "You really do look much younger and very handsome, now that you're cleaned up."

He grinned at me, but it wasn't as bright or dizzying as usual. "Now I just gotta lose…oh, fifty pounds or so, and I'll be in business." He slapped his belly.

I couldn't quite smile back, shaking my head. "You don't need to do anything."

He rolled a shoulder. "The doctor might think differently."

I tried a smile. "I'll see you later, okay?"

He nodded, smile gone, joviality fading. "Yep. Have a good hike."

I left his apartment, fighting back the disappointment that I knew I shouldn't feel. This is why I shouldn't let myself like him. We were different people, and our lives just didn't mesh. I was just courting more pain by pretending even a friendship with Lucas Badd could work.

I should stop the games and move on with my life.

Trouble was, that was easier said than done; I *liked* Lucas.

I shouldn't, but I did.

SEVEN

Lucas

GODDAMMIT.

I stood at my front window, watching Olivia walk out to her truck; dejection was evident in every line of her body, in her posture, in her walk. It had been written all over her face.

And it made me feel like shit—for letting her down and hurting her, which I clearly had done. I felt worse for being such a weakling. If I had been doing my rehab I wouldn't be in this position right now.

I watched her get into her truck, start it, but she didn't leave right away.

A hot knot formed in my throat and traveled down into my stomach. Since when was I so fucking weak? So willing to let an opportunity to be around a woman like Olivia Goode slip by, just because I had a bad knee?

Fuck that. It wasn't a bad knee, or a bad leg. It was laziness. Excuses.

Shit.

I growled a long string of curses under my breath, and hustled into my room. I tugged on socks and a pair of boots the boys had bought me when I first moved to Alaska. Found the backpack they'd also given me, and threw a few bottles of water into it, along with a handful of the protein bars Roman had made me buy the other day. There was also the big, thick walking stick Ramsey had made me—seven feet tall, thick as my wrist, with a spiky, bulbous knob on top. He'd sanded it and stained it and polished it, and had even worked a natural grip spot into the wood near the middle, where I gripped it. It was a beautiful piece of workmanship, and I hadn't used it even once.

I shoved my cheap drug-store sunglasses onto my face and hurried outside, not giving myself time to second-guess this decision.

"Wait!" I called out, just as Liv was getting ready to back out.

She heard me, and put the truck back into park. I did my best to keep the limp out of my walk as I approached the passenger side; she rolled down the window as I neared it. "Change your mind?"

I angled my walking stick into the backseat and then slid into the passenger seat. "Yeah, I did."

"For you, or for me?" she asked.

"Both."

Her smile was infectious—happy, joyful. "Good answer."

I absentmindedly massaged my leg where it still tended to throb sometimes. I watched Liv drive; she went an exact three miles per hour above the speed limit, used her turn signals religiously, and checked her blind spots at least three times before changing lanes.

She seemed content to let the silence stretch as she drove to the trailhead, and we didn't exchange a word the whole way, until she parked on the right side of the gravel road behind a row of cars, shut the windows, and got out.

Smiling at me with an eager gleam to her eyes, she donned her backpack. "Ready?"

I slung my own onto my back and stamped my walking stick into the ground. "As I'll ever be."

She laughed. "It's a little hike, Lucas, not a month-long excursion into the deep bush."

"Funny thing is, when I was young, I wouldn'ta thought twice about a trip like that—a month out there in the bush."

"Well, we change a lot as we grow older, don't we?"

I laughed gruffly. "Some of us more'n others."

I looked around: we were on a small, narrow gravel road lined with houses on both sides with the mountains rising up on our right. There were rusted out hulks of old cars in front of some of the houses, and power lines crisscrossed the road. A collarless dog, half-husky it looked like, trotted down the road away from us, its hind end on an angle following its front end. Liv set out down the road, her boots crunching in the gravel, and I kept pace beside her.

Within fifteen minutes, we were leaving the gravel behind and ascending quickly over rocky terrain, Sitka spruce towering over us, fragrant and massive; crows wheeled overhead, clicking and cawing in raucous conversation, discussing our presence with each other, alerting others ahead that we were coming.

Liv watched a crow hop and flutter from tree to tree, almost as if following us. "I've always been fascinated by crows," she said.

I watched the one she was focused on. "Did you happen to toss any food aside, last time you were here?"

She frowned at me. "Um, yes, actually. I was eating a granola bar and didn't want the last couple bites."

"Let me guess: you saw a crow watching you, and set it down, and it got eaten."

She nodded. "Yes. Why?"

"Well, crows are up there with dolphins and elephants when it comes to intelligence. They remember faces. Smarter than dogs, actually."

She blinked at me in surprise. "Really?"

I nodded. "Yep. Down in Oklahoma, I'd come home from work and plop down in my easy chair and…uh, well, I'd turn on the TV. National Geographic channel, usually. Just as background noise. I watched this special on crows, and it just stuck with me." I gestured at the crow still following us. "I'd bet dollars to donuts that that's the crow that got your food."

She slung her bag around to one shoulder and dug out a package of beef jerky, pinched a few pieces off of one end, and tossed them in the direction of the crow. "I wonder if I could tame one this way."

I chuckled. "Absolutely." I tipped my head to one side. "I mean, I don't know about *taming*, exactly, but you could teach one to get pretty close. When I was a kid, Liam did that. We had this big ol' murder of crows that lived in the woods not far from our cabin, and there was this one monster crow who liked to sit at the top of the tallest jack pine at the edge of the clearing, and it'd watch us play, and if we got too close to the edge of the woods, it'd set off an almighty racket—warnin' its family we were comin', I guess. Well, one day Liam got it into his fool head that he wanted that crow for a pet, and nothin' Pa or Grandpa could say would change his mind. So he set about doing what you're talking about—leaving food for it every day. It worked, sorta. The thing would hop down to within a hundred feet of Liam as he set out the food, which was usually bits of raw meat from a fresh kill. But that was as close as he could get it to come."

"Still, pretty amazing, I bet."

"Oh yeah, 'specially because that thing was damn near the size of a hawk. Big old beady black eyes, loud as anything." I laughed, remembering. "Well, Liam was getting frustrated because he wanted to pet the damn thing. So Grandpa told him how crows love shiny things even more than they love food. So Liam went around collecting coins and bolts and anything shiny he could find, and he'd leave a few shiny things with the food. That crow went nuts for him, after that. It'd hop right up to him, take the food the second Liam set it down, eat it, take the shiny stuff, and leave."

"Wow!" Liv exclaimed. "That's so cool!"

"He got the thing to let him pet it, and that ain't a word of a lie. In time, the crow started bringing Liam presents. It'd bring shiny stuff back, and once even a dead mouse it had caught. They exchanged presents."

"That's kind of crazy. I had no idea they were that smart."

"Some species more than others. They can use tools, pass information down to the next generation… they mourn when one of their family dies. Pretty fascinating critters, actually."

She smiled. "National Geographic, huh?"

I shrugged. "Somethin' to watch."

The hiking became a bit more strenuous, then, and I had to spare my breath for breathing. The trail twisted and turned, switched back on itself endlessly, climbing higher and higher. Soon, I was sweating and gasping, leaning on my walking stick, no longer trying to hide my limp.

Liv, of course, wasn't breathing hard or sweating at all, and it seemed like she was just enjoying a nice easy walk in the woods—while I was huffing and puffing and dripping sweat like I was trying to climb up the sheer face of a mountain rather than a minor incline on a well-maintained trail.

I felt ashamed of myself, truth be told. Once upon a time, I could've carried a hundred-pound ruck on my back and all but jogged up this trail. Now, every step set my big ol' belly jiggling and wobbling. My arms, too.

Well, pretty much everything on me jiggled and wobbled, as long as we're talking truth.

Eventually, stubbornness and pride weren't enough, and I knew I had to stop or risk another episode with my heart.

"Liv…" I gasped. "I need—I need a break."

She halted, wiping a few dainty, lady-like droplets of sweat off her brow, and glanced back at me. "Oh my god, Lucas! Are you okay?" Her expression was concerned, her voice full of worry.

A downed tree lay parallel to the path, and I slumped down onto it, stretching out my bad leg and massaging it, leaning my walking stick against the log beside me. I worked on slowing my breathing, and taming the resentment that was coursing through me.

She sat beside me, taking small sips from a big pink Nalgene clipped to her backpack via a carabiner. "Lucas?"

I didn't answer immediately, instead waiting until I could speak without gasping. "Fine…I'm fine."

Liv glanced at me sideways. "Lucas."

I groaned. "What?" I said with a harsh sigh.

"Tell me the truth."

"The truth is, I'm not okay."

"Should we go back?"

I shook my head. "No. I'm just being forced to face how badly I've let myself go."

She didn't answer for a long time, and I could

tell she was wrestling with what to say, and how to say it without insulting me.

I laughed, the sound a little bitter. "Liv, just say whatever's on your mind and quit worryin' about how it'll make me feel."

"I guess I'm just wondering if...if you were in denial?" She was quiet another moment or two. "With Darren, he knew he wasn't in the best shape. He knew he had a bad heart. He just...he thought if he stayed fairly active, it would counteract his atrocious diet. I told him otherwise, his doctor told him otherwise, but he just wouldn't hear it. He wanted to enjoy life and, for him, that meant eating what he wanted to eat, regardless of how it affected his heart."

"Meaning, you're asking how it's possible that I *didn't* know how fat and out of shape I am."

"I don't mean—"

"Liv." I grabbed a double handful of belly and shook it. "This ain't somethin' you can just pretend ain't there." I sighed, scrubbing my face. "I just...I guess I didn't care. It didn't matter."

"But, Lucas...you're...you're essentially dying."

I cackled. "Not essentially, babe. Reality—here and now, inescapable, undeniable."

"The heart attack?"

I nodded. "That was part of it."

"The car wreck?"

I nodded again, staring at the tree line, the blue sky beyond, and flexed my leg, testing the joint and the ache. "I woke up in the hospital, alive, and knew I'd only just barely escaped death…a second time. The first time, the heart attack, the fact that I survived it was…I don't want to say blind luck, but something very much like it. I shouldn't have survived it, but I did. Took a while to recover from the surgery. Forced me to retire early, because I just needed too much time off to recover, and I'd worked there nearly forty years anyway."

"What did you do?"

I shrugged, waved a hand. "Worked on the line in a manufacturing plant. Nothing super inspiring. It was just a job to pay the bills, honestly. I didn't hate it, but it wasn't nothin' I chose out of passion for the career. I just sorted of ended up there and never left."

"How do you mean, you just ended up there?" she asked, tilting her head to one side inquisitively.

"No end to your questions, huh?" I laughed. "Eh, you know, the way life does."

She smiled at me. "I'm curious—I don't mean to pry."

I sighed. "I guess I'm just not used to…well, to anyone caring."

She frowned. "Lucas, that's…that's awful."

"I mean, my boys love me, but they're my sons,

you know? Why should they care to ask about all this? They got their own lives to figure out, and they had all they could handle keeping my drunk ass out of trouble." I hissed, realizing what I'd just said. "Fuck. I…I mean—"

Her expression softened, turned compassionate—rather than judgmental. "Lucas, you have to know I've at least suspected that you're…um…"

"An alcoholic," I finished for her.

She nodded. "Yeah." Her eyes pierced mine, scrutinizing. "Are you…are you in treatment of any kind?"

I fished my year coin out of my pocket and handed it to her. "Clean a year. Go to AA meetings once or twice a month, just to stay accountable."

She nodded, examining the coin before handing it back, not looking at me, head down. "That's good."

I eyed her. "Don't wimp out on me, now, Liv."

Her head whipped up, eyes lasering on mine. "I'm not wimping out, I'm…piecing things together."

"Piecing what together?"

"What you've told me, and what you haven't." She paused. "So the wreck…"

I nodded. "I was wasted," I admitted, voice low and tense. "I…well, it's a long fuckin' story. And, if you want to talk about time sober, I was actually sober almost a year, and then I relapsed. Been another year.

So two, total, just with a bit of a fuckup in there." I growled. "One bad trip down memory lane was all it took to put me right back at the bottom of the bottle, and now…" I trailed off.

"And now, what?"

"Here I am, ground zero for memory lane. And honestly, staying sober would be a fuckuva lot easier if I wasn't living *here*."

"It's hard?" she asked, her eyes softer and more understanding than my sins deserved.

I nodded. "Yeah. Every single fucking day, I think, '*shit, I need a drink,*' just to try to stay above the memories."

Her head tipped to one side. "Stay above the memories."

"Yeah. I just mean—"

She cut in. "Oh, no. I know what you mean. I know exactly what you mean." She was silent a moment. "I used to be treading water in the middle of an ocean of memories, and losing the battle to stay afloat."

"How'd you get out? I mean, you seem like you're not in that anymore."

"I moved here," she said. "I was still living in the home Darren and I had built together—and I mean that literally. He and I hired a builder, but we were involved every step of the way. I helped build the frame, pour the foundation, hang the drywall, install lighting, paint, hang cabinets...everything. It was *our* home from the ground up. I hung every picture, chose every cabinet pull and light fixture, painted every wall...with *him*. And then he was gone. My kids were gone, moved out and living their own lives, and I was alone in that house. Alone with the memories."

"So you moved here?"

She shrugged. "Darren and I had gone on an Alaskan cruise, and spent a few nights here in Ketchikan. It was...it was actually the last trip he and I took together. He hadn't really liked it here very much, but I had. He was always more of a homebody and a city sort of person. He was happiest sitting outside at a downtown cafe somewhere, sipping espresso and eating crepes. Whereas I was always more at home..." She waved a hand around us. "Out here."

"Opposites, huh?"

She rolled a shoulder. "Sort of, in some ways." A hesitation. "He would never have wanted to move here, but the moment we stepped off the ship I was in love with this place. I loved every single minute we spent here and was actually truly sad to get back on the ship and continue with the cruise. I just felt at home here, immediately. Eventually, of course, the cruise ended and we went back home, and I daydreamed about living here, even though I knew Darren would never go for it. Just like I would never go for his dream of getting a little condo in uptown Manhattan. He talked about that, and I talked about a little log house in the mountains somewhere, and were trying to figure out how to compromise when he retired and we were ready to sell our house and move."

I couldn't help a laugh of bitterness. "I have the opposite problem. My boys moved here after discovering they had family here. I…well, I had this idea of doing some traveling again. I'd gotten sober after the heart attack, and the boys actually got a little sneaky, sold the trailer and the ten and a half acres I owned out from under me, bought me a truck and a little used Airstream. I was almighty pissed at first, actually," I said, laughing in amusement this time. "But then I hit the road and was thankful they'd forced my hand, or I'd never have left Oklahoma. I'd have been stuck there forever."

"So they did you a favor."

I laughed again. "Yep. I'm…well, I can be a little contrary sometimes."

"No, really?" she drawled, sarcasm dripping from her voice.

"Ha ha," I intoned drily.

"But then?"

I lifted a shoulder, flexing my knee again. "I was on the road for most of a year, just bumming around the country. Went over through Arkansas, Mississippi, Alabama, Georgia, up the coast to Maine, back down through New York and the Midwest, stopped for a while in Jackson Hole, and then headed up toward the Pacific Northwest. I was able to live off the proceeds of the sale of the trailer and acreage and not touch my retirement or savings, which was nice." I paused. Thinking. Trying to avoid having to remember too much. "I, um…I was doing great, you know? Feeling good, sober, seeing the country again. Out of Oklahoma, and feeling like maybe I had a handle on life for the first time in a long time."

"But then?" Liv repeated, prompting me to quit stalling and tell her what happened.

"But then I got to Seattle, and ran smack into a pile of bad memories. Some shit had happened in a certain park overlooking Puget Sound, and I…I thought I could handle it. I thought I could face… what had happened there. I thought maybe it'd help me to be there, to face things sober for the first time in…a long time."

"No?" she asked, her voice hesitant.

"Not so much." I swallowed, pausing. "I…well… it got the better of me. I couldn't deal, couldn't—facing it was too much. I ended up with a big ol' bottle of booze, drank it all, quit caring, and…got behind the wheel. Dumbest thing I ever did. Pure blind luck I didn't kill myself or someone else." My face burned, and I swallowed hard. "Woke up in the hospital, laid up with a broken leg, broken arm, cracked ribs, cut up, hungover, knowing what I'd done. What I could've done. How I'd fucked up."

"God, Lucas."

"One dumb decision, and…" I shrugged, lifted my palms up. "My boys brought me up here, rented me an apartment, gave me an allowance, took turns watching me like a hawk while I recovered, got out of the casts, worked on staying sober again. I built myself a little life here, but this is where I grew up. This is where things really started to go sideways a long time ago and that led me to that park on Puget Sound which, in turn, led me to…to being a fat useless old alcoholic bumpkin with a bum leg and no car."

"Hospital bills?" she guessed.

I shook my head. "Nah, I'm solvent enough. I had insurance—*have* insurance, through my retirement plan. I just…I can't bring myself to get behind the wheel again, even though I'm sober and a pretty damn good driver."

She eyed the sky. "You up for hiking some more?"

I nodded and heaved myself to feet, hauling myself up on the walking stick. "Let's go."

"Are you sure you're up for it?" she asked, the picture of concern.

"Yep. We're out here, on the trail, might as well finish the hike. A few more miles won't kill me. Probably."

She stopped, her face pale, shoulders drooping. "Lucas, I know you meant that as a joke, but I don't find it funny."

I cursed myself mentally. "Shit, Liv, I'm sorry. That was thoughtless of me, and I'm sorry."

She stared at me, eyes hard, fierce. "You know, you spend a lot of time talking about being a fat useless old man with a bum leg, but not a lot talking about what you could do to change that. You've been rather honest about not caring whether you lived or died, and I appreciate that honesty. But I have to be honest with you, Lucas—I can't be friends with someone with not only no will to live, but no will to improve themselves. To become better than they are." Her eyes bored into me, the compassion and concern gone, now replaced with something very much like anger. "Yes, you're overweight. Yes, you have a history of heart disease and alcoholism, a bad diet, and a bad leg. All that is true, I grant you. The real question is, what are you going to do about it?"

And with that, she turned and walked away with an angry stomp in her step, arms swinging, Nalgene bottle bumping her hip. I followed, a bit more slowly, both because my leg was aching something fierce, but also because my gut and my heart were aching even more.

The easy camaraderie we'd shared at the beginning was gone, and the rest of the hike was consumed by a hard, cold silence from Olivia, and a tense, thoughtful, uncomfortable silence from me.

She carried the anger with her all the way to her truck, and the entire ride back to my house. It wasn't until I was about to climb out that she spoke.

"Lucas…"

"Let me stop you right quick, okay? You didn't say anything but the truth. Now I gotta think on what you said. Did I like hearing it? Not s'much. Did I need to hear it? Probably. Definitely, if I'm gonna be honest."

"I wasn't going to apologize." Liv traced the stitching on the steering wheel leather with a fingertip. "I was going to say that what I said was borne more out of anger at my husband than you, but that doesn't make it any less true." A long, thick silence. "I want to be your friend, Lucas. But I'm not sure I can, if you're not able or willing to be healthy. To get healthy." She shook her head. "The way I lost Darren? Lucas, I simply *cannot* go through that again. I cannot, and will not."

I nodded. "I understand that. But you know as well as I do that changes like that have to come from me, not you. I couldn't have stopped drinking for you, and I can't change my diet and start exercising for you."

"I'm not asking you to."

I tilted my head. "Mmm, you sort of are. It's complicated, is what it is." I held up a hand to forestall her. "I want to be your friend. I like spending time with you. So what *I'm* saying is, I need to think on some things."

She nodded. "Okay. I have client meetings and designs to work on that will take up most of this week."

"I did enjoy the hike," I said.

"Until things sort of blew up?"

I laughed. "Yeah, up until that. But I bet you could get me on another hike, and maybe the next time, things won't go boom."

"I'd like that," she said, her voice low and quiet. "A lot."

"Me too."

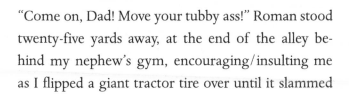

"Come on, Dad! Move your tubby ass!" Roman stood twenty-five yards away, at the end of the alley behind my nephew's gym, encouraging/insulting me as I flipped a giant tractor tire over until it slammed down, heaved it up and lifted it on end, and flipped it over again.

I was shirtless, clad in a pair of ragged, ratty, stained old shorts and a trashed pair of old running shoes. I was sweating like a pig, gasping for breath, and wishing I could heave this damn tire at Roman's stupid face.

"I *am* moving my tubby ass, you fuckin' annoying pencil dick punk!" I snapped back.

"You're lazy, is what are, old man," Roman bellowed. "Flip it faster!"

The asshole knew what he was doing, I had to give him that. Nothing could get me moving faster and working harder than being pissed off, and he was intentionally needling me. The more he teased, ridiculed, barked, insulted, and annoyed me, the angrier I got, and the angrier I got, the harder I worked to get this shit over with.

I had been recently cleared by my doctor for more vigorous activity like this, as I'd spent the last two weeks regularly working on my weaker leg, strengthening and stretching—it still got sore and achy, like it was now, but I could tough it out.

I'd already flipped the tire twenty-five yards one direction, and now I was flipping it back to where Roman stood; the bastard was built like a god, and that was as much motivation as anything he could say.

I used to be just like that, and I'd lost it. Wasted it. He stood there all six feet four inches of heavily muscled, ripped to nil body fat, toned, tanned perfection, looking like a blond mirror image of me thirty-some years ago.

It pissed me off.

I was determined to be that again.

So, with the giant-ass tire on the ground in front of me, heavy as hell, and me hot from the sun, I summoned willpower, summoned anger at myself, snarled like the fat shaggy bear I resembled, and heaved it up to shoulder height, reversed my grip, and pushed it forward until it slammed down with a ringing thud. I repeated it again and again without pause until it slammed down inches from Roman's toes.

He grinned at me. "Good job, Pops." He checked the stopwatch on his phone. "That's a record, by the way."

I controlled my breathing, wiping sweat from my eyes. "Yeah?"

He nodded. "Beat your best fifty-yard tire flip time by a whole ten seconds."

I looked down at myself: I wasn't willing to step onto a scale just yet, but I knew I was making progress: I could almost see my toes. Almost.

Roman watched me for a moment. "Dad, it's time."

My eyes snapped up to his. "Time for what?"

"To weigh in."

"Fuck that. I ain't doin' this to weigh less, I'm doin' this to get rid of the fat and look like I used to look."

He nodded, serious in a way he rarely was. "I know. But to do that, you need some kind of metric for your progress."

"Last time I stepped on a scale, I damn near barfed at the number. Ain't going there. I know where I'm at—still real fuckin' far from my goal. For now, the only metric I need is to look down." I slapped my belly.

Roman growled. "Pops. Listen to me, okay? Having more specific goals will help. Can you just trust me on this?"

"Why? Because you've ever had to lose eighty pounds?"

"No, but because I know what the fuck I'm talking about!"

I spun away. "I ain't havin' this conversation with you, goddammit!" I kicked the tire, and immediately regretted it, hopping around to alleviate the sting in my toe. "Just tell me what to do next."

I heard a door open, then, and my monster of a nephew sauntered out. "Yo, Rome. Maybe you two oughta let me take over. Some objectivity and all that." Baxter was four full inches shorter than both Roman and I, but was bodybuilder bulky, yet shredded like an athlete. It was ridiculous, honestly.

Roman eyed Baxter. "You think you can make some headway with the stubborn old grizzly, be my guest. I'm just getting pissed off."

Bax slapped Roman on the shoulder. "Go hit the bags or something. I got this."

Roman yanked open the door to the gym, frustration in every line of his body. "Dad, I'm just—"

I flipped him off. "Get outta here, Rome. Bax has a point. We're too much alike for this to work anymore today."

He nodded. "I just want to see you succeed at this."

"I will." I met his eyes. "I got no choice, you know? I ducked the hand of Death twice. I won't get a third chance."

He let out a breath, nodded, and then shot a grin at Bax. "All yours, cuz."

Bax eyed the equipment Roman had used for our session: the tire, a pair of thick ropes, some big weights shaped like balls with flat bottoms and a wide handle, and a small but heavy leather ball.

"Rome was on the right track," Bax said, nodding. "But let's get some basics down. First, I don't give a shit what you weigh. It's just a number. You want to cut the fat and build muscle, get back to being the big bad beefcake you used to be. Yeah?"

I nodded. "Yeah."

He dug a tape measure out of the pocket of his athletic shorts. "We're going to do a few things, okay? One, measure the girth of your arms, shoulders, waist, and thighs." From the same pocket he took something like a pair tongs or pincers. "This is a body fat caliper. There are some calculations involved, and I'll spare you that, but it measures your body fat, and that's what we need to know." He pulled a phone from his other pocket. "Third, we're going to take pictures—side and front."

I winced. "First two, fine. Third? Nuh-uh."

Bax lifted his chin. "Yes. You're doing it." He arched an eyebrow, hardened his jaw. "Like your kid said, it's a metric. It's a marker of where you are now, and when you get frustrated with your lack of progress—or rather, your perceived lack of progress, you look at the progress pics and realize, damn, I *am* getting somewhere. My experience as a trainer has proven that your shape changes before the numbers do."

I sighed. "I guess I gotta face myself so I can change myself, huh?

Bax nodded. "Truer words have never been spoken, Uncle Lucas."

So, we spent the next half an hour taking measurements with the tape measure and then using the calipers to pinch my fat in various places, after which Bax would type things into his phone and do calculations, and then, finally, I posed for front-facing and profile photos.

Bax set the calipers and tape measure on the ground, tapping his phone against his palm. "You wanna know?"

I nodded. "Yes."

"Your body fat is just over forty percent."

I winced. "That's...not good."

He scoffed. "No, Uncle Lucas, that's not good. At all. And I'm not gonna sugarcoat it for you."

I wiped my face with both hands. "Where should I be at?"

"Well, that's a relative and subjective question. Better question for you to ask is what's your goal?"

"Okay, then...what's my goal?"

He laughed, shrugging. "That's up to you." He slapped his belly—or rather, the twenty-four pack abs. "This is around eight to ten percent—I'm pretty good at maintaining at this point, so I don't measure it too frequently. I think for now, a good and reasonable goal—meaning attainable if you stay committed and consistent—would be around fifteen to twenty percent."

I scoffed. "So I just need to drop twenty percent of my body weight in fat."

He shrugged. "It sure as fuck was never gonna be easy. Hell, I do this for a living and it's not easy maintaining this body. What you've got to do, now? Shit, man. It's gonna be really fuckin' hard." His dark eyes bored into mine. "You gotta want it. You gotta *need* it. You gotta be a million, billion percent committed to it."

"I almost fuckin' died from not caring what happened to me, or what I looked like." I swallowed hard. "I didn't give a shit. I didn't even know I had nephews. Now I've got you, your brothers, all those women you fellas have snagged. And all of you fuckers look like Olympians and Greek gods, and here I am, fat a fuckin' walrus. But more'n that, I...shit. I just...I *care* now. I care if I live. I care if I look like shit. So yeah, Bax. I don't just want it, I really do honestly *need* it."

"Heard you may have another motivation on your mind, too." His eyes twinkled, a grin on his lips. "Of the variety which comes with curves and a sweet smile."

"Ain't none of your fuckin' business, Baxter."

"Sure it is. You want to stay alive, great. You want to be healthy to stick around for your boys and for the rest of us, great. But you want to look good for a lady love? Uncle o' mine, that there is a hell of a powerful motivator to do more than just live…that's where you get the motivation to get shredded."

I laughed. "At the moment, I just want to be able to go on a hike with her and not be red-faced and out of breath, huffing and puffing like a tub of lard."

"That's where it starts. Then you want to feel comfortable with your shirt off around her. And then you want to be irresistible to her because you're such a jacked old man."

I laughed. "I'll start with not dying."

"Baby steps, Uncle. Baby steps." He sidled up to the largest bell thing. "This is a kettlebell. This one weighs seventy-two-point-two pounds, also known as a two pood."

"A what?"

"A two pood. A pood is a unit of measurement unique to kettlebells." He pointed at the matching kettlebell beside the one he was standing in front of—his posture was loose, easy, but straight, hands at his sides, feet shoulder width apart. "Stand in front of it, like this."

I followed his lead as he showed me how to pick it up without hurting my back, how to swing it, clean it, press it…all sorts of evil torture which left me jellied from head to toe, drenched with sweat, and feeling more alive and more accomplished than ever.

For the first time in decades, I felt like just maybe there was a future ahead of me worth seeking.

EIGHT

Liv

WORK PICKED UP PACE OVER THE NEXT FEW WEEKS, becoming not just busy but downright hectic. When I moved up here, I'd had the idea of being semiretired, but once I made the move, I realized that even with the nest egg from life insurance plus the sale of our home, I would still need to work. Perhaps not entirely for financial reasons, but for mental and emotional reasons, too. I needed something to do, to keep busy—to keep my mind off the loss of my husband, the worry about my daughters, and just to simply keep looking forward.

So, to that end, I accepted new clients until I was working not just full-time, but overtime. Viewing spaces to be redesigned, coming up with sketches and plans and materials, dealing with the renovations and subsequent inevitable structural and architectural issues, making sure everything went as well as things can go, talking to contractors and resolving disputes…I was barely sleeping and only managed a few brief paddles down the channel with my friends from my standup paddleboarding club, and a short hike now and then.

Two weeks passed in a blur. I was sitting on my balcony sipping coffee one Sunday morning when I realized I hadn't seen Lucas or even spoken to him since the hike, and I felt a twinge of guilt. As well, I realized that the heavy pit in my stomach, and the ache in my chest were symptoms of missing him, things I'd been ignoring and attributing to being intensely busy.

Had I been too hard on him?

I didn't think so. I'd only spoken the truth. If he and I were to become closer and he were to, God forbid, have another heart attack I would…honestly, I wasn't sure I'd survive it emotionally.

But I just *missed* him. I missed his drawl and even his coarse manners and rough language. I missed his bluff bravado, which mixed so oddly with his self-deprecating humor.

I was supposed to meet a client in twenty minutes to go over some material revisions for her new kitchen, but…I didn't want to. It was a beautiful day, warm, sunny, peaceful. I wanted to be out on the water, paddling or canoeing. I wanted to be out on a trail with Lucas.

Argh. I shouldn't just cancel on my client, because she was in the final phases of her remodel, but she'd already changed her mind about the backsplash twice. Maybe if I rescheduled, she'd have more time to think and would end up wanting to stick with our current selection.

I dialed her number, explained that I needed to reschedule; she wasn't thrilled, but I suggested she stop by the store and look at other options for her backsplash, and we'd reconnect on Monday to discuss what she'd decided.

That taken care of, I felt a weight lift off of my shoulders. I decided that I wanted to be out on the water more than I wanted to hike, so I changed out of work clothes and into paddling gear—skintight knee-length leggings which compressed around the cuffs, a tight sports bra, a tank top, and a zip-up jacket which also compressed around waist and wrists to keep water out in case I ended up in the water. Some grippy shoes, polarized sunglasses, and a big floppy hat to keep the sun off my neck. I loaded my board into the back of my truck and strapped it down, and headed for the pier…

By way of Lucas's condo.

I buzzed his unit, and within a few seconds, got a buzz on the intercom in return. "Hello? Who's it?" He sounded sleepy, groggy.

"Wake up, sleepyhead," I sang. "Time to go paddleboarding!"

"Huh?"

"It's Liv," I said, laughing. "Can I come in?"

"Mmm. Yeah. C'mon up," he grumbled, and the door buzzed and clicked.

I trotted up the steps and into the building, and then to his unit, where he was standing in the doorway, looking bleary-eyed and groggy.

And shirtless.

He had lost weight—visibly, noticeably. His shoulders were more rounded with muscle, his arms were tighter, his belly was smaller, and his face was thinner.

"Liv," he murmured. "It's fuckin' early, babe."

I laughed. "It's nine o'clock, Lucas. I wouldn't call that early."

"Yeah, well, I'm retired, and I'm not working this morning, so it's early."

I felt a tremor in my stomach as he stretched, arms lifting over his head—his torso flattened and his arms bulged, and I got a sense of what he might look like in another few months of doing whatever he was doing.

Darren had never been very fit, let alone muscular. I'd loved him with all of my heart, mind, body, and soul, and always would, but in the deep, secret places in my soul, I knew I'd always felt a little twinge of desire for him to be…physically fitter. And seeing Lucas having made an obvious effort to change himself, I knew I was on the losing side of a battle to not like him even more.

Was I shallow?

"Just because you're retired doesn't mean you're allowed to lay in bed all morning. It's a beautiful day outside and I thought maybe you would like to go out on the water with me."

"What, like swimming?"

I giggled, shaking my head. "No, silly. Paddling."

"A boat?" He was obviously groggy, still.

I sighed, and headed for his kitchen, found his coffee maker and coffee supplies, and set about making coffee for him.

He plopped down at his kitchen table, and rested his chin in his hand, watching me. "Sorry, I ain't exactly a morning person," he said.

"It's okay," I said, leaning back against the counter near the coffee maker. "I am, and some people have found me to be a little much in the mornings."

He rumbled a laugh. "Naw, it ain't that. You're

all chipper and shit, and it's cute. I'm just kind of a grumpy bear in the mornings."

"As opposed to the sweet, easygoing darling you are the rest of the day?" I teased.

He snorted. "Yeah, well, we can't all be happy little angels all the time."

I felt a need to do something with my hands, something to occupy my attention. "Are you hungry?"

It was hard to tell under the beard, but he seemed to be blushing. "I, um. I'm actually not eating till lunch."

"Oh?"

He shrugged a heavy shoulder. "Part of my whole plan to quit bein' a fat walrus. I don't eat until lunch, then I eat lean, healthy food, and then I kick my ass with exercise at least three days a week."

"Well, it's definitely working," I said, meeting his eyes. "You look really good."

He seemed like he was trying to hide a grin. "You think so? It's a start."

"It's more than a start, Lucas. You really look great."

"It's not easy, but...I feel like it'll be worth it." He made a face, tipping his head to one side. "Hell, it already is. I feel better than I've felt in a long time."

I hesitated. "Lucas, about the hike..."

He held up his hands to stop me. "Liv, I needed

that. I can't say I liked hearing it, but I needed it. Sometimes, you just need a good kick in the ass to get yourself motivated."

"I just…I don't want you to think I don't like you for who you are, or that you have to be someone else in order to be my friend."

He sighed. "To be totally honest, I am doing this in part for you. I like you, Liv. I like you a lot. And I want to be a man you…" He shrugged, trailing off and restarting. "I want to be better."

"But you don't have to be anything different to be my friend, and I'm worried I made you feel like you do."

He shook his head. "You didn't know I was doing anything different these last couple weeks, yet here you are."

The coffee was mostly done brewing by then, so I hunted down a couple of mugs, poured us each a cup, and took one of the seats kitty-corner to his.

We sipped coffee in companionable silence for a few minutes, until it was broken by Lucas. "So, you wanna do what, now?"

"Paddleboard."

"What the hell is that?"

I laughed. "It's…it's kind of like a cross between canoeing and surfing."

He frowned, brow wrinkling. "Sounds hard."

I shrugged and tipped my head to one side. "Maybe a little at first. Basically, you have a big flat board like a surfboard, only thicker, longer, and wider, with a long paddle. You stand on the board and paddle around."

"Why?"

I couldn't help a cackle. "Ohhh, Lucas. Why? Because it's fun. It's challenging. It's great exercise, and it's peaceful, being out there on the water."

"When I called myself a walrus, it was in reference to my size and shape, not my affinity for water. That don't sound like somethin' I'd be too great at. I'd probably sink the damn board."

"They make them with varying capacities." I smiled at him with what I hoped was reassurance. "I wouldn't ask you to do anything I didn't think you were capable of."

He scoffed. "Now you sound like Bax."

"Who?"

"My nephew, Baxter Badd. He's been acting as my personal trainer. Kickin' my fat ass into shape."

I paused, trying to formulate how to say what I wanted to say. "Lucas, has anyone ever mentioned positive self-talk to you?"

He laughed with a derisive smirk. "No, I can say with complete certainty no one ever has, 'cause I ain't got a damn clue what the hell that's supposed to mean."

"It's exactly what it sounds like—positive self-talk."

He sipped his coffee. "Right. Sounds like frou-frou self-help mumbo jumbo for gullible sissies."

"Perhaps, but it's not. Some of the most success-ful people in the world—men included—use it."

"So? Break it down for me, then. What is it and why the hell would I want to try it?"

I topped off our coffee, and then sat again, con-sidering. "It just means, at the very least, not speaking of yourself or to yourself in derogatory terms."

He nodded, comprehension dawning. "Ahhh. I see. Not calling myself a fat walrus, you mean."

"Well, that's one way to look at it. But flip it, okay? Instead of thinking in terms of just *not* being insulting to yourself, go further. Reverse the impulse. You catch yourself saying something derogatory about yourself, and say something positive instead. That's where it starts."

"Where does it end?"

I laughed. "Oh, it doesn't, I suppose. But positive self-talk feeds into positive affirmations."

"More frou-frou self-help mumbo jumbo for sissies."

"Yes. This time, it's about naming what you want—claiming it as real, as yours."

"Now that just sounds idiotic."

"It feels odd, at first, sure. But it does help."

"For example?"

"When I moved up here, I felt lonely. I felt isolated. I felt like I would never fit in, like I would never have friends, like even though I was drowning in grief I couldn't escape my life back East. I thought I would have been better off staying there where at least I had a life and friends, and even belonged."

"Sounds familiar."

"I bet it does. So, I saw a therapist up here and she recommended self-affirmations. I would wake up every morning and I would look in the mirror and tell myself that I belonged here. That I was okay. That I was healing. That I didn't need to mourn anymore. That I would make friends, and find a life— make a life for myself without Darren... one in which I would eventually find my own happiness."

"Did it work?" he asked.

I smiled, sighed. "To some degree. It helped me focus on what I *could* do rather than what was done and had already happened. It helped me remind myself that I had to keep going, that I would be okay even if I didn't always feel like it."

"Bax is always talking about how I need to formulate a specific goal for myself. I've been telling him I just want to be healthy and in better shape, and he's always telling me that's not enough. I need a bigger goal, a more specific one to focus on. Sounds similar."

I nodded. "It is similar. What I'm talking about isn't so much about goals, though, as it is changing the way you interact with yourself."

He snorted. "Talk plain, Liv."

I sipped, and thought. "Okay, here. Plain talk. You're just reinforcing that you're a fat walrus by calling yourself that all the time. It's like negative reinforcement for dogs, or kids. If you tell a kid he's stupid frequently enough, what will happen?"

Lucas sighed, nodding. "He'll believe it."

"Even if it isn't true."

"Yeah, I guess that makes sense."

I rolled my hand. "Follow the logic, then. Adults are no different. We are just as susceptible to negative reinforcement as kids. So, if you refer to yourself as fat, or a useless old bear or whatever else, and you do so frequently, your mindset, then, is going to be one of believing that to be true."

"Because it is true."

I held up a finger. "But you're working to change that, yes?"

He nodded. "Sure."

"So you're working to change your body, which is amazing and wonderful. But you also have to work to change your mind. You have to believe you are what you want to become, or that you *can* be that. If you keep telling yourself you are what you have been, that's all you'll ever be."

He clutched his head in both hands. "You sound like a Buddhist or some shit. It's makin' my head hurt."

"This is basic positive reinforcement psychology, Lucas. Not Buddhism."

"I didn't even graduate high school, Liv. I barely went to elementary school, for fuck's sake. I learned how to read, write, and do basic math from my grandpa. Psychology is just a buncha nonsense to me."

"It's not nonsense, Lucas, it's just understanding how the mind works."

"You make it sound easy."

"You're not stupid, Lucas. You are perfectly capable of understanding what I'm talking about. You may not have a lot of formal education, but you have plenty of intelligence and street smarts. Don't act dumber than you are."

He growled. "So you're saying I'm telling myself I'm a fat useless old walrus with a bad leg, and if I keep telling myself that, I'll never stop believing it's true."

"Yes, exactly!"

"And the answer to that is to tell myself...what?

That I'm handsome and buff and my leg ain't fucked up?"

I felt my stomach flip. "You're already handsome, Lucas. And fitness isn't about being buff, it's about being strong and having endurance, eating healthy, and feeling good. It's about leading a healthy life, and protecting your body, so you can be there for your kids, your family, and yourself. And as you gain physical strength, you gain mental and emotional strength—it's a cliché but you become the best version of yourself. As for your leg, I don't know if it will ever stop hurting, because I'm not a physical therapist or a doctor. But I do know you seem to have done a lot of work toward strengthening it since we went hiking, and I also know you don't have to let it stop you from doing the things you want."

Silence, then. "Paddleboarding, huh?"

I grinned. "Paddleboarding. You'll enjoy it."

"I dunno about that, but I suppose I can try. Worst that can happen is I'll get wet and cold, right?"

My grin spread until my cheeks hurt. "Exactly!" I waved both hands at him in a shooing motion. "Go get dressed!"

"What should I wear?" he asked, eyeing me. "I ain't exactly got anything like what you're wearing."

I laughed. "I have an outfit for everything, Lucas. Just put on a shirt and shoes."

He nodded, and came back out wearing an Oklahoma Rodeo shirt which was huge on him, a ragged old Kansas City Chiefs hat, and beat-up old running shoes.

We headed out for my truck, and as I descended the three steps down to the sidewalk from his building, I felt his gaze on me.

My leggings *were* a little tight, I realized.

Actually, very tight.

I usually paddled with other women and ignored the attention of men, so I'd never thought about how tight these leggings really were. Or that my shirt and jacket didn't exactly cover my backside.

His gaze followed me down the steps and as I walked to the truck; I turned to catch his eyes, and he looked away, embarrassedly scratching his jaw—he knew I'd caught him.

Did I mind?

I don't think I did, even though what we had was simply friendship.

He'd said he liked me, though. A lot.

I tried to push that train of thought aside as we climbed into my truck and headed for my usual launch spot.

We parked, and I took him to the SUP—standup paddleboarding—outfitter, where he was fitted with a board suitable for his height and weight, a paddle, and a PFD—portable flotation device, which resembled a fanny pack but which could be inflated in case of emergency to keep him afloat, should he fall in.

When Lucas mentioned he'd never been on a SUP before, the sales assistant suggested a lesson.

"I mean, you get up there and paddle, right?" Lucas said, his voice gruff.

I sighed; men always resisted accepting help. "It's a bit more involved than that," I said, "and a quick lesson will make things a lot easier for you."

Lucas growled. "Fine. Whatever. Show me this shit, then, son."

The young man was tall and lithe, with sleek muscles and short messy blond hair, wearing colorful board shorts and an open zip-up hoodie. "Grab your board and paddle and meet me over at the docks. I'll grab my board and we'll hit the water."

In a few minutes, I was watching as Kyle, the SUP instructor, stood on the dock giving Lucas an overview of basic stance, paddle grip, and stroke mechanics.

"I've done plenty of canoeing," Lucas said. "This sounds a lot like that."

Kyle nodded. "It is. Just…standing up. This is a great core workout, so make sure to tighten your core when you pull. That will help with balance, too."

Lucas eyed the board that was leaning on its side

against the dock pylons. "You sure that thing will hold me? I ain't exactly a lightweight."

Kyle nodded. "I'm one hundred percent sure. It's a twelve footer, eight inches thick, and rated for up to four hundred and fifty pounds."

Lucas sighed. "Shit. I mean, I ain't light, but I don't weigh *that* much."

"Not by half," I said.

He tipped his head to one side. "Eh, not by half may be a bit generous. But it'll do, I guess, as long as you're sure of the rating."

Kyle set his board into the water, climbed down and sat astride it, kicking his bare feet in the water for a second before strapping the tether around his ankle. "So. Always put on your tether. The water is pretty calm today, but it's never worth taking a chance." He splashed a hand in the water. "Your turn. Set your board in, leave your paddle on the dock, and climb down on and sit on it like I am."

He hesitated a moment, and then Lucas stripped off his socks and shoes, and did as instructed. Somewhat awkwardly and with a good bit of uncertainty, he sat astride his board.

Kyle grabbed his paddle and used a shortened grip to paddle away from the dock; Lucas followed suit, and I got on my board and followed at a distance. Once we were out in the channel a bit, Kyle tucked his knees up on the board and under his butt and sat upright.

"If the water gets choppy or you're unsure of your balance, you can always go down to your knees. This is your safe position." He stood up in a smooth, lithe movement. "Try standing up, facing forward. Take your time."

Lucas went to his knees first, and spent a few minutes like that, getting used to it. And then, slowly, lumbering, he got to his feet, arms waving to catch his balance.

"Tighten your core, and stand straight. Get used to just standing on the board at first."

Lucas took a deep breath and held it, glancing back at me. I saw resolve harden on his face, and he stiffened, but that didn't' help. If anything, it made it worse.

"Relax, Lucas," I said. "Remember, the worst that can happen is you go for a swim."

"Relax, she says," Lucas snarled. "Easy for you to say. I feel like a walrus balancing on a toothpick."

"A-*hem*," I coughed.

He rolled his eyes. "Yeah, yeah." He closed his eyes briefly, and let out a breath. "I can do this."

"That's better," I said. "Try it again, this time with feeling."

He loosened, and his balance improved. "I can do this." This time he sounded like he almost believed it.

Kyle was just drifting, paddle blade resting on his board, watching the two of us. He grinned at me, and paddled back to the dock.

Once Lucas got the hang of things we paddled for a while, staying fairly close to the shore. The more he did it, the better he got and by the time two hours had passed Lucas had established an easy style and was paddling easily, keeping his balance effortlessly. He was even grinning.

Eventually we returned to the dock, returned his board and paddle, and headed for my truck—Lucas insisted on carrying mine for me, which only made me the tiniest bit melty.

Sitting in my truck, engine idling, I looked over at Lucas. "So. Paddleboarding."

He leaned his head back against the headrest and groaned. "I'm sore in places I didn't know could be sore." He swiveled his head to grin at me. "I had a lot of fun, though. A little weird and scary at first, but it ended up being fun."

I shouldn't be this giddy; we were just friends. "So…you'd go with me again?"

He smirked. "If you'll be there, yeah."

"But not by yourself?"

He snorted. "Not by a long shot, Liv."

I laughed while sighing. "Baby steps, huh?"

He glanced at me, one eyebrow brow arched.

"Getting a three-hundred-and-some pound, six-foot-four, sixty-two-year-old redneck out on a paddleboard? That there is a hell of a big step, sweetheart."

"I suppose when you put it that way…" I said.

He glanced at his palms, which had the beginnings of blisters. "You want to get some lunch with me?"

I smiled, heart thumping hard. "Yes, I do."

"Know where Badd's Bar and Grill is?"

I shrugged. "I've heard of it. Pretty popular local hangout, from what I hear."

"My nephews own it. My dad opened it a few years after I left Alaska, and my brother bought it a couple years after that, and then took over when Dad's health started failing." He sighed, as if something in that statement was painful.

"What aren't you saying?" I asked.

He shrugged. "A lot, probably."

"Start with something small?"

He groaned, rubbing his temple. "I wasn't there when Dad passed. Or Gramps. Or Liam."

I wasn't sure what to say that—he wasn't so much mourning their loss or expressing sadness over it, but that he hadn't been there; condolences didn't seem appropriate right now.

"Why not?"

"Some grudges are impossible to get over."

"Against them?"

He rolled a shoulder, staring out the window. "Liv, I…" His sigh was more of a growl. "It's history. No sense digging it up. They're all in their graves, now."

I recognized his need to let it go, and nodded. "Okay."

"Just like that, huh?"

I shrugged. "If you don't want to, or can't bring yourself to talk about it, I understand. I'm not going to push or pry."

"I…well, I appreciate that," he said. "More'n you know."

"Badd's Bar and Grill, then?"

He nodded. "Bax said he'd be there this afternoon. Sunday lunch with the crew is a thing, I guess. Should be some good grub."

I felt a little woozy at his suggestion. "The crew, meaning…your family?"

He gazed at me. "Didn't think of it like that. We can go somewhere else."

I shook my head, resolved to not make more of it than need be. "No, it's fine. It sounds like fun."

It sounded like a date, is what it sounded like… with his extended family.

It turned out we were just down the road, so the drive there was short. The parking spots along the street near the bar were filled with trucks of all sizes and colors. A big motorcycle was parked out front, and there was a giant yacht in the harbor down on the quay which something told me belonged to someone in the bar. There was music thudding from within, and a sandwich board was placed outside the propped-open doors which read in neat block lettering: *"Closed for a private event. Open to the public Monday!"*

We found an open parking spot a dozen or so feet down the road from the bar, and made our way toward it. I sensed nerves jangling in Lucas, but wasn't sure what to say. We paused at the open doors, and Lucas seemed hesitant to go in.

"Are you okay?" I asked.

He nodded, and then shook his head. "I shoulda been straight with you. The whole gang meets here every Sunday, but this is the first time I've been to one of these gatherings. I kinda invited you because I need some moral support."

I frowned. "They're your family."

He nodded, glanced at me. "Yeah. But…" he trailed off.

"What?"

His head ducked. Shoulders slumped. "I didn't even know I had family other than my kids and my estranged brother until a couple years ago."

"Really?"

"I was hiding down in Oklahoma. Drinkin' my-self into a goddamned stupor every fuckin' day... didn't know Liam and Lena had had any kids, let alone fuckin' *eight* of 'em." His drawl was pronounced, and his language saltier than ever. Signs of agitation, as if I needed any further proof other than his overall demeanor.

"Lucas..."

He huffed, half growl, half sigh. "Rome found out, dragged his brothers up here. Never left. Now I'm here, and I don't know my own kin from Adam. They all got wives and girlfriends and fiancées and kids, and my own boys are settlin' down, and I..." He swallowed hard. "I can't bring myself to go in there."

"Why not?"

"I was a fuckin' coward, Liv. Hid from my own brother because of...shit. Not goin' there. Point is, they don't know me. I don't know what I was thinkin', draggin' you into this damned mess."

I smiled at him, resting my hand on his shoulder. "There's never any time like the present for mending things with family." I was standing close enough to him that I could feel his body heat and his anxiety. "Do they hold ill will toward you?"

He scoffed. "Hell, no. The opposite. They've been badgerin' me to get to one of these gatherings for months. I've just been too damn chicken. And now I'm hidin' behind a woman." He growled, slapping himself in the forehead. "God, I'm such a fuckin' tool."

"Positive self-talk, Lucas. Remember?"

"That shit may work for stayin' on a paddleboard, but this here is serious emotional baggage."

"This kind of situation is exactly what it's most needed for." I saw his hands opening and closing, trembling. "I…I don't know how to ask this tactfully, so I'll just ask. This being a bar, is that going to be an issue for you? Considering…"

He nodded. "Another reason for being nervous—I've avoided these for that reason. I ain't been sure I was strong enough to be around drinking without falling off the wagon."

"And now you are?"

He shook his head. "Hell no. But if I want to get anywhere with my kids and my nephews and all of them, I gotta figure out how to be okay."

"Another reason for my presence, I imagine."

He nodded. "Yeah. Thought maybe if you were with me, I'd have that much more of a reason for stayin' strong."

I turned away, sorting through my myriad of emotions. "I will say that I wish you'd been more forthright about your reasons for asking me here. I feel somewhat blindsided."

"I'm sorry."

"I am willing to be here with you, for all the reasons you've stated, and simply because I enjoy spending time with you." I turned to face him. "I am a woman who appreciates honesty above all else, Lucas. Just…talk to me. Don't blindside me, and don't use me."

He nodded, and then jerked his head in the direction of my truck. "Let's go. I'll do this another day, on my own."

I shook my head and grabbed his hand, pulling him back before he could walk away. "No."

He halted, eyeing me with astonishment. "No?"

"We're here. I smell food, it smells good, and I'm hungry." I smiled at him as brightly and reassuringly as I could. "No time like the present."

He blinked at me, and then slowly shook his head. "I wonder if God misses you up there."

I frowned, tilting my head in puzzlement. "What?"

"Well, I figure heaven lost an angel when you came down here, and I wonder if God misses having you up there with him."

I laughed, leaning into him. "Ohhh, Lucas. What a pickup line."

He winked at me. "It wasn't a line, sweetheart. You really are an angel."

"I'm not an angel."

"Then tell me your biggest flaw."

I laughed. "Just one?"

"How many can you have?"

"Just as many as the next person, Lucas. I'm far from perfect."

"Then name one."

I sighed, thinking. "I'm great at figuring out other people, and expect honesty from them, but I am not always so great at figuring out myself and being honest with myself."

His expression was musing. "Hmmm. Interesting to note."

I frowned. "What does that mean?"

He shook his head, grinning. "Nothin'. Let's go in and party." He paused, waving a hand. "Party clean, for me." He gestured at me. "You better not feel any kind of obligation to not drink just for me. My issue is mine and mine alone. Okay?"

I smiled. "I have never really been much of drinker, truthfully. A bit in high school and college, and maybe a glass of wine or two here and there with Darren, but I never really enjoyed being drunk, so it's really not a big deal for me." I grabbed his arm and held on. "So, rest assured, if I don't drink, it's because I don't want to, not because of you."

He nodded. "Okay, then." He took in a deep

breath and stepped between the doors. "Let's go meet my family."

I sucked in a deep breath, shunted my own nerves way down, and pasted on a smile. I didn't entirely have to fake it, because just being around Lucas tended to put a smile on my face. But nonetheless, if I was being honest with myself—which, like I'd told him, I wasn't always very good at—I was feeling as if a large cloud of butterflies were dancing in my stomach.

Lucas's family.

This had suddenly gone from a fun, low-expectation morning on the water with Lucas, to feeling very much like a date. A serious one.

With a man I knew I was developing feelings for.

I shook that thought off, and refused to consider it.

Friends. Just friends. We are here as friends.

I'm just meeting my *friend's* sons and nephews. Nothing else.

Nothing else.

I wondered if he knew I was as nervous as he was.

NINE

Lucas

HER HAND WAS SHAKING.

I squeezed gently, and felt her squeeze back. My heart thudded, realizing I was holding her hand. Electricity arced through me, buzzing in my veins, setting me on fire. A simple thing, but for a man who'd been alone as long as I had, it was huge.

Once we passed through the doors, I let go; everything I was getting from her signal-wise was telling me she liked me, but there was resistance as well, and I wasn't sure if she was ready to hold my hand, let alone hold it in front of my family, which would be giving them—and me—the wrong idea.

She smiled at me as I let go, knowing why.

The interior of the bar was fairly dark, but it was buzzing with conversation, and humming with music. One of my nephews and a stunningly gorgeous young blonde woman were on a little stage in the back corner, creating the music. My nephew was sitting on a wooden box that he was slapping to create a drumming sound while the girl strummed a guitar, and they were singing in harmony. It was amazing music, although god knew I didn't know shit about music. I just knew it sounded great, and it was my nephew making it. The rest of the crew was clustered around the bar, standing, sitting on stools, a few in a booth near the kitchen, and others milling around.

I tried to identify the ones I'd met, and the names I remembered. I leaned close to Liv and pointed them out. "The big dark-haired one with the tats is the oldest of my nephews, Sebastian. He goes by Bas or Bast, or some stupid shit like that. Next to him is my son Roman, who you met. The one with the buzz cut and a permanent scowl on the other side of Rome is Zane, the next oldest of my brother's set. He was a Navy SEAL, which explains the scowl, I'd say. On the other side of the bar opposite of Zane is Bax, he's the big fucker built like a bull on steroids. Next to him is the pretty boy of the bunch, Brock. I think Brock is actually the next oldest after Zane, and Bax is after him."

Liv laughed, standing with me just inside the bar.

"You know I'll never remember all this, right? Even for me, this is going to be a lot of names and faces to memorize."

I chuckled. "I'm telling you for my own sake. Quizzing myself on my own family."

She bumped me with her shoulder. "There's a lot of them, so be nice to yourself."

I had no answer for that, so I went on with my inventory. "The young skinny kid with the glasses is the baby of the family, Xavier, the one with the long ponytail is Lucian, next oldest to Xavier. The one on stage is…Canaan? I think? Not sure. He's an identical twin to the one in the booth, and I'm not sure which is which. Only met 'em twice. I know the ones on stage are married to each other, and are pretty successful musicians."

Liv frowned at them, listening. And then her expression brightened. "Oh! I know them! They're Canary. My daughter Cassie is a huge fan of theirs. She also was a fan of…oh gosh, Bishop's Pawn, I think it was?"

I shrugged. "Honestly, fuck if I know."

She laughed. "You have a lot to learn.

"No shit," I growled. "Um. So, my other two boys are in the booth over by the kitchen. Ramsey is the one with the beard, and Remington is the other one, obviously."

"What about the women?"

I sighed. "I'm not as sure of them, who's with whom, or their names." I pointed at the bar, where three women were seated in a line, engaged in a three-way conversation with each other and the men behind the bar. "I know Dru is the one with the reddish hair on the end, married to Sebastian, with the tattoos. Next to her is…oh god. Um…she's with Zane. Marie? No, that's not it. Close, though." I squinted, thinking. "Mara? That sounds right. Mara. On the end of the three sitting at the bar is Kitty, who's with Roman. Not married, but living together serious, permanent-like, whatever you want to call that." I surveyed the bar. "The native chick is Juneau, who's with Remington, and next to her, the tall blonde with the huge…ahem. The tall blonde is Izzy, who's with Ramsey."

Liv giggled, slapping my arm. "Lucas. Really. I know what you were going to say."

I shrugged. "I meant it as a general description."

Liv bit her lower lip, stifling a laugh. "I mean, she *is* rather prominently endowed, isn't she?"

"Right? That's all I'm sayin'. Don't mean nothing disrespectful by it."

"You don't owe me any explanations, you know," Liv said.

I swept a hand at the bar in general. "That's

about all I can identify for sure. You can guess who's with who based on where they're standing for the most part, but I don't know all the women connected to my nephews, and I sure as shit don't know the names of the forty-seven kids running around." I winced. "Which would be my great-nieces and great-nephews. Which makes me feel old as fuck."

Liv shook her head. "You really do swear a lot, you know that?"

"Does it bother you?"

She tipped her head side to side. "I generally find it unnecessary to swear every other word. But I certainly won't tell you what to say or not say."

I laughed. "But you don't like it."

She shook her head. "I didn't say that." She smiled at me. "I'm just not used to it, that's all. Darren was raised in a rather conservative Christian home, so he rarely swore, even though we weren't really devout or practicing Christians, and my mother raised me to be...proper, you might say." Her voice took on an arch, hoity-toity tone. "'A lady has no need for vulgarity.'" She laughed. "That was her favorite phrase to use if I ever even used a word, like gosh or darn."

I arched my eyebrows. "So the way I talk would burn her ear hairs right off."

She burst out laughing, and god*damn*, her laugh

had a way of shooting right down south. "Oh my. Ear hairs. She would be apoplectic at the very suggestion that she had *ear* hair."

"That was a phrase Gramps liked to use. He would bust out with a long string of curse words if he got hurt or frustrated, and then talk about his sergeant in the war, who could swear fit to singe your ear hairs."

"Uncle Lucas!" I heard a deep, booming voice call out. "Get your ass in here, old man!" I saw Sebastian waving at me, a grin on his face.

I headed in, more than a little hesitant, now that all eyes were on me. Even the music had stopped. "Well, shit, kids, don't everybody stare at me all at once. Jesus."

That drew a few laughs, but the attention didn't go away. Suddenly, everyone was clustering around me.

Sebastian had slid over the bar and was standing in front of me, eye to eye; this seemed to be some kind of unspoken signal, because everyone went back to their conversations, and the kids on stage went back to playing and singing.

"About damn time you showed up for one of these," he said.

I rolled a shoulder. "Well, here I am."

Sebastian clapped me on the shoulder. "Welcome.

Seriously. We're all glad you're here." He glanced at Liv. "Who's your friend?"

I put my hand on her lower back, drawing her forward. "This is Olivia. Liv, this is Sebastian."

Sebastian took her hand in his. "Call me Bast. Welcome to Badd's."

"Hope it's okay I brought her," I said.

Bast grinned. "The more the merrier." He gestured at the bar. "Drinks are free for the asking, food's laid out in the kitchen buffet-style. Help yourself, and have fun."

I saw Rome eying me, eying Liv, and then eyeing the taps for the beer, and I saw concern in his eyes. So, I figured I'd better get the awkward shit out of the way right off the bat. "I'll help myself to food, but I'm sure my boy Rome may have mentioned that I have a tiny bit of a problem where booze is concerned, so I'll just stick to water, or iced tea if you have it."

Bast nodded. "There's always someone pregnant these days, so there's as many different nonalcoholic options as there are boozy ones." He pointed at the bar. "There's a big ol' Yeti over by the service bar with a bunch of different kinds of fancy bubbly water on ice."

"Ooh, LaCroix!" Liv said, clapping her hands. "I'll go see what they have."

She headed off by herself, and I saw at least four

of the women angling toward her. Sebastian chuckled. "I hope she's ready for an interrogation. She's about to get drilled by the Gossip Girls."

I chuckled. "The Gossip Girls?"

Sebastian pointed them out as he named them. "Claire, Izzy, Tate, and Harlow." He rumbled a gruff laugh as the four women circled Liv as she examined the contents of the cooler. "They're always the ones who want to know everything about everyone's business, so Zane and Rome and I have been calling the four of them the Gossip Girls."

"I know Izzy, and I know Tate is the one with the twin," I said. "Which is Claire and which is Harlow?"

He shot me a look rife with skepticism and humor. "Seriously? You don't know who Harlow Grace is?"

"How should I? I ain't never met her before."

Sebastian laughed, scrubbing his stubble. "She's famous, man. Like, household name famous."

I looked at the four women, who were now standing in a circle of which Liv was the focal point, and realized I did recognize one of them.

"Ohhh, yeah. I remember, now. Your youngest brother, Xavier. He's dating that actress." I pointed at the one I recognized. "Her."

Sebastian nodded. "Yeah. That's Harlow. We all call her Low." He pointed at the tiny blonde. "That's

Claire, obviously, by process of deduction. And, just so you know, Low and Xavier got engaged last week. Pretty big news in the entertainment world."

I watched Liv engaging in a lively conversation, a can of…whatever she called it, something French sounding, in her hand. She had a huge grin on her face, and occasionally laughed at something one of the other women said.

"She's a beautiful woman, Uncle Lucas," Sebastian said.

I nodded. "That she is."

"You guys dating?"

I shook my head. "We're just friends."

He glanced at me skeptically. "Just friends don't go to family get-togethers together."

I sighed. "I sort of didn't tell her that's what this was until just before we walked in."

"And she's still here?"

I shrugged, gesturing at her. "Obviously."

"She digs you."

I frowned at him. "Mind your business, son."

He growled, a deep in his chest sound. "Not your son, Uncle Lucas. Don't much care for that term."

I held up my hands. "Just a phrase. Sorry."

He was quiet a moment. "I have a lot of questions."

I growled, sounding a lot like he had a moment

before. "I guessed you would. This may not be the best time or place for that, though."

He nodded. "Agreed. I'm just saying. My brothers and I…there's a lot we don't know. About you, about Dad. Mom."

My sigh then was long, low, slow, and contained a note of pain audible even to me. "That there is a hell of a big topic, Sebastian."

"Call me Bast. You're my uncle. Only strangers call me Sebastian…and my wife if she's pissed."

I laughed at that. "Bast. Funny name."

He rolled a heavy shoulder. "Xavier couldn't say Sebastian when he was little, so he started calling me Bast, and it just stuck."

I shoved my hands in the pockets of my shorts. "You guys have a good bunch of kids, here."

Bast nodded. "Sure do. Dru's at the tail end of her pregnancy, as a matter of fact. Doc says it could happen in the next week or ten days."

My eyebrows lifted. "You're havin' a baby?"

He grinned. "Yep. She's thirty-six weeks, and doc says she's carrying a big ol' baby boy, so they're thinking they may induce her early just to make it easier."

I felt a surge of guilt. "Damn. I didn't even know."

He glanced at me sidelong. "I can't give you a polite response on that one."

I waved a hand. "I've been pretty self-absorbed."

I laughed bitterly. "Or, rather, avoiding all of you because I don't know how to handle any of this."

"Hey, at least you're honest." He patted my shoulder. "Enough serious bullshit. Let's introduce you to eleven of the most beautiful women in Alaska."

I laughed, following him further into the bar. "I know some of 'em. Izzy, Juneau, and Kitty, mainly."

What followed then was a whirlwind of introductions and conversation. I chatted with Dru, who looked like she was about to pop any day, and a breathtaking young woman named Eva, who was married to Baxter, and Claire, who was almost as foul-mouthed and inappropriate as me. I talked to Brock, the twins—both sets: my nephews Canaan and Corin, Canaan being the one who'd been playing on stage when we arrived, and their wives, Aerie and Tate. Bast made me feel welcome and at home, and at the end of an hour or two, I felt like I knew everyone by name and face, and felt a growing kinship with most of them. Liv had somehow gotten dragged into my orbit at some point, and was never far from me, although she was always engaged in lively conversation with someone, perfectly at ease. Her eyes followed me, though, as did Roman's.

She angled over to me when we'd been there at least an hour and a half, cornering me against the service bar, placing a hand on my forearm and disarming me with a sweet smile. "You promised me food, Lucas."

"My stomach is about to eat me from the inside out, I think," I said, trying to pretend I wasn't melting inside from the feel of her hand on my arm and the blistering heat of her sweet smile. "Sorry. I got caught up in gettin' to know my nephews and...nieces-in-law, I think they'd be."

We went into the kitchen, a brightly lit industrial space of polished stainless steel. The smell of food was mouthwatering—there were trays lined up on the counter containing chicken strips, mozzarella sticks, cheeseburger patties, hot dogs, French fries, sweet potato fries, and chicken wings, each tray kept hot with those cans of fire. There was a salad bar: a bowl of mixed greens and bowls containing diced green, red, yellow, and orange peppers, carrot, cucumber, celery, and tomato slices, bacon bits, shredded chicken, and shredded cheese; there were other trays containing baked salmon steaks, grilled chicken breasts, several racks of barbecue ribs, even slices of perfectly cooked prime rib.

Liv and I loaded up our plates, and we found spots at the bar and dug in.

Zane was on the other side of the bar from me, sipping a dark beer, eying me. "Uncle Lucas."

I nodded at him. "Zane." I gestured at the

kitchen with my fork. "Hell of a spread ya'll put out."

He nodded. "That would be compliments of Xavier, Ramsey, and Dru. They spend all day Saturday prepping all that food, and most of Sunday morning cooking it."

I blinked at him. "Ramsey?"

Zane snorted, a small grin on his face. "Yeah, Ramsey, your son. He's a hell of a cook."

I leaned back on my stool. "Ram! C'mere, boy."

He moved to his feet gracefully, and swaggered toward me, leaning his forearms on the back of my stool—it wasn't actually a stool, it was a tall chair with a high back on a swiveling seat. "What's up, Pop?"

"I didn't know you cooked." I indicated Zane. "He says you help put out the spread of food in there."

He shrugged. "I do okay."

"What did you make?"

He reached over my shoulder, stole my fork, and speared a chunk of salmon. "I do the meat. Grill the burgers, dogs, and chicken, season and bake the salmon, and the prime rib. Xavier does the fried stuff, and Dru does the salad bar."

I took my fork back and sampled the salmon, and then the prime rib. "Well damn, son. I had no idea."

He tried to hide it, but his expression darkened. "I had to learn."

I kept my gaze on the food on my plate, noting the sudden silence around me as those listening in to the conversation held their breaths at the subtle but definite dig at me.

"Yeah, you did," I said. "I never was much of a cook."

Ramsey's hands tightened on the chair back. "Hard to cook when you're wasted all the time."

I gripped my fork so hard I felt it bending. "Ram, c'mon. Not here, not now."

Liv bumped my knee with hers. "Lucas, you know…it's none of my business, but sometimes you just have to face things head-on, whether it's a good time or not."

Zane crossed his arms over his chest, and his eyes narrowed. "Well shit, then. If you're facing things head-on, I'd like to know what the fuck happened between you, Dad, and Mom. Rome seemed to know something, but it was nowhere near as much as we deserve to know."

I scrubbed my face with both hands. "God fucking damn it."

Liv rubbed my shoulder gently. "It's okay, Lucas."

"The fuck it is," I snapped, and then sighed. "Sorry. But I been avoiding this shit for decades. And now everyone wants to know everything all at fuckin' once."

Bax's woman, tall end of medium height, incredible body, jet-black hair, green eyes, a gentle expression on her face, spoke up. "This is a lot of pressure to put on him all at once. I don't think it's fair."

I managed a wobbly grin at her. "Thanks. You, I like."

Zane was an immovable force. "Fair? You want to talk about fair? How about I never fucking knew I even had an uncle or three cousins. My whole life, I thought Dad was an only child. When Mom died, he went to fuckin' hell. Shut down, willed himself to die. If you had fuckin' *been* here," he said, stabbing a finger at me, "maybe he would've figured out how to go on, how to keep living for his *eight* goddamn kids. Maybe he'd be here to be a grandpa to his grandkids."

"If you'd been around, maybe when he did die, we would have had you to lean on," Bast added. "I'm with Zane on this one."

I found myself staring at the wall over Zane's shoulder, at the bottles of whiskey lined up. Wishing for a drink. Almost able to taste it. My teeth gritted, and I felt the fork bend in half in my fist.

A small warm hand touched my shoulder. "Lucas? Breathe."

"I've never wanted a drink so bad in my fuckin' life." I growled.

"You don't need it," Liv said. "Don't give it

another thought. Just face it. Deal with it. Tell the truth."

"The truth sucks."

"It sometimes does. But you'll feel better talking about it."

I stared at her. "You must be nuts."

She frowned. "Why would you say that?"

"To be here? Gettin' tossed in the middle of some seriously heavy baggage of a family you don't know from Adam?"

"You're my friend, Lucas. This is what friends do."

"I ain't had a lot of experience with friendship, Liv."

"Never too late to learn," she said with a smile.

I twisted on my chair, glancing in turn at the many faces watching me . There were twenty-two people surrounding me, not including Liv. All of them listening, waiting.

I felt sick.

"Fuck." I sucked in a deep breath. "Fine. Here goes. I ain't told this story in its entirety to anyone— not ever, not once."

The room quieted and you could hear a pin drop. I paused, thinking back, summoning the painful old memories.

"First thing all ya'll oughta know is that what I'm

gonna tell you ain't gonna leave your mom and dad squeaky clean. Yeah, I'm a bastard and I got a hell of a lotta skeletons in my closet, but they ain't innocent in what went down, neither of 'em. You all want to know what happened? Fine. But don't go jumpin' down my throat when I tell you shit you won't want to hear."

"Just tell us," Bast growled. "We get it."

I let my gaze snap up to his, my eyes blazing. "You think you get it. But you don't. You're gonna want to take a swing at me before I'm done, I guarantee you."

"I've wanted to take a swing at you since the moment I knew you existed," Bast said. "Doubt your story will make much of a difference."

"Shows how much you know," I muttered. "Anyway, here it goes. You are probably all aware that Liam and I were identical twins, as alike as you two are, Canaan and Corin. Except we never changed our appearance—we came into town once every few months for a haircut, and we got the same thing, so there wasn't any easy way to tell us apart unless you knew us really well. We were poor, too, so we had basically the same clothes, cheap ones from thrift stores and surplus stores. We grew up by Ward Creek, out in the bush. We hunted for food, and if we missed our shot we went hungry. We pumped water from a well every day of our lives. We shit in outhouses and in the woods more often than not. Life for us was a matter of survival. We grew our own veggies, and the only way for us to stay warm was to chop wood for our fires. No gas, no electric heaters, just a fireplace. It was backwoods rough. We barely ever saw other folks than Gramps and Dad, most of the time. Mom—our mother was a local gal named Tanya. I don't think she and our dad were ever married, and she passed on of cancer of some kind when Liam and I were three or four."

I held up my bent fork, set it aside, and accepted the one Liv had been using and I took a moment to eat a few bites and wash it down with the weird-ass fancy flavored bubbly water shit.

"None of that really matters, though. Just background. We were roughnecks, wild, barely civilized, barely educated, spent more time in the woods than in a building." I shoved more prime rib into my mouth, and then continued. "Liam and I met Lena when we were…oh god, fifteen, just shy of sixteen? Gramps took us into town for haircuts and some supplies. Usually he'd pay for our haircuts and then give us a couple bucks to spend how we wanted, which was usually on cheeseburgers, fries, and a milkshake, 'cause that shit was a serious treat for backwoods bumpkins like us. Well, we were at our usual place up on Tongass, north o'here a ways. Ain't there no more, and I don't remember what it was called, just some greasy spoon kinda place. We were chowin' down on our food, chattin' about whatever, and then we saw her. Both of us, at the same time. She was walking past with a group of friends, but I know for me, there weren't no one else on the street the moment I saw her."

I stopped, sighed, scrubbed my face with my palm, and then spent a minute eating before continuing.

"Lena Dunfield was goddamned gorgeous." I glanced at Eva. "She looked a lot like you, matter o'fact. Black hair, green eyes…" I hesitated. "The, um…the same figure."

Eva blushed, smiling at me. "You're sweet."

I shrugged. "She was wearin' a short pleated white skirt and a red sweater, black boots with weird little heels." I was losing myself in the memory, now. "She, uh. Damn, she was so beautiful. Filled out that sweater like nobody's business, and the skirt was just short enough to make you think you might get a glimpse of somethin'. Never did, but you'd hope and look and hope. She stopped in front of the cafe for some reason—and that was the moment it all started. She was standing just a couple inches away on the other side of the window, and she looked at us. Now, this part was the subject of argument between Liam and I for fuckin' *years*, but Liam ain't here no more so you're getting my side of it. She looked at me first. She stopped, saw us, and her eyes went right to me. Then to Liam, and then back and forth between us. And let me tell ya, those big green eyes went wide, and she smiled, and god, right then, she was smitten. With me, with Liam, who the fuck knows anymore? We was twins, and she liked what she saw."

"Sounds like the start of a Hallmark movie," Claire said.

I scoffed. "Coulda been, I bet. Not that I've seen a Hallmark movie, mind you." I rolled a hand. "So, she came in, pulled a chair up at the end of our booth, and that's how the friendship started. For us, she might as well have been a fuckin' movie star. She was from the city, drop-dead gorgeous, funny, easy to talk to, and she seemed to like us, despite us bein' the kinda boys we were—no manners, uneducated, all kinds of rough around the edges, basically." I finished the food on my plate and pushed it back, sipped at my water. "We kept finding all kinds of excuses to come down here, then, and we always managed to track her down. Then, one day, she talked us into letting her follow us up to the cabin."

"From the way you've described things, it sounds like that took quite a lot of courage on her part," Liv says.

I laughed. "She was a city girl, through and through. If you could call Ketchikan a city at that time but, to us, it was the big city. Never been anywhere else up to that point, so this was *it*." I shook my head. "That was Lena, though. Absolutely fearless. Barely knew us at that point, but she jumped in the truck and sat between us all the way back to the cabin. Didn't even blink at how...rustic it was, and just to be clear, rustic is bein' generous. Dad and Gramps were shocked as hell when she climbed outta that cab, lemme tell ya. Coulda knocked Dad over with a feather."

"I bet," Bast said. "What was she like? Mom, I mean."

I sighed. "Your mother was...one of a kind. Ballsy as hell, but all woman. I mean, when she got outta that truck, Dad was standing there in denim overalls and no shirt, a shotgun in one hand, a hatchet hangin' from his belt, a dead rabbit in the other hand that was drippin blood all over his bare feet. Keep in mind, Dad was a monster of a man. Ain't no Badd man ever been small, but Dad was probably the biggest. Stood, oh, six-six, I'd say, and was damn near four hundred pounds of mostly muscle, though by that point he'd put on some weight around the gut. Big ol' beard, black as night, gone to gray in spots. Scary motherfucker, I'll tell you, even to grown men. He'd go with us to town on rare occasions, and grown-ass men would cross to the other side of the road." I couldn't help a laugh. "Gramps wasn't any less intimidating—he was like Dad, only older. Not quite as burly, but hard as nails and cold as ice. One of those old guys who you just knew, just lookin' at him, that he'd seen some shit and done some shit. He had those old soldier eyes, the permanent thousand-yard stare, even fifty-some years after the war." I shook my head. "And Lena, she just walked right up to 'em and shook their hands, never minding the blood on Dad's hand."

All was silent and absolutely still as I told my story. I felt everyone around me, clustered, hanging on each other, sitting on stools and chairs, and even perched on the bar. Gramps had been a storyteller, taught us history and the Bible by telling stories to us, so I guess I'd learned the art of drawing out a story from him.

I mused in silence for a minute, maybe two, and no one spoke, waiting.

"Get to the good shit, already," Zane growled.

I gave him a hard glare. "There is no *good shit*, punk. We're talking about history that turned me into a reclusive alcoholic, and resulted in my twin brother and I not speaking for the last forty years of his life." I couldn't help a snarl. "So have a little fuckin' respect, would you?"

"Sorry," he mumbled. "Just impatient. I've waited my whole damn life to hear this."

I frowned. "What do you mean? You didn't know I existed until what, almost three years ago?"

"Whatever happened with you and him affected him, too. He turned to drinking after Mom died, but he was a pretty heavy drinker before that—Mom's death just made him drink himself to death." This was Bast answering. "He wrestled with somethin', our whole lives. He'd sit out there," he pointed at the door, "on a chair, a bottle of Jack in one hand and a rocks glass in the other, staring out at the water, drinking, clearly thinking hard about something. Never would talk about what, though." He shrugged. "Now we understand…or at least, we're beginning to."

I nodded. "Alcoholism runs in the family, sad to say. Dad and Gramps, both. Great-Gramps too, but I didn't really know him. I just remember Dad talking about Gramps in not exactly glowing terms. So all of you boys best keep a weather eye on your drinking. Just be aware, you got it in your blood to end up like me, if you ain't careful." I noticed the way Dru glanced at Sebastian, and gestured. "You have thoughts on that, don't you, sweetheart?"

She palmed her belly with both hands, rubbing gently in circles, her eyes on her husband, loving and affectionate in a way that made my heart twist. "He gets…maudlin, sometimes, and turns to drinking to deal with it."

"Don't know what the fuck maudlin means," I murmured.

"Means I get stuck thinking about things, and sometimes a little depressed." Bast crossed his big tattooed arms over his chest. "Shit. If I say I don't have a problem, it'll sound like denial."

Zane rumbled wordlessly, pointing at me with a thick finger. "We ain't talking about you, Bast, we're talking about Uncle Lucas."

I sighed, nodded, scraping at the grains of the wood bar top. "Fair enough." I fiddled with the fork. "Forgot where I was."

"You were telling us what Mom was like when she was young," Lucian said. "I'm very curious. I barely remember her."

Lucian was the quiet one, from what I knew. His woman, wife, girlfriend, live-in significant other, whatever—I wasn't sure—was an exotic-looking young thing with dark caramel skin and dreadlocked hair and stunning eyes. She was hanging on his shoulder, nuzzling into his neck as he sat sideways on the stool to face me, his arm slung low around her hips in a casually possessive curl.

I rubbed my jaw. "Lena…god, how do you describe an entire person?"

I felt my gut twisting, my heart hammering, my entire being reacting with a physical, mental, and emotional wrench in trying to recall Lena for all these family members, when I've spent every day of the last forty years trying to forget her.

"She was…" I glanced at Liv, an apology in my eyes.

She rubbed my shoulder. "Go on."

"She was magical. No other way to put it." I scraped my hand through my hair. "It ain't a physical thing, either. I mean, sure, she was damned beautiful. But you kinda stop seeing that after a while, you know? That ain't quite accurate because you don't stop *seeing* how beautiful someone is, you just…get used it. She wasn't someone you could ever take for granted, though. She was smart, smarter than just high school learnin'. She would go to the library every week and check out as many books as they'd let her. She carried around this bag, a big old sack she'd made out of old jeans and flannel shirts and that ugly green canvas the Army uses to make rucks out of. It was always full of stuff—it was more than a purse, it was…I don't know how to put it. She lived out of it. Didn't register to Liam or I right off the bat because she was shy and quiet about it. But the fact was she had a terrible home life, and she was basically a runaway. And you know it had to be pretty fuckin' terrible if she preferred to be at our log cabin, which barely had running water and electricity, rather than her own home."

Bast, who'd been perched on the same stool as his wife, shot to his feet. "Wait, hold on. Hold on, hold on."

I blinked at him. "What?"

He shook his head. "I was organizing the basement the other day and..." He shook his head again. "No fuckin' way. Hold on—I'll be right back."

He jogged to the very back of the bar—to a door that led into the storeroom, and down to the basement. He vanished down the steps, was gone a couple of minutes, three at most, and reappeared with something in his hands.

He stopped in front of me and tossed it on the bar in front of me.

My heart...it hurt almost as bad as when I'd had the heart attack—I felt so bad I literally clutched at my chest, unable to breathe. My eyes misted, my throat closed.

It was Lena's bag.

My hands trembled, shaking like rusty, papery oak leaves in a fall wind. I lifted the too-familiar, long-lost shapeless bag up to my nose and inhaled—it still smelled of her. Mints, dryer sheets, and the faint scent of perfume. I smelled the woods. The ocean. The pine trees.

Lena.

The bag was not empty. I fished inside and withdrew…books, of course: *The Unbearable Lightness of Being*, *Remains of the Day*, *I Know This Much Is True*, *The Things They Carried*, *All the Pretty Horses*.

There were bookmarks in each, along with library slips indicating the books were now decades overdue.

"Damn," Bast murmured. "Guess we owe the library some money."

"Sebastian," Dru whispered. "Hush."

There was no sound in the bar other than breathing and the occasional cough or sniffle.

"This is it," I said, eventually. "Her bag. Her satchel of essentials, she called it. She came over one Saturday with a paper bag full of old clothes, some scissors, and an old tin box full of sewing supplies. She sat down cross-legged on the big old stump outside the front door of the cabin, and she made that bag. She didn't look up once, didn't speak, didn't do nothing except cut and sew. She did accept a pull of Dad's hooch, though. Took her maybe two hours, and then she held up this bag. Liam and I had just got back from chopping wood and digging a hole for a new outhouse."

"She made this herself?" Dru asked, running her fingertips over the fabric.

I nodded. "This was about…oh…six months after we met. After that, she was never without it. She kept a couple changes of clothes in there, food, a canteen, a carton of cigarettes, needful girly sorts'a things like makeup and whatnot. Sewing stuff. A big ol' hunting knife Gramps gave her. Sometimes she'd have a bottle of somethin' in there, or a baggie of dope. You could find just about anything you needed in this bag."

"Cigarettes? Dope?" This was Xavier. "I was not aware that Mother was a smoker of anything."

I waved a hand. "She wasn't, except socially. Meanin', us three'd go hiking up the creek, catch some fish, go swimming, eat, get a little tipsy, smoke some dope or a few cigarettes. None of us were smokers in the sense that we smoked regularly. It was just… something to do. Something you did, I guess. I dunno. It was the same with the dope."

"By dope, you mean…?" prompted Brock.

"Dope. Pot. Mary Jane. Weed." I waved again. "I ain't seen this thing in…god. Since the last time I saw her…that day at the park in Seattle."

"Tell us about that?" said Corin.

I shook my head. "I'm gettin' there, kiddo, gettin' there." I let out a breath. "The three of us were inseparable. We did everything together. She basically lived with us, after a while. Stopped going to town, except when we went. She'd occasionally vanish for a few days, maybe a week at most, but that was a once a year sorta thing." I paused a moment. "Liam and I were both stupid for the girl. Head over heels in love. We didn't ever talk about it, but for the two, three years she was with us up at the Ward Creek cabin, it was simmering between us. We knew it was gonna have to get dealt with at some point, but we were hopin' it would sort itself out somehow. I dunno. I know I…I loved her."

I closed my eyes and ducked my head. "Always have. Always will—she'll always be a part of me." I shook my head, rubbed my eyes. "We were always vying for her attention. One-upping each other. Who could get a bigger buck, skin it faster, chop more wood, run faster, jump higher, grow a bigger beard. Make her laugh. Buy her somethin' fancy. For her part, she was careful, mostly. I think she was just as confused as we were, if not more so. Liam and I were a lot alike, but also very different. She didn't want to choose, I don't think. Who would, though, y'know?"

"She picked Dad, though, obviously," Bax said.

I nodded. "Yeah, she did. Not easily, though." I thought a while. "Not sure what all I told you, boys," I said to Roman, Remington, and Ramsey. "Probably only partially the truth, knowing me."

"You said she gradually started favoring Uncle Liam, and it all came to a head when you took a trip to Seattle," Rome answered.

I nodded. "That's the truth, but only the vague outlines of it." I paused again, got up to refill my plate from the kitchen with more salmon and prime rib, and I allowed myself a few French fries and a mozzarella stick. "It got complicated. She liked us both, that much was obvious. But who she liked more was...less obvious. Liam and I, by the time we were eighteen, were gettin' antsy. We wanted to get off the Ward Creek property and see more of the world. Cast out on our own, the usual coming of age sorta shit. So we each got jobs down here, Liam at a bar, me at a lumber mill outside town. Lena would spend time with whichever of us wasn't working, and that was when things got complicated, because before we got jobs, it was always the three of us. When it was just me and Lena, I was on top of the world. When I was working and I knew Liam was off, I knew he was with her, and I was jealous."

I hesitated, not sure how much of this next part I should tell.

"Don't hold out on us," Zane rumbled, as if reading my mind, or my hesitation. "Tell it all."

"Fine. But remember, you asked." I ate a few bites and then continued. "Liam got sucked into the bar life, started working a lot, so I was spending a lot of time with her. I worked early mornings, so we would meet up after I got out and spend all day together, hiking, fishing, walking around town, just sitting on the dock and talking."

I thought of those days, and a smile crossed my face. "That lasted about three months, and those were the happiest days of my life." The grin faded. "We went hiking one day, way up off the trails. We stopped at this little pond, and we went swimming. Skinny-dipping. Things got a little…steamy. It was my dream come true. I thought that was it, she and I would be… together. That she'd chosen me." I swallowed hard, and summoned the resolve to continue. "It happened a few times. Her and me, usually on a hike, late afternoon or early evening. She…her favorite time of day was sunset. We would hike up to a hill somewhere, and…yeah."

Bast was sipping beer from a pint glass, and slammed the last half of it so fast he nearly choked, and then slammed the glass down on the bar hard enough to crack it. "You're tellin' me our mom slept with you…*and* our dad?"

I shrugged. "Who was first, I don't know. Was she goin' from one of us to the other? Don't know that either, not for sure. I want to say no." I couldn't look at him, at any of them. "I…all I know for sure is me and her spent just about every single day together for three months."

"What changed?" Brock asked. "What happened?"

"Liam…noticed. Saw us getting closer. Saw himself getting pushed to the side a little, not being in on jokes. So he cut back his hours at the bar and started seeing her while I was working. He'd get up early and take her to breakfast, or…I dunno. Shit like that."

"So she was messing around with both of you?" Zane asked, anger tingeing his voice.

I held up both hands palms up. "Told you, I don't know for sure what was goin' on with her and Liam. I know that once she and Liam started spending more time together, her and I were over. She still went hiking and stuff with me, but anything physical was over. Which is why I figured she started having feelings for Liam and stopped things with me." I swallowed hard, staring at my plate. "I want to think the best of her as much as you boys do, but you want the truth, so I'm tellin' it."

"Keep going, Uncle Lucas," Lucian said. "Good or bad, tell it."

I nodded. "She was tryin' to balance us both for another month or two. We'd basically moved into Ketchikan by that time, Liam and I living in a little one-room apartment. I dunno where Lena was living, to be honest. She was…she was hard to get to know. Very private. Kept her past locked down tight as a drum. All these years later, I don't know shit about where she came from, other than I suspect her family life was rough. Brutal, even. But she never let it keep her down. She was…sunny. I dunno how else to put it. She was just…sunny."

Bast cleared his throat. "Yeah, that's a good word for it. That's how I remember her." He blinked hard, and I watched him dash at his eyes without any hint of embarrassment. "When I think of Mom, I think of sunlight, and…warmth. She was quiet, never raised her voice."

"She was always humming," Zane murmured. "I remember that."

I laughed, nodding. "Yeah. She was. She'd find something to do, knitting or sewing or a crossword or whatever, and she would just hum. Not a melody I ever recognized, just…a constant musical hum."

Bast tipped his head backward. "Yeah."

I let out a harsh, fast breath. "So. It started to become obvious to me that she was choosing Liam. More of her time was with him. When the three of us were together, she would sit close to him. Address most of her comments to him. She still talked to me, we were still…friends. But that…magic, I guess, was gone. Whatever we had, it was gone. And I…"

I had to pause for a long time to summon the courage to tell the truth, out loud, for the first time in my life.

Absolute silence.

"I got bitter. Angry." I clenched my fists, hid them under the bar—tried to hide the shaking. "I started resenting Liam. Even her. I was still in love. She'd chosen him, but my heart hadn't gotten the message. Things kept going. I started seeing them holding hands, whispering. I got more and more angry, and bitter."

I glanced at Liv, and her face was a mask of sadness and compassion. I couldn't figure out why she'd look at me like that now, how she could feel anything for me.

"I, um. I figured I may as well try and move on, you know?" I shook my head. "Caitlin. God, that girl deserved a hell of a lot better than she got from me. I was usin' her, plain and simple. Relief, you might say. Plus, either revenge, or an attempt to make Lena jealous. To this day I dunno why Caitlin put up with it—she was a smart, beautiful girl, a good person. She had to know what was going on. But she hung around with me for a couple months. Called it goin' steady, back then, and I guess it sort of did help me stop pining over Lena in an obvious way." I laughed bitterly, shook my head. "That's a lie, though. At best, all it did was mask my hurt."

"You guys ended up in Seattle," Rome said. "The four of you."

I nodded. "Yep. All four of us were born-and-bred

Alaskans, never been south of Ketchikan, so we decided to take a trip down to Seattle. Just for the weekend, for fun." I stretched my arms over my head, then dropped my hands onto the bar top. "We ended up staying a week. Had two little rooms in a motel, three doors down from each other. Liam and Lena, and me and Caitlin."

"Was that hard?" Remington asked.

I nodded again, staring once more at a single spot on the bar, a whorl in the grain. "Fuckin' agony. Thank god my room wasn't next to theirs. I knew by then which way the wind was blowin', what was happening with them behind closed doors. They weren't crazy with public displays of affection, but it was still obvious they were a couple. I was tryin' my damndest to pretend I was over her, but…" I rolled my shoulder. "I wanted her. I thought I was the better man for her. I thought…stupid romantic kid that I was; I thought we was meant to be together. That she'd see the error of her ways and be with me, at some point. That there was somethin' I could do, somethin' I could say that would make a difference. I knew deep down I was foolin' myself, but at that age, when you're that lovestruck, you don't know jack shit."

"There's no convincing a lovesick nineteen-year-old of anything," Liv said. "There's no logic powerful enough, no argument convincing enough. The love, or obsession, or infatuation of a nineteen-year-old is an invincible, all-powerful force."

I laughed bitterly. "Got that right, Liv."

"I remember what I was like when I was nineteen and lovesick myself…and I've got five daughters who have all been through that."

"The lovesick me was a blind fool, and the king of all dumbasses," I said. "Things all started boiling up toward the end of the week. Caitlin and I were flaunting things, I guess you could say. And so Liam and Lena started to do the same. I kept seein' Lena look at me sometimes, sorta hurt. Confused. I don't know. Just these weird looks when she thought I wasn't paying attention."

"You said you and Uncle Liam came to blows about it," Ram said. "Over Lena."

I nodded. "Yeah, but I'll get to that in a minute. The week was awful. I was with Caitlin and lovesick over Lena, watching her get cozier and cozier with my brother, watching her look at me like she didn't know me, like seein' me with Caitlin was somehow painful for her even though she didn't want me. I was confused as hell. We went to this park, the four of us. Sat there watching the sun go down, smokin' dope and sippin' whiskey from a bottle. One of those rare beautiful sunny days in Seattle, where it's just…

magical. And Liam ended up sittin' off by himself, and Caitlin went over and talked to him, so that left me and Lena. She sat down with me on this bench. Didn't say nothin' for a minute or two. Maybe longer? I don't know. A long time, anyway. It was an uneasy, tense silence. Like, we both knew there was a fuckin' world of shit we both needed to talk about, but neither of us wanted to start. Eventually, Lena turned and gave me this look…I knew it was goodbye.

"I remember what she said as clearly as if it was yesterday. 'Lucas, I know you're in love with me.'"

Silence.

I swallowed past the lump in my throat. "'You're my best friend, Lucas. And I love you, but…like a best friend. I don't want to lose our friendship, but you need to understand that I love Liam in a way I'll never be able to love you. I'm *in* love with Liam. It wouldn't be fair to you if I wasn't totally honest. I know this is going to hurt you, and I'm sorry. I wish I knew how to make it hurt less, but I just can't. I understand if you can't be my friend anymore, but this is just how things have to be.'"

"Wow." This was Claire. "That's some brutal honesty for you."

I nodded. "Hit me like a fuckin' knife to the gut."

"What'd you say?" Ram asked.

"I didn't say a damn thing. Didn't know what to

say. Didn't have a single word in my head. Just…emptiness. Pain. Rage. Confusion. I don't fuckin' know, just…mainly it was just pain." I hung my head. "So I did somethin' then that set me on a course that would end up defining me as a person. I went out, bought a handle of Jack, and got obliterated. Alone. In the motel room. I just walked away from that park, went straight to the nearest liquor store, bought a handle, went to the room, locked it, chained it, put out a do not disturb sign, propped a chair in front of it, and sat and drank that whiskey outta the fuckin' bottle until I couldn't hear Lena's voice in my head no more."

Liv sniffed. "Oh, Lucas."

I glanced at her. "What?"

Her smile was gentle. "That doesn't define you."

"Maybe it don't no more, but it did. For forty years, that shit defined me. If I wasn't drinkin', I was thinkin' about it. Every waking moment of my life I spent running from her, from those words—*I love Liam in a way I'll never be able to love you.* I heard it on repeat, on a loop. Over and over. Getting blasted was the only way I could think of to make her voice stop."

"It still hasn't stopped, has it?" Liv asked.

I sighed, a long slow sad sound. "No, it hasn't. Being sober, I've learned to ignore it, but I still hear her. I can move past it now, though. I'm workin' on it. But yeah, you're right."

Liv rubbed my shoulder. "You'll get rid of her voice, Lucas."

I shrugged. "Maybe. Hopefully." I hesitated a while. "So, to finish the story, when I woke up I was in the back of the truck, in the bed of it. The truck was moving, and I just lay there in the back for a long, long time, staring up at the sky and listening to the wheels on the road, my head aching, heart cut to ribbons, what Lena had said running through my head, cutting deeper and deeper with every second. I sat up, and Liam was driving, with the women in the cab with him. We were just outside of Seattle."

Another long silence.

"He stopped the truck, got out, came around, and stood facing me. 'I ain't babysitting your ass no more, Lucas.' That's what he said. His first words to me. I told him I don't need him to babysit me. We argued. Fought about me drinking, about all the shit we'd been stuffing down for years. About Dad, about living in Ketchikan. He wanted to open a bar of our own; I wanted to get the hell out of Alaska. Finally, after a fuckin' hour of bickering like little bitches, he came out with it. 'You're just jealous,' he said. 'Jealous of me because Lena chose me instead of you.'"

"Ouch," Bax said. "That had to hurt."

I chuckled. "You could say that. I decked him. Knocked him flat on his ass. Truth be told, it was kind of a sucker punch, but I was pissed off. 'I ain't jealous of you,' I told him. 'She belongs with me. She oughta be with me, she oughta be mine. She *was* mine, but you stole her.'"

"And she was in the truck listening to this?" Bast asked.

I nodded. "When I shouted that at Liam, she got out, told me that wasn't fair—he hadn't stolen her, they just fell in love."

"Bet that helped," Bast said, obviously sarcastic.

"Yeah, tons," I responded, equally sarcastic. "Liam just looked at me with this pity in his eyes. I mean, I was a fuckin' mess. I'd passed out and I don't know what all I did after I blacked out, but I had a black eye and there was barf all over me and my clothes were ripped…never did find out what I'd done after blacking out, and don't want to know. But man, that pity in his eyes?" I shook my head. "That was the thing that made me snap. I just…I dunno. I snapped. I attacked him, and it turned into a hell of a fight. Neither Caitlin or Lena could stop us. I was operating on pure rage born out of pain. He was just defending himself, for the most part, but it turned into its own thing. How long it went on, I don't know. Till we were both bloody and bruised and couldn't stand up."

The sadness in Liv's eyes was haunting.

"He got in the last hit. Socked me in the jaw,

knocked me on my ass." I swallowed hard. "Last thing I saw of my brother was him turning away. He tossed my bag onto the side of the road. Got in the truck and drove away. I never saw him again; never saw Lena, or Caitlin either. Never saw my dad again. I watched them drive off, my twin brother and the woman I loved. Once they was out of sight, I stood up, grabbed my bag, and started walking."

"Where'd you go?" Rome asked.

I shrugged. "Nowhere, really. Just walked south, away from Seattle, away from Alaska. I walked until I couldn't walk anymore, and then I hitched a ride with a trucker as far as Oregon. He dropped me off in some little one-light town, and I got a room. And a bottle. I'd taken all of my money with me when we left Ketchikan for Seattle. I think deep down I'd known I wouldn't be back." I traced a pattern on the bar top. "Six months of wandering, odd jobs for cash or food or a place to crash for the night…I ended up in a podunk town in the middle of fuckin' nowhere, middle of Oklahoma. Saw a sign on a factory looking for help, no experience required. I went in, got the job, started working right there and then. It was summer and I slept in a field behind the factory, under an old oak tree. A few weeks later, I got my first check, used it as a deposit on a trailer. Figured I was about as far from Alaska as I could get, and I was sick of walking. Might as well stay there. Which is what I did. I never left that town again, except for goin' to Walmart two counties over. Forty years, I worked in that factory, drank myself stupid every night thinkin' of Liam and Lena, and Dad."

I shrugged, swallowed hard. "And that there is the story. First time I ever told it all to anyone, and probably it will be the last and only time." I stood up, trying to remember how to breathe. "Ya'll excuse me. I need to...I gotta go."

I walked out of that bar, alone.

TEN

Liv

H E WALKED OUT, AND I LET HIM GO.
There was a long silence after he left.

"Damn," I heard his son, Roman, whisper.

"Yeah," another of his triplets said, "Damn."

One of the women—the quiet, elegant one with auburn hair, involved with the enormously muscled man who was training Lucas—moved to stand near me. "What's your relationship with him? Pardon my bluntness, but I'm curious."

I let out a laughing sigh. "I'm not sure. We're… friends, at the very least."

Roman eyed me. "Friends, huh?"

I nodded, gazing at him steadily. "Yes, friends. Why?"

"He's just starting to get his feet under him," he said. "Last thing he needs is to fall off the wagon because he got his heart broken."

I wasn't sure how to answer that. "Roman, I...all I know is, he's a good man. Or he's trying to become one. I like spending time with him. Could there be more than that? I don't know. Maybe. But I'm struggling to get my feet under me as well, following a life-changing tragedy of my own. So I don't know, in answer to the question you're almost but not quite asking—will we become romantically involved? The answer is, I don't know. I don't know if I'm ready for that, with anyone, least of all with someone with his..." I hunted for the right word.

"Baggage," the bearded triplet filled in—Ramsey, I think it was. "You got yours, he's got his. Problem is, his baggage can kill him. If he drinks again, he's *gonna* die. That ain't a question, that's a fact."

"I'm aware of that," I said.

"And you're still interested in him, in being his... friend?" This was Roman's girlfriend, Kitty.

I shrugged a shoulder. "Yes, I suppose so. I'm not going to hold his past struggles against him. We have all done our share of making mistakes in this life, me included."

Roman nodded, as did his brothers, and most of their cousins. "Just...don't lead him on, okay?"

"I appreciate your concern for your father, and that you're merely looking out for him, but—"

"You understand, that in a lot of ways, he's still the nineteen-year-old kid on the side of the road, watching everyone he loved drive away from him, right?" This was Remington. "He never got over that. He aged, but he never grew out of that person, never stopped being that."

I sighed. "I think I'm starting to understand that," I said. "And unless he can find some healing and move beyond it, I think all we are capable of being is friends."

Roman held out his hand, and I took it—he shook my hand gently but firmly. "Sounds like we're on the same page, Olivia."

"I think we are," I said, offering him a smile. "But if you'll excuse me, I'm going to go catch up to Lucas. He needs a friend right now."

"He wants to be alone, I can tell you that much right now," Roman said.

"I understand that," I said. "But I said *needs*, not *wants*."

"It was good to meet you," Roman said.

"You as well." I scanned the crowd of Lucas's family. "All of you. It seems to me like you all have created something wonderful for yourselves, here. A gathering like this, every week? Amazing."

Sebastian's wife, the pregnant one…Dru, I think it was? I'd heard so many names so quickly, and it was hard to keep them straight all at once. She reached over and drew me in for a hug.

"You're welcome here anytime, Olivia," she said. "I mean that."

"Thank you," I answered, feeling a warmth in my stomach. "That means a lot."

I gathered my purse and headed out the door, with one last backward wave—I heard conversation erupt behind me, the gathered clan discussing what had just happened. I glanced both ways down the road, at the docks across the street, looking for evidence of which way Lucas had gone. The answer was, not far. I spotted him down the wharf a ways, leaning on a post, watching the waves curl and ripple, the seagulls playing. He looked lost and morose.

I made my way over to him; stood beside him in silence, content to let him break it.

"So. That's the story," he said, not looking at me. "Now what?"

I glanced at him, puzzled. "What do you mean, now what?"

"You've heard all the dirty details." His eyes lifted to mine, finally. "I expect you have some feelings on it."

"I do." I leaned closer, so our arms were brushing.

"I think you're still holding on to Lena. You're scared to move on. Scared to let yourself heal."

"I don't think I know how."

"You need a counselor, Lucas. A therapist. Someone who can help guide you past this."

He growled. "A shrink? Hell, no."

"You have the wrong impression of what a therapist does, I think." I hesitated. "I saw one—I'm still seeing one, as a matter of fact. All that happens at therapy is you talk about things that cause you pain, past or present. And the therapist listens, asks questions, and suggests ways you can help yourself heal from those things. There's no magic, no weirdness, no judgment."

"I'd have to talk about it all over again."

I nodded. "You would. A lot, I imagine. But that's part of why it works. Talking about it removes the power of it. The more I was able to talk about Darren's death, and my many and varied feelings on the subject, the easier it became to simply talk about it. When you refuse to talk about things, you unwittingly give them even greater power over you."

He rolled his shoulders uncomfortably. "I dunno."

"There is nothing unmanly or weak about asking for help, Lucas," I said. "In fact, I would argue that asking for help when you need it is, rather, a sign of strength of character."

"Strength of character." Lucas laughed, a bitter bark of a sound. "That ain't somethin' I've ever been accused of having."

"Then perhaps now is the time to develop it."

He eyed me. "Why do you care, Liv? Honest answer."

I was silent a moment. "Because I like you. A lot. I think I could develop…feelings for you. Perhaps I already have. But in order to protect myself, I have to be careful about who I let into my life, into my heart. And unless you are willing to do what it takes to heal yourself, to find your confidence and strength, I cannot allow myself to get involved with you." I swallowed hard, hating the taste of honesty. "I want to, I really do. But you're…you're still wallowing in toxicity, though you are not drinking any longer. The toxicity remains, and it will win in time, if not addressed. And I can't…I just can't, Lucas, no matter what my heart may want."

"Just your heart?" he asked.

I shrugged. "It all starts with the heart, and leads back to it," I answered, knowing I'd correctly divined his meaning. "For me, there is no separating my heart from my mind or my body."

He stared at me, and I couldn't read his expression. "I see."

"I want to be your friend, Lucas."

"But that's it."

"That's not what I'm saying."

He hissed, frustrated. "I think I need time to…to figure things out."

"I'm not going anywhere, Lucas." I met his eyes. "Literally or metaphorically. I am your friend. I want to hike with you, paddle with you. Have lunch."

"But not dinner, or breakfast?"

I frowned, trying to parse his meaning. "Lucas…"

"Meaning, dinner as a date, and breakfast the morning after."

I closed my eyes, wishing I knew better how to answer. "I…I told you. I can't separate my mind or my body from my heart—despite parts of me wanting something deeper with you, I can't go there unless I know I'm getting all of you. I won't settle for leftovers, Lucas."

He hissed again, and then groaned. "No, you won't. And you shouldn't." He looked at me, sad beyond expression. "I need to think."

"Lucas…"

He smiled at me. "I'll be okay."

I watched him walk away, and felt a heaviness. A reaching of my heart. A yearning of my body. I wanted to comfort him, and to be comforted.

I longed to be able to have dinner with him… and even breakfast the next morning, someday. But I knew I'd done the right thing. I just hated how much it had hurt him to do so, when he'd already suffered so much.

I went home, pretending it hadn't hurt me as much has it had Lucas.

"Mom?" This was Cassie, my second-oldest daughter, when I answered the phone Monday morning at 2 a.m.

"Cassie? What's going on, baby? It's two a.m., here."

"I know, I'm sorry. I just..." she sounded shaken.

I sat up in bed, turned on my bedside lamp. "Cass, baby girl. Talk to Mama."

"There was a wreck, Mom."

My heart stopped. "Oh no, oh god. Who—"

"Rick, my fiancé. He's in a coma."

I blinked, trying to be fully awake process what she was saying. "Wait—Rick...your *fiancé*?"

"Yes, Mom. Jesus."

"I'm sorry, I just..." I shook my head. "He's in a coma?"

"Medically induced. But now they're not sure he's going to be able to come out of it. Or if he does, that he'll...that he'll be..." She couldn't finish. "He proposed three weeks ago. We were going to come up and visit you and tell you in person. That's why you don't know, yet. No one does."

"God, Cassie, I'm so sorry." I let out a breath. "Are you hurt? Physically?"

"I broke my leg."

Oh. Oh no. Oh god, no. "Cassandra, no."

"Shattered it in three places. I'll need plates and screws."

"Cass—"

"I'll never dance again. Not professionally."

Cassie was a dancer—she'd gotten a full ride to Julliard, had graduated with honors and had been hired immediately by a dance troupe which toured internationally. Dance was her life. It was *her*—who she was, and who she had been since she was a little girl.

"I'll be there as soon as possible."

"You don't need to come, Mom. You have clients and things."

Silly, silly girl. She's always been the tough one, the show-no-weakness one. "Cassandra Danielle Goode, you don't really think you could stop me from being with you right now, do you?"

"Mom—" her voice broke, and that was, for Cassie, the equivalent of a body-racking sob, an ear-piercing scream. "I...I—"

"First flight out, Cass. Where are you?"

A long, long pause. "Paris."

"France?" I asked, stupidly.

"Yes, Paris, France." I heard her gathering her strength, her courage. "That's why you're not coming. You don't need you to spend that kind of money on a ticket all the way here. I'm getting the surgery the day after tomorrow, and I'll be on a flight home to New York once I'm cleared for travel. You can meet me at the airport. Okay?"

She wasn't the only one with a spine of steel—where did she think she'd gotten it from? "Cassandra, you will have your mother in that hospital with you."

"Mom."

"Cass?"

"Don't. Please."

"Stop, love. Just stop." I quieted my voice, knowing with Cassie the only way to get through to her was with gentleness; aggression would only stiffen her pride and stubbornness. "I'm coming. I'm your mama. This is what mothers do, Cassie-lassie."

She groaned a laugh. "Cassie-lassie? You haven't called me that in like ten years."

"First flight I can find, baby girl. Hang tight and be tough. Mama's coming."

She sniffled. "Mama, I…" she cut off with an audible gulp.

"I know, sweetheart. I know. Keep it together a little longer. I'll be there as soon as I can."

"Mom, flights here are, like, thousands of dollars. Plus a hotel—"

"Let me worry about that. You just stay strong."

"I know I'm supposed to be the tough one in the family. But I...I'm scared."

"You don't have to be tough all the time, Cass. We'll figure this out together."

"I'll never dance again."

"Cassandra, put that out of your mind. That's not your priority right now. And don't you dare put limits on yourself. Neither you nor the doctors nor anyone knows anything for sure. Right now, you just breathe like I taught you."

She did as instructed—took a deep breath to the count of four, held it for four seconds, and let it out for a four count, and she did this four times: it was square breathing, which I had learned from a yoga teacher as a way to combat anxiety and panic, and I had taught it to all of my girls.

Once done, she was steadier. "I'm sorry, Mama."

"Nope. Not a word of that."

"But you don't know—"

"I don't care. You can tell me when I'm sitting there with you."

"Okay. I love you, Mom."

"I love you too, Cassie-lassie."

Once the call was ended, I tossed my phone aside on the bed and did some square breathing myself. Calmer, I snagged my phone up again and looked up flights. The soonest one was tomorrow—or rather, today—at five a.m., but it was a flight with several long layovers, so it ended up being fastest to take a flight at nine-forty, but which only stopped in Seattle and went directly from there to Charles de Gaulle airport. And it cost almost seven grand for a round trip. Yikes.

But this was my daughter, and I'd have given her a kidney, or my very life if needed, so a few thousand dollars was a small enough price to pay to be there for her when she needed me. I booked the flight, checked in, saved my boarding pass to my phone, and set about packing. There would be no more sleep tonight, so I may as well get busy.

By first light I was packed for a month. Once it was a decent hour, I began calling my clients, explaining that I had a family emergency. In a couple of cases, I emailed them my designs and an invoice, and told them they could either wait for me to return, or take my design proposal and let their contractor create things from there. I suppose it was a testimony to my clients' loyalty to me that they all chose to wait until I was able to return.

I called a cab to take me to the ferry to the airport but, on the way, we passed my favorite hardware store.

"Excuse me," I said to the driver. "Could we stop here for a moment?"

He glanced at me over his shoulder, puzzled. "The hardware store? On the way to the airport?" He shrugged laconically, and pulled over into the parking lot. "Whatever, lady. Keepin' the meter running, though."

"Thank you. My friend works here and I need to speak to him before I leave. He doesn't have a cell phone."

"Who the shit doesn't have a cell phone, these days?" I heard him mutter, but it was to himself rather than to me, so I ignored his comment as I headed into the store.

I was greeted by Bill. "Hey-a, Liv. What can I get for you this fine morning?"

I smiled back at him, but it was strained. "I actually need to see Lucas."

Bill's eyebrows raised a tiny bit, but then lowered again. "Sure. I'll page him." He grabbed the phone, pressed the intercom button, and spoke into the mouthpiece. "Lucas to the register, please. Lucas, to the register."

Lucas arrived in a minute or so, wearing an

apron, carrying a handful of boxes of screws. He was sorting through them as he walked, not really looking up. "What's up, Bill? I never work register, so—" He saw me, then, and halted, mouth clicking closed. "Liv. What's up?"

I glanced at Bill, simply because this was a pretty private conversation—fortunately, Bill caught the hint, and muttered something about getting more coffee from the break room.

When he was gone, I shifted from one foot to the other. "So, my daughter, Cassie, the second oldest. She's a dancer with an international dance troupe, and she got in a car wreck in Paris. Broke her leg, and her fiancé is in a coma. They're not sure if he'll wake up. So, I have to go to Paris."

He cleared his throat. "Paris, like, France?"

I nodded. "Yeah. Her troupe dances all over the world."

"She must be pretty talented."

"She is."

"Broke her leg, huh? Not good, if she's a dancer."

I let out a long breath. "No, it's not. She says she needs plates and screws and things, which is probably going to be the end of the line, as far as professional dance goes."

He shook his head. "God dang, Liv, your girls

are goin' through it, ain't they? Sorry to hear." He fiddled with the boxes. "Is there anything I can do to help?"

I shrugged. "I don't know."

"Check on your condo?"

I shook my head. "I don't have any pets or plants, so there's nothing to really check on, but thanks. I just wanted to let you know that I'll be gone…I'm not sure how long."

"Appreciate the heads-up. Have a safe trip, yeah?" He shuffled his feet, fiddled with the boxes of screws, making them jingle as they shifted. "Liv, I…" he trailed off with a sigh. "Nah, not the time. You gotta go be with your girl."

"What were you going to say?" I asked.

"Just that I appreciate you being there yesterday. That was rough, and unexpected, tellin' that story like that, in front of all that family I barely know. You being there, not judging me…" He rolled a shoulder. "It meant a lot to me. More than you know. So…thanks. That's all I wanted to say."

"You're welcome, Lucas. That's what friends do, you know."

"Well, I want to be there for you like that, if you ever need anything. So please, don't ever hesitate to ask."

I felt something inside me melt a little further,

and I leaned forward, into him, wrapping my arms around him. I buried my nose in his neck, and felt his arms close around my shoulders, enveloping me in warmth and strength. For a moment, I just enjoyed the feeling—the feeling of being sheltered like that…something I missed dearly. More than I had known, I realized. I inhaled his scent—hardware store scent, soap, and something woodsy and male. Heady. Dizzying.

I backed away, unsteady on my feet, my heart doing flip-flops. "I needed a hug. Thank you."

He cleared his throat, a gruff, blustery sound. "Yeah. Well." He rubbed his nose. "You smell amazing."

I couldn't help a grin. "I was thinking the same thing about you."

He scratched his beard. "Ramsey got me some sorta oil to put in my beard, makes it softer and smell good."

"I…it's nice." I felt so stupid, feeling so off-kilter and heady just from a hug. "I have to go. Flight is in a couple hours and I need to be on it."

"Go. Be with your girl. It'll all work out, okay?"

I nodded. "Yes, I'm sure it will. She's a tough girl."

"She's got a great mom."

I backed away, breathing slowly and deeply

through the flutters in my stomach. "Thank you, Lucas. Hopefully I'll back soon, and we can…talk more."

"Don't worry about that. We'll catch up whenever it works out. Go mom the hell outta that girl."

I smiled at that turn of phrase, and then waved as I headed out the door and climbed back into the cab.

The whole way to the airport, through security and check-in, and while I sat waiting to board, all I could think of was how his arms around me had felt, how his scent had made my stomach tight. How being in his arms had just felt…right.

Then finally my flight started boarding, and I did my best to put Lucas out of my mind while I started researching places to stay near the hospital—Cassie had texted me the address of the hospital, so I should be able to find a room close by.

Charlie had broken up with her boyfriend and was likely going to quit her job, Poppy was likely going to quit school without a definite plan for the future, and now Cassie was facing a career-ending injury, and a comatose fiancé…and I had not known they were even engaged.

God, please, can we make sure Lexie and Torie avoid any life-changing crises? Thanks.

ELEVEN

Lucas

A WEEK TURNED INTO TWO, AND THEN LIV SENT ME A postcard from Paris at the start of week three, telling me Cassie's surgery had gone well and that she was healing and going through physical therapy before attempting the journey home. Cassie's dance troupe was paying for Liv's stay in Paris, while insurance was taking care of the medical bills.

I was working out with Baxter six days a week, resting Sunday and treating myself to a cheeseburger and fries; the rest of the week, I was working out, intermittent fasting from eight in the evening until noon, eating clean, lean foods, consisting mainly of salad, turkey and chicken, brown rice, sweet potatoes, fish, avocado, eggs, and berries. Funny part of it was, I felt better than I had…pretty much ever, even as a young man. The fat was melting off, and I was getting stronger by the day. My limp was gone, and that leg was back to full strength. My gut was vanishing by the day, my muscles were gaining shape and tautness, and my confidence was soaring.

I'd even taken up running every morning with Zane who, it turned out, lived in a converted warehouse just down the street with his wife Mara and their son Jax. Zane was an early bird out of habit from his years as a Navy SEAL, so we met outside his warehouse at five every morning, ran three, four, or five miles, and then I would shower and go into work, meet Bax at his gym for an hour of torture known as HIIT workout and weight lifting, and then I'd usually spend the evening at home.

Alone.

Sometimes, Roman, Remington, or Ramsey would come by and hang out with me, or take me to dinner. Occasionally I'd go hiking with Ramsey, and those hikes turned into one of my favorite things.

It was halfway through the third week of Liv's absence, and I was on the trail with Ramsey, hiking up in the wilderness off-trail near Deer Mountain. Ramsey was ahead of me a ways, out of sight but within shouting distance—we'd hiked together enough by this point that we had a system: he'd lead the way in a general direction, and we'd hike that way separately but always within shouting distance of each other. He'd long-since gone beyond the need to stay on maintained trails, preferring instead to head into the real wilderness, trusting in his knowledge of the terrain and a compass, while I trusted him…

And my own recurring memories.

Lena, Liam, and I had spent endless hours in these woods surrounding Ketchikan, and while the terrain had obviously changed somewhat, the basic landmarks were the same, and even some of the older trees I'd used for specific landmarks were still there.

I caught up to Ram as he topped a rise, pausing to sit with his back to a tree, sipping from his canteen.

He glanced at me, a long, speculative look. "You know, Dad, I gotta admit, I was kinda skeptical there for a while, but it really does look like you've turned your shit around."

I pulled a small pocketknife from my hip pocket and picked up a stick, whittling at the end of it. "You got every right to be skeptical," I said, slowly. "But yeah, this ain't a fluke. I feel good. I like being sober and healthy. I like working out, feeling myself getting stronger, looking less like a tubby fuckin' walrus and more like I used'ta look." I laughed. "Well, used to look, plus forty years of hard living."

"You look great, Dad." Ram grinned at me. "Honest answer, though—how much of this is for yourself, and how much of it is about Olivia?"

I sighed. "Honest answer is complicated, son. I'm doin' it for me, *and* for her."

Ram frowned. "Want to elaborate on that?"

"Well, she's sort of the motivation. I want to look good, feel good, *be* good, for her. I want to be able to go on hikes with her and not be out of breath in less'n a mile. I want to be a man she'd be proud to be seen with and, the truth is, I wasn't that when I met her. I was a sad sack of self-pitying shit. And yeah, she was the motivator to get my shit figured out, because I like her, and I want to see more of her, but she's too wary and too proud to be sucked into the mess that is my life, and with reason, damn good reason. So, if I start havin' some pride in who I am and what I look like, maybe she'll let herself like me more, and we can be more than just friends."

"You want that with her?" Ram asked.

I nodded, watching an eagle soar in wide, lazy circles. "Yeah, I do. She's an amazing woman." I dug deep, grumbled something that took a lot of courage to speak out loud, which I realized I could only have said to Ramsey, my most temperamental but insightful son. "I want to deserve a woman like her."

Ramsey was silent a while, and I could feel him

thinking; that's why I could only have said to him—he'd think, and respond with care, when it was something serious like this.

"I think you're definitely getting there, Dad."

"Not there yet, though?"

He shook his head, breaking a twig into small pieces; a warm breeze blew, ruffling his thick beard and shaggy blond hair. "You haven't dealt with things. Not really. Talking about it was a big step, and I recognize what it took for you to do that, especially in such a big setting. But that's not the same as doing the work to deal with it on a deeper level."

I growled. "Before she left, Liv told me I should see a shrink."

Ram poked into the soil between his toes with a bit of the twig he'd snapped into pieces. "You should. There ain't the stigma in seeing a therapist that there used to be."

I sighed. "Yeah, I guess you're right." I took a deep breath of the wild air, smelling pine needles and earth and sunshine—a commingling of scents that meant Alaska to me. "Ram, I...I know I've hinted at this in the recent past, but I don't think I've ever said it outright in so many words." I met his eyes. "I'm sorry. For all the ways I wronged you and your brothers. Neglected you. Made you take care'o me when it shoulda been the other way 'round. I gotta say this to your brothers, as well. But I'm sayin' it to you, now. I'm sorry."

Ram clapped a burly arm over my shoulders. "Forgiven, Dad. You making the effort you are to turn things around is all I needed to see."

My throat closed, and I blinked hard. Ducked my head. "Let's—uh. Let's keep hiking."

Ram didn't let go of me, though. "Nuh-uh. Don't bluff past this moment, Pop. You gotta live in the moment. Something I've been learning from Izz—emotions ain't bad things. Feel 'em. Let 'em breathe inside you. Don't shove 'em down, or run past 'em, just 'cause you're feeling something strong."

"I been drinkin' my way past strong emotions for forty years, boy. Don't rightly know what the fuck it even means to let emotions breathe inside me. Shit sounds like Yoda Buddhist bullshit, if you ask me."

"Yoda was wise, for a funny-talking little green puppet, and Buddhism isn't bullshit. Just 'cause it's a little mystical or deep doesn't mean its bullshit."

I laughed. "Fine, whatever."

My eyes were still stinging, but I tried to just let the mess be there instead of shoving it down. After a while, it all kind of morphed into…something else. Not sadness, or depression, just a sense of…deeply powerful gratitude that I'd been able to have this moment, here, with Ram.

Ram eyed me sidelong. "All right?"

I nodded, breathing deeply. "Yeah. Really good, actually." I shot a grin at him. "Just really glad we had this."

He nudged me with his shoulder. "Me too." He stood up. "Rome and Rem may not be as easy, though. Just fair warning."

I nodded and stood up. "I know. Rome still harbors a lot of resentment toward me."

"Remington, too, but he hides it better. He may actually be the hardest to win over." Ram took another sip of water from his canteen, and then clipped it back in place on his pack. "Ready?"

I did the same, taking a drink and then settling my gear into place. "Let's go."

We circled back down and around toward town again, taking several more hours before we reached the place where Ram had parked, at the end of a little dirt road. He slung his pack onto the backseat of his truck, and I did the same, and then Ram paused, resting his forearms on the lip of the truck bed, eying me speculatively.

"You know, I've been running guided tours and hunts for a while now, just on word of mouth, cash-only. Been putting off the process of creating an actual business out of it." He kept his gaze on mine.

"Okay?"

"Issue is, I can't really run things the way I'd want to without at least one other person. I need someone to do shorter local hikes, hunts, and fishing trips, hold down the office and shit like that." He arched an eyebrow. "It'd have to be someone who knows this area like the back of their hand, someone comfortable out in the woods, hunting and fishing and hiking. Someone I trust."

"You gettin' at somethin' specific, or you just yammerin' to hear yourself talk?"

He rolled his eyes, laughing, and shook his head. "You, you big dumb lummox. These hikes we've been going on together…it's something I've been thinking about for a few weeks now."

I let out a shocked breath. "You serious?"

He nodded. "As a heart—" he cut himself off with a bark of laughter. "Bad choice of words, sorry. Yeah, Dad, I'm serious. You and me. Badd Outdoors, or something like that."

"A Badd Day in the Woods," I suggested.

He cackled. "Funny. Too many words, though. Gotta be quick and catchy." He glanced at me. "That mean you're in?"

"I'd probably need to spend some time brushing up on my skills. Haven't hunted or fished in years, and while I'm getting back to knowing where I am in these woods, I'd need to get my dead reckoning skills back up to par before I'd feel comfortable leading folks." I stared at him across the bed of the truck. "You really want to go into business with me?"

He nodded again. "Yeah, Dad. I do. I need a business partner, and I know you're a damn good woodsman. You know this area better'n I do, and you haven't lived here in decades."

"Used to be you could blindfold me, drop me in the woods anywhere between Clover Pass and Beaver Falls and I'd know in a few steps where I was and how to get where I wanted to be." I laughed. "Even now, I could get us to the old homestead up by Ward Creek from here."

"Been up there since you been back?" Ram asked.

I shook my head. "Nope. Probably nothin' there but rotting logs and broken glass, now."

"Should think about it. Might help you get past the old shit."

I nodded. "Fair point." I let out a long sigh. "Let's do it, Ram. I'm in."

Ram grinned, slapping the lip of the truck bed with both hands, and let out a loud whoop. "All right! Badd Outdoors, here we come!" He climbed behind the wheel and glanced at me as I slid in as well. "You're wasting your time at that hardware store. You belong out here, Dad."

I nodded. "It's served me well, that job. Got me on my feet, introduced me to Liv, kept me busy...I needed time to get to this point, Ram. Nothing's wasted."

He nodded. "Good point."

We chatted easily as Ram drove us back downtown, and when he was about to drop me off at my condo, he tapped the steering wheel with one hand. "You know, you'll need to start driving again. You still have a license, yeah?"

I nodded. "Yeah. I dealt with all that already. Despite my history of alcoholism and overall terrible decisions, I rarely drove drunk and never got popped for it the few times I did, living in the boonies where we did. Wasn't anyone on patrol to see me swervin', and the bar I drank at was only a few miles down the road. Not excusin' nothin', just...anyway, the point is, that was my first offense, anywhere, ever. So I paid some fines, took some safe driving classes and mandatory AA, shit like that. I'm legally allowed to drive, I just..." I shrugged. "Haven't wanted to."

"The wreck shook you up more than you're willing to admit, I think."

I nodded. "Yeah, probably true." I sighed. "So I gotta get a set of wheels."

"And probably a cell phone made in the last, oh I don't know, twenty years?" Ram said with a laugh.

I pulled out the flip phone I'd had since the mid-90s. "What's wrong with this?"

"It's a dinosaur, Dad. Belongs in a museum. I need to be able to reliably contact you, preferably by text."

I faked a cranky growl. "Whatever. A phone *and* a truck?"

"I'll help you pick 'em out, if you want."

I answered with an uncertain noise. "I'll think about it." Then I turned to Ram and said, "I may need a ride somewhere."

The next major event was the conversation with Rome, a few days after my hike with Ram. I'd bought a phone, and was still on the hunt for a decent used pickup, and decided to call Rome for a ride to go check out a truck I'd seen an ad for on a corkboard in my little supermarket.

He picked me up within a few minutes of my call, and I gave him the address. Once we were on the way, he eyed me. "Got a phone, gettin' a truck…movin' on up, huh?"

I nodded. "That's the idea."

"What prompted it?"

I wasn't sure if Ram was ready for everyone to know our plan to go into business together, and

I wasn't sure Roman was ready to hear it, so I just shrugged. "Time to deal with it, you know? The accident shook me up, shook my confidence as a driver. I dunno. I guess the way everything happened, being immobile and the bum leg and moving up here after all these years, it was a lot of change all at once."

Rome didn't respond right away. "Which you brought on yourself."

I sighed, trying to keep the bitterness out of my voice when I responded. "I know, Roman. I know. I'm working on fixing all of that."

He had his window open, trailing his hand out in the breeze. "I do see you making an effort. Don't think I don't see that, Dad."

I had to dig deep again, summoning the wherewithal to say what was needed. "Rome, I…part of fixing myself and my life is addressing my mistakes."

Rome's fist gripped the steering wheel tighter. "I'm listening."

"So, uh…I just wanna say I'm sorry, and ask you to forgive me for bein' such a bad father to you and your brothers." I swallowed hard, cleared my throat, and continued. "For all the horrible shit I've done, all the ways I neglected you boys, and made you fend for yourselves growin' up, seein' as I was too drunk most of the time to…to be a real father to you. I didn't do right by you boys, and I'm sorry."

I wanted to duck my head and close my eyes and swallow the pain and the embarrassment, but I didn't. I kept my eyes open and on my son. Rome glanced at me, at the road, back to me again, his brow furrowed, his expression hard to read. He turned his gaze back to the road, and was silent for a long time.

Abruptly, he yanked the wheel over and pulled off the road onto the shoulder, shoved his door open and lurched out, rounding the hood to pace up the road a ways. I gave him a minute or so, and then got out of the truck as well, following him down the road.

He braced his hands on his hips, staring at the sky. "You know how long I've waited to hear that?"

"You shouldn't have to hear this. But, to answer your question, thirty-some years, I imagine."

He nodded. "I used to sit outside the trailer at night, waiting for you to pass out, trying to imagine what it would be like to have a dad who wasn't a drunk."

My eyes blurred with hot salty tears. "Fuck, Rome."

He whirled on me. "What? You think I'd make it easy on you, old man? One apology and all's forgiven?"

"I guess I was hoping for…" I shrugged, holding my arms out wide, palms up. "I dunno."

"We learned to fight, defending you—defending ourselves because of you. I was cleaning up your vomit and keeping you from choking on it by the time I was six years old. Keeping you from burning the fuckin' house down." He closed his eyes, shaking his head. "I dreamed of running away, but I never did because you'd've fuckin' died if we had. Truth is, I used to have these awful fuckin'…nightmares, fantasies maybe, I don't know what the hell to call 'em— that we would come home one day and you would be dead, and we would only have ourselves to worry about. You know, we'd steal money from your wallet just to go buy groceries because all there was in the house was booze."

I choked. "I know."

"So…you getting sober, getting healthy, apologizing…all that is great. It's progress. But I can't just snap my fingers and get over all of it."

"I'm not expecting you to just get over it. Or even for you to forgive me. I just…I needed to say it."

He nodded. "I appreciate that. I really do." He swallowed hard. "And I forgive you. It'll take time to stop being bitter and angry about some of it, but I can see you trying."

"Thank you, Rome. That's all I need to hear."

We got back in the truck, finished our trip to look at the used truck—it was an '11 F-150 with a hundred thousand miles on it, but it had recently replaced belts, spark plugs, alternator, brakes, and shocks. It was ten grand, so I bought it and drove it home. And on the way I tried to figure out how to have the last hard talk…with Remington.

A bell was attached to the doorframe over the door of the tattoo parlor Remington and Juneau ran together in the touristy area near the cruise ship docks in Ketchikan. Rock music was blaring from speakers in the corners of the ceiling, the walls were decorated with native Alaskan tribal art, abstract tattoo designs—totems, stylized wolf heads and bears and beavers and crows—along with a series of floor-to-ceiling mirrors that ran the length of one wall, in front of which were a row of tattoo chairs—six of them. Three of them were occupied, Remington at one, Juneau at another, and a thin, lean young man was at the third, his hair cut long on top and shaved on both sides, tattoos covered his arms, and he had three rows of earrings in each earlobe. He was wearing black jeans and a black Opeth T-shirt. There was an island counter in front of the door, with an iPad on a mount in the center and several books of tattoo designs stacked haphazardly—on the front of the counter. Facing the door was the business logo: *Badd Ink*, in lettering designed to resemble abstract native Alaskan tattoos.

Remington didn't glance up immediately when the bell dinged—he remained focused on his client's arm. "Be right with you."

"I can wait," I said.

Remington pulled the tattoo gun away from his client's skin and glanced up at me, then, upon hearing my voice. "Dad—you're…here."

I chuckled. "Yep."

"What's up?"

I was standing at the counter, and I tapped a tattoo design book. "I want you to ink me."

He laughed, rubbing his forehead with the back of his black rubber-gloved wrist. "I'm booked for a month, Pop. Make an appointment now, and I could get you in…three weeks at best."

I frowned at him. "I'm your father."

He went back to work. "If you don't need anything big or elaborate, I have about forty-five minutes after this client and before my next one. I was gonna take my lunch then, but I can skip it, if this tat is important to you."

"Sounds good," I said. "This is something that is important to me, or I wouldn't have showed up here like this. I know you're busy."

It was a week after my talk with Roman, and I'd gotten another postcard from Liv, saying she was heading back here the following week, with Cassie.

I was looking forward to seeing her—I'd missed her more than I was quite ready to admit, but I was glad to have had this time to get my shit in order.

One thing I hadn't told any of my boys, or her, was that I'd been seeing a therapist twice a week since my conversation with Ramsey, and I finally under-stood why Liv had pushed me to do it. My therapist had gotten me to talk about things from my child-hood that I had honestly forgotten, things that had clearly left more of a mark on me than I could have ever imagined. He'd delved into my relationship with my father, with Gramps, with Liam, with Lena...I had gone balls to the wall, telling him everything, all the dirty, ugly, sordid details of my life, and in turn he'd recommended various ways of moving past the roadblocks to emotional health—number one was apologizing to Roman, Remington, and Ramsey. I'd started that on my own, as part of my AA process, but I recognized the need for it beyond just sobriety.

I was down at least ten percent body fat since my first session with Baxter, and my endurance was way up, my overall energy levels were through the roof, and for the first time since leaving Alaska all those years ago, I could see some muscle definition. Baxter had told me the gut would start vanishing pretty quickly, but I'd see the most immediate results in my face, shoulders, arms, and chest, but that the visceral fat around my belly would take a while to get rid of entirely.

I was excited for Liv to come back, to see my progress. I wanted to talk about all that had happened in my life since she'd left. I wanted to simply breathe in her presence, in a way I hadn't known was possible.

Lost in my ruminations, I jumped when Rem clapped me on the shoulder. "So. You want a tattoo, huh?"

I stood up and rubbed the back of my neck. "Yeah. Something to commemorate this new phase of my life."

He kept his expression neutral. "Got an idea what you want?"

I shook my head. "Not really. Something that works in three R's, for you and Ram and Rome. Doesn't have to big or elaborate. Just three R's with a cool design or whatever. You're the artist. Surprise me."

He had a pad of paper and a mechanical pencil and he leaned over the counter and began sketching. "Sure. I think I can work up something. Give me a minute or two."

I nodded, and went over to a long narrow table up against one wall, with folders full of photos of previous works done by each of the tattoo artists— work by Remington, Juneau, and the young man who was here, Tomás, and two more, whose names were Rip and Anya. I spent a few minutes perusing the folders, and then Rem called me over.

"So, here's what I was thinking." Ram spun the pad around to show me his proposed tattoo.

It was an equilateral triangle with the words "wisdom," "courage," and "serenity" in calligraphy inside the triangle; I recognized this design as a fairly common one among recovering alcoholics, and I appreciated what he was doing by incorporating it. Around the outside of the tattoo, on each face of the triangle was a large, stylized R, each one slightly different from the others.

Using the pencil, he tapped the R that matched up to wisdom. "That's Ram." He tapped the R that corresponded to serenity; "that's me," and finally, the last R, above courage, "and that's Rome." He shrugged. "At least, that's how I envisioned it. Each can mean each of us, or whatever. Meanings are usually more in the eyes of the beholder."

I let out a breath, looking at it. "Wow. That's perfect, Rem. I love it."

He eyed me. "Yeah?" He glanced down at it. "I wasn't sure if you'd want a sobriety tat, or if it was just a general new phase of life thing."

"It's everything, Rem. Sobriety, health…you boys." I traced the words inside the triangle. "Those are the center points of AA, but I guess the further down this path I go, the more those three ideas, wisdom, courage, and serenity, become important to me beyond just being sober."

Rem glanced at the back of the room. "We have a private room, if you'd rather go in there than be out here."

I shook my head. "Nah. Out here is fine. Nothing I have to say can't be said while you're inking me.

The man in the chair getting inked by Tomás nodded at me, and lifted his arm; he had a full sleeve, with Tomás working on the other arm. He tapped a spot on his bicep. "That tat, there—the triangle. AA and NA. How long you got?" He was a burly, bearded guy wearing a biker gang cut on a leather vest; he was about twenty years younger than me, but looked like he'd lived just as hard as I had.

"A little over a year," I said.

He nodded again. "Six years for me. Best thing I ever did. I'd be dead or in jail if I hadn't gotten clean. Good work, brother."

"Thanks. You too."

I sat down in Remington's chair while he transferred the design to tracing paper, and then moved to sit on his rolling stool.

"So, where you want it?" he asked, holding up

the tracing paper. "It's kinda big. Had to be, to fit the words and the R's."

I held out my right bicep. "Here? Nice classic spot."

Rem nodded. "Easy enough."

And so, he got to work tracing the design onto my skin in a tattoo artist's marker, showed it to me for approval, and then began inking it.

I waited a while, until I'd gotten used to the stinging of the needle and the noise of the gun. He was leaning close enough that I wouldn't have to speak too loudly to be heard over the gun or the music; I waited, too, because it was Rem I was most worried about, in terms of reaction and potential rejection.

After twenty, almost thirty minutes, Remington paused, pulling the gun away and looking at me. "This really about the tat? Or you got something on your mind?"

I sighed. "Obvious, huh?"

"Well, you said it was important."

"It's about the tattoo, but there's other stuff I want to say to you. Things I've had on my mind for a while." I hesitated. "Having you do a tattoo on me, that one in particular, it's…it means a lot to me, son."

Remington took his time answering. "I'm glad to see you staying sober."

"Had doubts it'd stick, huh?"

"Of course I did," he said with a shrug, wiping ink away. "Who are you sober for?"

I watched him work as I answered. "Myself. Had to be. But it is also because of you three."

"So it ain't about that woman? Olivia?"

"Rem, I couldn't have gotten sober for anyone if it didn't start inside me, not even the three of you boys, let alone a woman I barely know. Yeah, she may have been part of the inspiration to start workin' out and getting healthier, but I was a year sober when I met her."

"You could still relapse, though."

"I wish I could be bitter about that statement, but I don't have that luxury," I said, sighing. "You got every right to feel that way."

"Yeah, I do."

"Let me ask you this, though: how many times did I ever try to get clean?"

He paused, wiping ink away, and then glanced at the ceiling. "Ummm...none, that I know of."

"Exactly. I never tried. I never cared. I was...too fucked up in the head to even think about sobriety."

"What's your point, Dad?" Rem asked, going back to inking.

"My point is, this isn't an *attempt* to get clean, this is *me*, now. I don't ever want to go back to how I was. Living alone in that shitty fuckin' trailer in the middle of fuckin' nowhere, drinkin' my fuckin' life away. Killing myself. You boys hating me, me hating myself." I growled. "I feel good now for the first time in my life."

"Good, huh?"

I nodded. "Damn good. I'm losing weight, getting strong again, I got ideas for what I want to do in the future, and shit, I *have* a future, now. Something to look forward to besides an endless retirement of bein' wasted and alone."

"What future?" Rem asked.

"Ehh, that ain't important now. What matters right now is that I got ideas. I'm healthy, I'm sober, I'm...well, you're the only one I've told this to, but I'm actually seeing a therapist."

Rem jerked the needle away from my skin, glancing at me in shock. "No shit?"

I nodded. "Yep. Talkin' through all the bullshit I put myself and you boys through, my childhood, the story I told ya'll. All of it. Getting down into the nitty-gritty and workin' on being a better person, not just the same fucked-up bastard I've been."

"Admirable goal," Rem said, his voice still neutral.

He spent a while in silence, then, working on my tattoo, and I let the silence stand, digging deeper for the apology, to gird myself for the harsh and unwelcoming reaction I was anticipating. I watched him finish the lettering inside the triangle, and then when he paused to wipe ink away, I caught his eye.

"Remington."

He set the gun down, sitting upright and stretching his arms and back. "What." His voice was flat.

Third time, last time…the hardest one of all. "This is a me thing, not just an AA thing, or a therapy thing. Okay? Keep that in mind. I owe you an apology, Rem. I was a terrible person and a worse father to you boys. I…" I swallowed. "Shit, this is hard. Sayin' I'm sorry isn't enough. Asking you to forgive me…that ain't enough."

He stared at me, eyes hard, unforgiving. "No. It's not."

"I can't change the past, can't undo what I've done." I blinked back emotion, swallowed it, remembered Ramsey's advice about letting emotions exist instead of choking them down all the time. "All I can do is fix what I can fix—meanin' me—and move on with my life, try to be a better person, and…and hope you can forgive me. Someday."

Remington rubbed his forehead with the back of his wrist, eying me with a carefully blank expression. Then, without a word, he went back to inking me. I sighed, closed my eyes, leaned my head back against the headrest, and let the silence ride.

Another fifteen minutes of silence as he finished the tattoo—agonizing, excruciating silence. When he was done, he set his gun aside, wiped the ink away, rolled his stool backward, and gestured at the mirror.

"Take a look," he said.

I examined the tattoo—he'd embellished it beyond what he'd sketched out for me, making the calligraphy work on the R's more elaborate and stylized, turning the triangle into braided knots, and doing for the lettering inside the triangle the same as what he'd done for the R's.

"It's amazing, Remington. I love it. Thank you."

He indicated it. "It ain't done—needs some finishing touches, shading, shit like that, but that'll be a separate session. I got a client waiting. Come back next week, Wednesday, say, maybe…three o'clock. I'll finish it then."

"Rem—"

He glanced up at me, frustrated. "I need time, Dad."

"I just—"

He held up a hand. "Dad, please. I heard what you said, and I know you're looking for an 'I forgive you' or something, some sort of immediate resolution, but I can't give you that. I just need time, okay? You're trying, and I recognize it. But you fucked things up for us so bad, and I can't just wave that away.

This shit runs deep for me, okay? Real deep." He gestured at my new tattoo. "That there…that's a big step for me. Putting that on your body. Take it for what it is—it's the most I can give you right now."

I nodded. "Yeah, okay. I get it."

He wrapped the tattoo, handed me a salve of some kind, and gave me basic care instructions, and then I stood up and headed for the counter.

"Tat is free, Dad," he said when I dug out my wallet.

I stared at him. "Your time is valuable, Rem—I wasn't angling for a freebie just because I'm your dad."

He nodded. "I know. And like I said, I heard you. I can't give you what you want right now, but I can give you that much," he said, gesturing at my arm. "And coming from me, that's a lot."

"I'll take it. Thank you, Rem." I swallowed hard. "I love you. Ain't been great at sayin that or showing it, but I do."

"I know."

Nothing back.

But then, I'd gotten far more than I had ever expected.

I went home, then, and thought about…a lot of things.

TWELVE

Liv

I SAT IN THE WAITING AREA OUTSIDE OUR GATE AT CHARLES de Gaulle airport, sipping an espresso, munching on *pain au chocolat*, reading a New Yorker article. Cassie was beside me, head tilted toward my shoulder, snoring softly, a paperback copy of *American Gods* by Neil Gaiman in her hands, her thumb holding her place, the book slowly slipping out of her hands. We had arrived at the airport three hours early, anticipating a heavy line for security and check-in, but there'd been nearly no one here for international departures, so we'd breezed through and arrived at our gate with more than two hours to spare. We'd shopped the duty-free stores, had a leisurely breakfast and then, still with forty-five minutes before boarding even began, we'd gotten coffee and a pastry; Cassie had devoured her pastry and slammed her coffee, then promptly fell asleep.

Which she definitely needed—in the month and a half I'd been in Paris with her, Cassie had only been able to sleep sporadically, a few hours at night and cat-naps throughout the day. She claimed this was normal for her, but it made Mama worry.

She had needed plates and screws in her leg, and weeks of physical therapy before she was able to regain full mobility, or anything close to it. Because her dance troupe was based in Paris, her surgery and subsequent PT needed to happen here in Paris, where the union doctors and therapists were located. Now, however, she'd regained enough mobility that she only needed to continue the protocol and have follow-up sessions with a physical therapist in the States. She was officially retiring as a dancer, however, and with no backup plan in place, was moving in with me until she could figure out what she wanted to do with the rest of her life, now that professional dancing had been taken away from her—even Rick, her fiancé, had been taken away from her. First by the coma, and then, once he had come out of it, he hadn't been the same and had broken up with her shortly after emerging from the coma—to focus on healing and being with his family, he had said. A devastating blow to Cassie, just to add insult to injury.

I was worried about my Cassie. She was depressed, angry, bitter, confused, and prone to emotional outbursts. Being a passionate, high-octane, high-energy, highly emotional person anyway, this wasn't entirely unusual, but she had always been a relentlessly positive person, able to find the good in just about any situation. Now, though, she seemed to be slipping faster than I knew how to handle.

She was leaving her friends in the troupe—as much a family to her as her sisters and I—leaving her life as a dancer, losing her career and the one thing she'd worked for since she was three years old. She was leaving Europe where, from the age of seven, she had always insisted she would live.

Basically, her life was as shattered as her leg had been. But, rebuilding her life wouldn't be as simple—not to say *easy*—as a couple of surgeries and a few weeks of PT.

I sipped my coffee and munched on my pastry, worrying about Cassie instead of reading.

I was worrying about my life, now that I would have a daughter with me again. I was just starting to adjust to life as an empty nester. Selfish of me, I know, but it was reality. My life was going to change, at least until Cassie figured out a new life for herself, and was able to find a new normal.

I also worried about Charlie, and Poppy. On top of being with Cassie all day every day, helping her to PT, and helping her move through the basics of day-to-living with the challenge of limited mobility, I had spent a lot of time on the phone and video chatting with each of my daughters. Charlie had officially left her position with the law firm, had sold her condo, and was living in a loft apartment on a month-to-month lease, living off the savings she'd been socking away for a house in the suburbs—or that had been the plan, she said, assuming she and Glen were going to get married and have children.

Now, though, she was living off her savings, doing a lot of yoga, running, and what she called "introspection", and which I called pouting and feeling sorry for herself. Which, I assumed, meant she was going to find her way to Ketchikan, at some point.

Poppy had decided to finish the semester at Columbia and reassess after that—which, again, I assumed meant finish the semester and then move to Ketchikan until she decided to pursue art full-time like I'd told her she should do months ago.

The only two daughters I wasn't currently worried about were Lexie and Torie—Lexie was at a liberal arts college in upstate New York, majoring in journalism and women's literature, and very literally burning bras and marching for women's equality and social justice campaigns of various kinds. She'd settle down eventually, I figured, but for now, she was a social justice crusader with a burning passion to right all the wrongs in the world, all by herself.

Torie…was the exact opposite. Laconic, easy going to a fault, difficult to rouse to excitement about anything, she was still living back in our erstwhile Connecticut hometown, living an apartment with four other girls, attending community college, working at a cafe as a short order waitress, and probably smoking a lot of pot and watching indie films at the local theater. I wasn't sure at all where Torie would end up in life, and while I wasn't worried about her in the sense that she wasn't currently in crisis, she was the child I worried most about in general, because she seemed to have no passions and no particular talent, nor any kind of drive to find one. She was content to wait tables, take two or three classes a semester at the community college, smoke pot with her friends, and watch movies. Which, being just barely nineteen, was fine for now, especially since she was supporting herself. But I just worried that she would never find her niche, and while I wanted to push her to look, I knew I couldn't. Torie was like water—you couldn't force her to do anything, or to go anywhere; the harder you pushed, the more she would slip and shift away from where you wanted her to go.

I sighed, wondering if I was going to end up with all five daughters around me again. While I relished the thought of having them near me again, as I missed them each dearly, and missed our camaraderie as a family, I had been enjoying my independence.

Which I felt guilty about, in a lot of ways. My independence had come at the cost of my husband's life—not that I'd wanted to trade his life for my independence, but I'd only found it after his death. I missed him dearly, and I'd trade my life now—or rather, how it had been before Cassie's accident—to have him back. In a heartbeat.

But I couldn't have him back—I couldn't go back, so I had to move forward and try to find joy in my life where I could.

Cassie stirred, murmured in her sleep, and her book flopped to the floor between her feet. I left it, and gently eased her down so her head was resting on my lap; she folded her hands under her cheek, on my thigh, stretching her still-healing leg out along the empty seats.

I'd sent Lucas another postcard the day before yesterday, letting him know I was finally coming back to Ketchikan…with a stowaway.

I had been shocked to discover how much I ended up missing that man. How much of my mental space and emotional energy had been spent on wishing I could see him, wondering what he was doing, hoping he'd continued his journey toward health and wellness, and that he was repairing his relationships with his sons.

Truth be told, in the deepest darkest parts of the night, when I was more asleep than awake, and my mind spun impossible fantasies that were more than dreams yet not really daydreams, I thought of Lucas. In the last several years I had purposefully forgotten about the importance of sex, and what having a physical relationship could mean to me. I'd woken up more than a few times with my thighs clenched together, my core aching, nipples hard, and mental images of him and me entwined and naked dancing through my mind.

The feeling of his hand in mine was seared onto my soul.

The sound of his rough, gravelly, southern drawl and vulgar expressions were emblazoned on my heart.

I'd managed to keep such things under some kind of control when I'd been around him every day, but now that I'd spent nearly two months away from him, all I could think of was him.

And the longer I went without seeing him, talking to him, being around him, the more intense my feelings grew …and the more wild my thoughts.

I sighed, staring into space, letting my mind wander:

How long had it been since I'd last had sex? It had been with Darren, obviously, and he had died three and a half years ago…closer to four, now. And, before his death, things had been…sort of cool between us, sexually. I don't mean cool in a colloquial sense, but in a temperature sense. We'd gotten lazy and complacent, and he'd thrown out his back putzing in our garage a good six months before he passed, which meant it had physically hurt him to have sex. So… nearly four years since his death, plus probably four or even six months before that?

I tried to recall specifically the last time I remembered having sex with Darren.

It had been a Tuesday, a spring morning. He'd woken up early, feeling good, not much back pain, and we'd had a nice breakfast on our back patio, sharing a pot of coffee and chatting about our various plans for the day. I'd headed back to our room to shower and get dressed for my client meeting later that morning, and Darren had surprised me by following me back, and kissing me with a passion I hadn't felt from him in weeks, if not months. The sex that had followed had been passionate and quick. He'd fallen asleep soon after, and, if I was being brutally honest, I had been left somewhat unsatisfied. It had felt great to connect with him, and I had deeply enjoyed the way he made me feel…

But I hadn't reached climax.

Which, admittedly, I rarely did.

I shook myself out of that train of thought as Cassie stirred and sat up.

Her white-blond hair—a recessive genetic trait inherited from Darren—was loose and fine, sparking with static as she ran her hands through it, stretching with a groan.

"Still not boarding yet?" she grumbled, her voice scratchy and muzzy.

"Nope. Ten minutes or so, I suppose."

She nodded, picked her book up off the floor, and smiled at me. "That was a good nap. Thanks."

I leaned over and kissed her cheek. "You need to sleep more."

She sighed. "I just can't. My hours have been so crazy for so long that I just don't know how to sleep more than four hours at a time anymore."

She had been recruited by the troupe before she'd even graduated, which she'd done early, through insane hours of practice. She had all but literally lived in the dance studio and practice rooms, sleeping a few hours a night at most, attending classes early in the morning and dancing before, between, and after classes until late at night. And then, once hired by the company, she'd worked relentlessly to stay at the top of her game—the troupe was a competitive environment, viciously so, and to attain and retain status and seniority required constant practice and commitment.

And now she was at odds, with nothing to do and nowhere to go.

We both read in silence for a while, until the announcement for boarding blared over the PA system first in French, and then in English—"Flight DL1234 with service to Seattle, now boarding at Gate 81…"

As the first class cabin passengers lined up, Cassie and I began gathering our things, throwing away paper coffee cups and pastry bags, arranging carry-ons and purses, tucking books and magazines away.

In another fifteen minutes, we were seated in our business economy seats—her by the window, me in the middle, a middle-aged man on the aisle.

It wasn't until we were in the air that Cassie turned to me. "Mom, are you mad that I'm moving back in with you?"

I frowned at her. "Of course not! What kind of a question is that, Cassandra?"

She shrugged. "Poppy only left for Columbia last year, and you just moved to Ketchikan." She eyed me. "Would you tell me if you were?"

I sighed, knowing she was perceptive enough to know if I hedged. "I'm not mad. I wish this hadn't happened to you, I wish I could give you your career back, and yes, living with you again will be an adjustment, just when I was starting to adjust to being alone. But you're my daughter, and there is nothing in the world more important to me than my daughters. You will stay with me until you're ready to move out again, once you've figured out what you want to do."

"What if I never do?" she whispered.

"You will. You're too restless, you have too much energy and drive to stay idle."

"I'm scared I'll just go crazy. I've never thought about doing anything *but* dance, for my entire life."

"I know. That's what this period of time will be about—exploring your other passions."

She laughed bitterly. "I don't have any."

"Nothing? There's nothing, literally *nothing* you like or love or are even interested in other than dance?"

"Dance history?" Another bitter laugh. "Can't do much with that."

I patted her thigh. "You don't need to figure it out right this moment, Cass. Take your time. Give yourself grace—you've suffered a major setback, and no one, least of all me, expects you to bounce right back."

She nodded. "I know. But…I guess I do. I expect that of myself."

"Which you need to address."

"I can't just give up dancing entirely. I may not be able to dance professionally, but it's…" She shook her head and sighed. "It's part of me. It's part of who I am as a person. I just don't think I'd know who I am without it."

"It'll take time, Cass."

She shook her head yet again. "Time in which I do what? Sit around watching TV? Wait tables and do drugs like Torie?"

"That's not fair," I scolded.

She sighed. "I'm angry, and bitter."

"I know. You may need a therapist—for your emotions as well as your leg."

"I'll figure it out."

"Cass—"

She opened her book. "Let it go for now, okay, please?"

I plugged a pair of earbuds into the TV screen in the back of the seat in front of me, and chose a movie to watch for the flight back.

Since our flight out of Paris had been booked two weeks ahead, I'd sent my flight info to Lucas with the last postcard. At the time, I hadn't been sure why, but I hadn't been able to talk myself out of doing so. I didn't expect to see him at the Ketchikan airport, but a part of me hoped he would be there.

We deplaned for the second and final time at the Ketchikan airport, fought through the foot traffic to the luggage claim, and then hauled all of our stuff to the ferry dock—or rather, all of Cassie's stuff. She had her entire life in four suitcases and two carry-ons, while I had packed fairly minimally, leaving with one stuffed suitcase and returning with two, as I'd purchased quite a few things during my seven weeks in Paris, and had ended up needing an additional bag.

I dreaded the cab ride home—we'd probably need two cabs, just to accommodate all of our luggage.

Cassie was all wide eyes as we struggled off the ferry with our luggage, gazing at the mountains all around, at the wide rippling gray-green water and the clear blue skies with a few puffs of clouds here and there…and, as if welcoming her, a bald eagle soared over the channel in the distance, screeching that iconic call.

"Wow," Cassie breathed. "I always wondered why you moved here, of all places."

I smiled. "Starting to understand?"

She nodded, blue eyes wide and sparkling. "Yeah, I get it now. I really, really get it."

I was trying to figure out how to get us back to my condo, how to fit all this luggage and the two of us into a couple of cabs. I wished I'd just driven and parked my truck in long-term parking, but I hadn't felt safe doing that, not knowing how long I would be away in Paris.

I felt him first. Just a sixth sense. I set my suitcases down and looked around—he was standing down the sidewalk a good fifty feet, looking in the wrong direction completely. I let out a sigh—a mixture of relief, joy, and anticipation.

I bumped my daughter with my elbow. "Wait here a minute, Cass."

She set her things down and frowned at me, leaning down to massage a sore spot on her thigh. "Why?"

I shook my head, not knowing how to even begin explaining. "I...my friend is here to pick me up... pick *us* up. I wasn't sure he would be, but he is."

Cassie's radar honed in on something in my voice and expression. "A friend?"

I gave her a Mom special—the look that says *don't push me, child*. "Yes. A friend."

"We'll be talking about this later, Mother." Cassie, ever impertinent, always did like to push; especially when she knew I didn't want to her to.

I snorted but otherwise ignored her as I weaved through the crowd disembarking the ferry, and the family and friends welcoming them.

I was within a dozen feet of him, and he still

hadn't noticed me. I finally reached him, stood close enough to smell the cedar and pine of his beard oil— close enough to see that he had indeed not been idle the last two months. He was…wow. Well on his way to being jacked, as Lexie liked to put it. His arms stretched the short sleeves of his T-shirt, which was also stretched taut around his mammoth shoulders and chest. There was still a hint of a belly behind the shirt, but it was nearly gone. He'd gone down several jeans sizes, his hair was short and clean cut, and his beard was gone, replaced by a short, neat, silver-and-black goatee, his jawline shaved. He'd had his ears pierced, I noted, simple silver hoops in each ear—it was a look I'd never cared for, generally, but on him somehow just…worked. He had on a necklace as well, braided black leather with bits of what looked like bone—teeth or claws sandwiched between cylinders of polished metal. He also had tattoos, an indigenous, tribal, totem sort of thing on the bicep facing me, obviously a work in progress, and as he reached up to scratch his hair, I saw another tattoo on that forearm, but couldn't quite make out what it was.

His jeans were loose but not baggy, a faded light wash, his T-shirt was a plain black V-neck, and he wore expensive-looking hiking boots.

My heart skipped a beat at the sight of him.

Something else further south in me also sat up

and took notice of this new and improved version of Lucas Badd. It was, all in all, a remarkable physical transformation.

My mouth was dry, my hand trembling as I reached up to touch his shoulder. "Lucas."

He whirled, and those deep, dark, expressive brown eyes of his fixed on mine—his eyes lit up, warming from surprise to sheer joy and excitement.

"Liv!" His voice was pure Lucas Badd, a sound I'd know anywhere—a voice I could pick out of a crowd—rough, gruff, gravelly, weathered. "You scared the shit outta me, woman."

I couldn't help a laugh, staring up at him, a cheesy, happy, breathless grin on my face. "Hi."

He growled, a sound of…god, I don't know. Pure male exuberance, maybe. "Damn, girl. Sure is good to see you." He let out a short, sharp breath. "You're a hell of a lot more beautiful than I remember. You somehow get sexier, livin' in Paris?"

I shook my head, laughing again. "No, Lucas. I'm just me."

He hesitated, and then wrapped his arms around me. I froze for a split second, and then his scent and his warmth enveloped me and I had no choice—my arms went around his neck, my fingers buried in his hair, my nose pressed against his skin. I inhaled him, the scent that was Lucas—the beard oil, deodorant, and another deeper, earthy scent layered over that, the smell of the forest, maybe.

When he finally let me go, I couldn't breathe—the essence of Lucas had me wrapped up and tangled and twisted. I made myself step backward, away from his scent, although I couldn't take my eyes off of his.

"I missed the shit outta you, Liv." He scratched the back of his neck as he said this, a sure sign that he was nervous to be admitting it.

My stomach flipped. "I missed you too," I said.

We'd parted on uncertain terms, acknowledging the attraction between us, but no sense of resolution in terms of what to do about it—him knowing he wasn't in a place to start any kind of a relationship, and me knowing I couldn't allow myself to draw close to a man I was worried would only hurt me in the end.

Now?

The attraction that had been there when I first met him was still there, but the flickering flames of it were now a raging inferno. I felt shallow, my physical attraction to him being cranked so far up simply due to a few changes to his appearance, but it was a fact I couldn't ignore. I had already been attracted to the man as he was when I met him; I left for Paris for two months, and he was drastically altered. Fit, powerful, clean cut. It was more than the mere physical fact of him losing weight and gaining muscle, though, it was what it represented: hard work, determination, a dedication to health and fitness—a pride in himself.

It gave me a sense of hope that, perhaps, he was a man I could let myself feel things for after all.

Or, perhaps more accurately, let myself act on the feelings I already had.

I realized we were just staring at each other, and any questions my daughter might have had were bound to increase exponentially with every second we spent just staring at each other.

"I...my daughter—" I let out a breath and started over, gesturing back at Cassie. "My daughter is with me."

He smiled. "You mentioned that in your postcard." He waved at Cassie, who waved back with a reserved expression. "I figured you may want a ride home."

I blinked at him. "Wait...you drove here."

His grin was huge. "Yep. Big changes in my life, but that's the most relevant one at the moment. I got a truck, so we can fit all your shit into it." He glanced at the pile of luggage surrounding Cassie. "Good thing too—looks like you two have a hell of a pile of it."

I laughed. "Yeah, I guess we do. I came back with more than I left with, and Cassie is bringing her whole life with her."

He nodded. "How's your girl doin'?"

I shrugged. "It's difficult." I headed toward her, and he stayed beside me. "We can talk more later. She can't be on her feet for too long, so we need to get off the sidewalk."

We reached Cassie, who stood with her purse in both hands, eyeing Lucas with something of a mixture of awe, skepticism, and hostility.

"Hi there, Cassandra. My name's Lucas. I'm a friend of your mother's." Lucas stuck out his enormous paw, and Cassie shook it, her tiny, delicate hand lost in his.

"Call me Cassie. Only Mom ever calls me Cassandra, and only then when I'm in trouble."

He nodded. "Cassie, then. I didn't want to assume a familiarity, since we're just meeting. Your mom's told me a little about you. Pleased to meet you, darlin'."

Cassie's eyes narrowed at the term. "Told you a bit about me, has she?"

"Just that you're a hell of a dancer, and that you had an accident."

"I *was* a hell of a dancer," Cassie said. "Not sure what I am, now." Her voice dripped bitterness.

"Sure as fuck ain't my place to talk about any of that, but I happen to know from personal experience that things are never as permanently fucked as we tend to convince ourselves they are. Ask your mom about what I come through, sometime."

"I think that's your story to tell," I said.

He shrugged. "Whatever. Ain't the time for heavy shit. Let's get you two home."

"Home." Cassie sighed, long and deep and confused.

She and I both watched in amazement as Lucas took the two huge matching duffel bags Cassie and I had bought on the Champs-Élysées—both of which were stuffed to bursting and less than half a pound each under the maximum weight limit for checked luggage—and slung them each on one side. He then stuffed a suitcase under each huge arm, clutched the handles of the other two, and set off for the parking lot, easily carrying our luggage as if it weighed nothing. He'd left each of us to bring our carry-ons and purses. We followed him, watching him stride across the parking lot with a bounce in his step.

"You know," I said to Cassie. "He was in a pretty bad wreck himself. Messed up his leg, needed surgery and therapy." I indicated him. "You wouldn't know it, watching him."

Cassie rolled her eyes. "Yeah, well, he wasn't a professional dancer, was he? I'll heal to the point that you'd never know what happened, but that's a far cry from being able to dance eight to twelve hours a day, seven days a week like I have for five and a half years."

"I know, Cass, I know." I couldn't quite keep the frustration out of my voice—frustration at how she seemed to be giving up already.

She sensed my irritation, or just heard it, and huffed. "Don't, okay? It's been a long day and I'm not in the mood for lectures on persistence or whatever I can see you winding up for."

I clicked my teeth together on exactly what she'd accused me of being about to say. "Okay. I understand."

"I'll get through this, Mom…just, in my own way."

I nodded. "I know. But I'm your mother, and I—"

"You're prone to lectures, is what you are. And I'm exhausted."

I chuckled. "I don't lecture."

Lucas, a few feet ahead, turned to not quite look back at us. "You lecture, babe. You gave me a hell of a lecture when we were on that hike—remember?"

Cassie narrowed her eyes me. "Babe? Is there something I need to know?"

"It's just how he is," I said under my breath. "It doesn't mean anything specific. It's not what you're thinking."

"I'm thinking I saw the way you two looked at each other," Cassie muttered.

"Cassandra. *Don't.*"

She just grinned. "All I'll say is that I'm okay with it. It's time—past time, if anything."

"Cassandra Danielle—"

She held up her hands, grinning at me. "That's it, I'm done. That's all I've got to say."

"We'll talk later, young lady. In private."

Lucas chuckled. "Ooooh, you got the young lady. You gonna get it later, sweetheart."

Cassie hobbled a little faster, a more familiar fire sparking in her eyes. "Let's get one thing straight, Lucas—we just met. You don't get to call me 'babe' or 'sweetheart' or 'darling' or any of that. Even if we hadn't just met, don't call me that. I realize you may identify as a good old boy or whatever, but—"

Lucas eyed her, unperturbed by her snappish outburst. "Hey, I'm sorry. Just a habit from way back, all right? I didn't mean nothin' by it." He frowned. "I ain't a good old boy, though. Don't go accusin' me of that."

Cassie halted as Lucas reached a black F-150 with a lift and aggressively treaded mud tires, and set our suitcases and duffel bags in the bed one by one. She eyed the truck with a skeptical grin. "You sure? You've got the look down pretty pat."

He glared at her. "It ain't a fashion statement. The truck, I mean. I live and work off road and in the woods. The lift and the tires are necessary. The drawl is from livin' in Oklahoma for forty years. And the look…well, that's new."

I nudged Cassie's shoulder. "Don't be antagonistic, please. He's doing us a favor. We'd never have gotten all our luggage and both of us home in one car, or in one trip, otherwise."

She rolled her eyes again, but said nothing.

Lucas lowered the tailgate and climbed up into the bed in a single lithe movement that was lighter and easier than his size and bulk should have allowed, securing our baggage into the truck bed with a few bungee cords, and then he hopped down and closed the gate. He unlocked the doors with a key fob, and rounded the hood to open the front passenger door.

Cassie took the rear driver's side seat without a word, so I climbed up through the door Lucas was holding open for me.

"Nice truck," I said, examining the clean, fresh-smelling interior.

Lucas started the motor, and glanced at me. "Thanks. It ain't fancy, but it's mine and I like it. It gets the job done."

"What job?" I asked. "You're not working at the hardware store anymore?"

He grinned, shaking his head. "No ma'am."

"So, what do you do now?"

"Me and Ram have a business, now. He's been

running hunts and hikes and the like for a while now, usually deep in the bush. He was doing it sort of unofficially, by word of mouth recommendation only, but now we got a real deal business, with a website and everything. He's still doing the long-term, deep bush trips, and I do the local ones. I guide hikes for the kind of tourists who want a more challenging experience than the usual day trip, but don't have the time or resources to plan anything more involved. I also do a hike from downtown Ketchikan into the forest, off-trail to a staging area we've built, where we can canoe through the forest a ways, and then hike back. It's a nice little trip that takes most of a full day."

I blinked at him. "For real?"

He nodded. "Yeah. For real." He glanced at me. "Why? That seem impossible to you or somethin'?"

I shook my head. "No, I just...when we first met, I had to convince you to go on a short day hike with me. "

He nodded. "I started going on day hikes with Ram after you left, and I sorta got back into who I used to be, to a degree. I told you some of how I grew up—hiking wasn't a once in a while thing for fun, it was part of how I lived my life. Hunting, fishing, canoeing, all that—I was doing all that as soon as I could walk, lift a pole or a paddle or a rifle. Once I started, it was pretty easy to relearn the old skills, you know?"

He paused, shrugging. "Not totally there, yet. Still got some work to do, but I'm making progress."

I couldn't take my eyes off of him. "Lucas, you've done more than just make progress. You're...I don't want to say a totally different person, but close."

He glanced at Cassie in the rearview mirror—I'd almost forgotten she was back there, I realized guiltily—and then at me. "Maybe once you're settled, you and me can meet up for coffee, or lunch."

I realized what he was getting at—he wanted to talk in private.

I resisted the urge to run my hand over his shoulder, over his thick bicep, over his forearm to his hand—resisted the urge to hold his hand. "I think I could fit you into my schedule."

His grin was playful. "Well that there is mighty kinda'ya, sweet thing," he said, pulling his natural drawl into a caricature. "I surely do appreciate it."

He winked at Cassie in the rearview mirror, eliciting a sound from my daughter which resembled the snarl of a trapped wildcat.

He just chuckled. "Yikes. Don't piss off that one, huh?"

I cackled. "Oh my, Lucas. If you think Cassie has a temper, you should meet my daughter Lexie. She'll scalp you, skin you, and castrate you faster than you can blink, and she can do it with nothing more than a few words." I laughed, imagining her meeting a man like Lucas. "In your case, she might try to literally scalp you, skin you, and castrate you."

"Well, warn me if she comes to town. I'll hide in the woods till she leaves."

Cassie's laugh was unexpected. "Oh dear god, if Lexie were to ever meet you, Lucas, I would sell tickets. That would be quite a show."

Lucas nodded, musing. "If you sell tickets, I'll go in with you fifty-fifty, and turn up the charm a notch or two just to really piss her off."

Cassie frowned, but it was meant to hide a grin she couldn't quite help. "This is your idea of charm, is it?"

Lucas winked at her again. "Darlin', you ain't seen charm yet."

"Call me *darlin'* again, and see what happens," Cassie snapped.

"Sure thing, sweet pea."

This got Lucas another snarl from Cassie, which just made Lucas chuckle.

I frowned at Lucas. "Don't antagonize her, Lucas. Please? She's been through enough."

Lucas sighed. "I'm just teasin', Liv. I don't mean nothin' by it."

"I know that, Lucas, but—"

"Mom," Cassie cut in. "I can handle it myself. I

broke my leg, I didn't have a nervous breakdown. I'm fine."

"You're in an emotionally vulnerable state right now, Cassandra, and you don't need to be—"

"*Mom*," she hissed. "Stop."

I sighed. "Fine. I'm sorry."

The rest of the ride home was tense, more specifically between Cassie and me. Lucas seemed oblivious to it, humming under his breath as he drove, taking us to my condo.

Cassie's questioning glance as he pulled up to my building asked why he knew where I lived, if we were just friends, and my answering look told her to keep her mouth shut about it and mind her own business—my daughters and I have developed a rather complex set of looks over the years, so we can have entire conversations without a single verbal word being exchanged.

As we pulled into a visitor spot near the door, Cassie eyed the four-story building nervously. "Which floor do you live on, Mom?"

"Third," I answered. "But there's an elevator."

Cassie suppressed a sigh. "I never take an elevator unless it's more than five floors up. Haven't for years. I hate elevators."

I winced. "You may have to make some concessions for the time being, honey."

She nodded. "I know. But…" she huffed. "I'll be fine."

Lucas waited until she slid out of the back seat and headed for the front door, watching the limp in her step. "Stubborn one, ain't she?"

"All of my girls are violently allergic to dependence on anyone for anything. Even Torie, my most laid-back child, started working at fourteen, bought her first car the day she turned sixteen, moved out at eighteen, and refuses to ask for help unless she's literally starving. I visited her once and her apartment, which she shares with four other girls, contained nothing but a package of hot dogs, two boxes of Kraft Macaroni and Cheese, and a six pack of beer. Oh, and ketchup." I sighed. "They had plenty of money for pot, though."

"I mean, priorities, right?" Lucas said, his voice wry.

I groaned, watching Cassie standing on the steps up to the door, spinning in a slow circle, taking in the view—which even from here was magnificent. "I'm worried about her, Lucas. She's independent to a fault. I don't know how this is going to work."

"One day at a time, one hour at a time, one minute at a time," Lucas said, as if reciting something he'd told himself a million times. "That's how I got sober, how I got into shape, and how I'm repairing my relationships with my boys."

I eyed him, full of curiosity. "I have a million questions for you."

He grinned. "Well, I'm hoping we'll have time to answer them all, Liv." He opened his door and hung his foot out, but paused to look at me. "For now, though, that girl needs you. She may not be able to say so, but it's written in every line of her body and every word she says. She needs her mama."

"I know she does."

"You just call me when you've got a few minutes. I don't aim to get in the way of your time with Cassie."

I frowned. "I don't have your number.."

He opened the console armrest and pulled out a new iPhone. "I'm even learnin' to send text messages. My boys find it funny, for some damn reason. My big old sausage thumbs don't like to hit the right keys and I spell shit wrong, seein' as my education is spotty at best."

He unlocked the phone, laboriously hunted through the apps until he found the contacts, and eventually figured out how to add a new contact... watching him mistype three times in the process of entering my name, which was only three letters, was funnier than it had any right to be, and I had to suppress laughter as I watched him struggle.

He huffed. "Okay, now what's your number?"

I reached for the device. "Want me to just type it in?"

He kept it out of reach, snorting. "Nope. I gotta learn." He glanced at me, amused. "Roman says watching me try to use this thing is the most frustrating experience in the world."

I laughed. "It's…something." I told him my phone number, and again, watching him type the ten digits was comically frustrating, as he had to back up and retype at least a dozen times. Finally he had my number in correctly, and he sent me a message:

This heer is lucas.

I bit my lip. "Got it."

He eyed me. "What?"

I shook my head. "Nothing."

He flushed, ducked his head. "Look, I told you I don't spell too good. Liam and I quit school when we was, like, nine. Or if you want to know the truth, my dad quit takin' us. Closest school was almost an hour drive from our homestead, and he just didn't have the time, so Gramps took over our learnin', but he could barely read, write or add himself."

"Lucas, you know I could—"

He shook his head. "Liv, if you're about to suggest you could teach me to read and write…well, just don't. What I know works fine for me."

I nodded, sighing. "Okay."

He grinned at me. "It bugs you, don't it?"

I laughed, shrugging. "I just want to help."

He gestured at Cassie. "Right now, she needs your help more than I do."

I reached across the console and wrapped my arms around his neck, inhaling his scent once more. "I'll call you, okay?"

His hand slid up my back to curl around the back of my neck, and I felt his nose against my cheek, his breath on my jaw; all I'd have to do is twist my head ever so slightly and his lips would brush against mine—

I yanked away from him, my heart hammering in my chest. I dragged my fingers through my hair, clearing my throat.

"It's good to see you, Lucas. You look amazing. You should be proud of yourself."

He nodded, rubbing his thumb across his lips. "I actually am pretty proud of myself."

I swallowed hard. "Would it sound condescending if I said I was proud of you?"

He lifted a shoulder. "I know what you mean, and…it means a lot to me, comin' from you."

"MOM!" Cassie bellowed.

I sighed. "I have to go."

Lucas slid out of the truck, heading for the bed of his truck. "I'll bring your luggage up."

"You don't have to."

He grinned. "Don't you know I been dyin' to see the inside of your condo?"

I laughed. "It's not that exciting."

"Maybe I'm easily excited."

I giggled. "I think it's best I don't follow that line of conversation."

He wiggled his eyebrows at me—silly but suggestive—as he set our luggage on the ground. "Scared of impropriety, are you?"

"I'm not *scared* of it, Lucas, I'm just…proper."

He snorted. "Over-fucking-rated." He settled the duffel bags crossed over his chest, tucked a suitcase under each arm and one suitcase in each hand, and headed for the door. "You need to loosen up a little, Liv. Life is too fuckin' short to be proper all the damn time."

I couldn't get his words out of my mind as I opened the door for him, called the elevator, and led the way to my condo. He waited until I opened the door and followed me in, setting the luggage on the floor just inside the door, and then taking a long look around at the open concept floor plan.

Cassie limped slowly inside, taking it in as well. "Nice place, Mom."

Lucas nodded his agreement. "Funny—it's pretty much what I would have imagined your place looking like. 'Course, I don't have the imagination to see exactly this, but it just fits you, I guess." He gave my place one last look around, waved at Cassie, and then paused next to me, brushing his cheek against mine in a ghosting tease of a not-quite cheek-kiss. "See you," he whispered.

I leaned against him for the briefest instant, and then pulled back. "Bye."

He was gone, then, leaving a lingering breath of woodsy male scent in his wake.

Cassie perched on the edge of my couch and smirked at me. "A friend, indeed."

I pointed an index finger at her. "Not a word, Cassandra."

In typical Cassie fashion, she ignored me. "You don't have to talk to me about it if you don't want to, but I say go for it. He's huge and crude and vulgar and uneducated, but he's clearly smitten with you."

"He is not smitten," I muttered.

Cassie shook her head at me, snorting gently. "Mom, he's bananas for you. If you don't see that, you're being willfully blind to the obvious."

I rubbed my forehead. "Cass, please."

She lifted her bad leg and extended it across the ottoman that matched the couch. "Mom, *you* please."

I stared at her. "I have no idea what you mean."

She closed her eyes tiredly, spoke without

opening them. "You're as goo-goo for him as he is for you. Why you're pretending to be oblivious, I don't know, but it's not like you. You were the one who taught the five of us to face facts head-on."

I had no response to that, so I set about unpacking my things, and then Cassie's, while she fell asleep on my couch.

Goo-goo?

Was I goo-goo for Lucas?

Was he bananas for me?

Was I pretending to be oblivious?

Too many questions, not enough answers.

Maybe it truly was time to face facts head-on.

THIRTEEN

Lucas

I LAY AWAKE AT TWO IN THE MORNING, UNABLE TO SLEEP. Liv had been home for two days already and I hadn't heard from her. I didn't want to bug her—not with her daughter newly arrived and trying to recalibrate her entire life, but I couldn't stop thinking about her. She was so near, yet she might as well have been on the moon.

I missed her, and the brief reunion on the way home from the airport hadn't been anywhere near enough for me. I needed more. Needed to smell her, see her, feel her. God, I'd thought I had my feelings for her kinda locked down, but from the first moment I laid eyes on her at the ferry dock, I'd known I was in trouble.

It wasn't that she looked any different, because she didn't. She smelled the same, spoke the same—she was just Liv, as she'd been since we first met in the hardware store. I was different, though, and her being gone while I'd been working my ass off to revamp my life and myself meant I saw her in a whole new way.

Or maybe the absence really had made my heart grow fonder. I'd always kind of thought that saying was a bunch of bullshit, but maybe it wasn't after all. I'd missed her more than I cared to admit, and I found myself wondering if she'd missed me as much—if her feelings toward me had changed or grown at all.

Unless I was misinterpreting her body language cues, it sure did seem like she'd missed me, and that she'd liked seeing me again—and this new and im-proved me—had helped her feelings along.

But was there a future between us?

Could there be?

Did I want there to be? That one, at least, was easy to answer: yes, I did. I deeply wanted to know what life could be like with Olivia Goode in it day in, and day out. To know her inside and out. To feel her affection, physically and emotionally and mentally.

When she smiled at me, I felt like I could fly. When she'd told me she was proud of me, I had been on top of the world. That moment where it had seemed as if she'd been resisting the urge to kiss me,

I could have wrestled a bear, could have shouted with joy.

If I were to have the privilege of kissing her, I would never, ever, take it for granted. I would never take *her* for granted.

My phone rang, a jarring, shocking digital warbling sound—Roman had told me I could change the ringer, but I couldn't figure out how.

I stared at the screen for a moment, shocked breathless—*liv*, it read.

I clumsily swept my finger across the screen to answer it before it stopped ringing, as if the fact of her calling me would somehow vanish. "Hello?" I murmured.

"Did I wake you up?" Her voice was quiet, nearly inaudible.

"Nope. I was awake." I must have been delirious with lack of sleep—it was the only way to explain my next words. "Just laying here trying to convince myself I shouldn't call you."

"Why would you convince yourself of that, Lucas?"

"It's two in the morning, and your daughter is with you."

There was a long hesitation on the other end. "I haven't been able to sleep since I've been back."

"Jet lag?" I asked.

"Yeah, that's part of it—France is several hours ahead of here." Another pause. "But that's not the only reason I haven't been able to sleep."

"What's the other reason?" I asked, feeling something tense and thick in the air between us, even though we weren't even in the same room.

"You." This was a whisper.

"Me?"

"Yes, you, Lucas. I can't stop thinking about you."

"I ain't been able to stop thinkin' about you since the moment I met you, Olivia." I wasn't sure what prompted my actions, but I found myself tugging on shorts and a pair of running shoes, grabbing my keys, and heading for my truck.

My hands and feet operated on autopilot as I steered the truck across town. I still had Liv on the line, but most of the trip was spent in silence.

Finally, she spoke. "You told me how you felt two months ago, and I think maybe I was a little unfair to you."

"No, you weren't," I said, my voice brusque. "I needed a kick in the ass, and you saying what you said was it. You got me to realize that I wasn't taking myself seriously. That I hadn't really given a shit about *me* in fuckin' decades."

"I wasn't trying to change you."

"I needed to change, Liv. Desperately. Inside and out. For myself. So don't ever think what I done— gettin' rid of the belly and all that, the tats, cutting the beard, a new job with Ram...none of it was *for* you, or *because of* you. It was for me, because I wanted to be a better person."

"Lucas, I..." She swallowed hard. "You were already a good person. An amazing person."

I snorted. "The fuck I was. Getting sober was nothin' but survival. I'd have died if I didn't quit. And starting to lose weight was the same thing—I'd have had another heart attack if I didn't, and the next one woulda been fatal. A doctor flat out told me as much. The real work I been doing is what's made me a better person."

"Like what?"

I pulled my truck into a parking spot and shut off the engine. "Come outside."

"What?"

"I'm in your parking lot. I drove here while we was talking."

"Oh. Okay...um. Give me a minute to change into something appropriate."

"Liv?" I spoke without thinking—without letting myself think. "Don't."

"Don't what?"

"Change. Just come out here like you are." My

next words tumbled out unbidden: "Unless you're naked."

"I'm not naked, Lucas." A beat of silence. "You wish."

I barked a laugh. "Damn right I do."

Silence then, as we both realized what had just been exchanged between us. "Lucas..." A hint of disapproval tinged her voice.

"You know what, I ain't gonna take it back, and I ain't gonna apologize. You are a goddamn beautiful woman, and I ain't gonna sit here and pretend I ain't crazy fuckin' attracted to you. Yes, Olivia Goode, I *do* wish I could see you naked. And a whole lot more than that, but I won't shock you with the details."

The silence from Olivia then made me wonder if I'd gone too far.

"I'll be right down," she whispered.

"I can't wait."

Click.

The wait was interminable, even though it couldn't have been more than a minute. When I saw her, my heart stopped, and my lungs seized, and things got almighty tight between my legs. She was coming down the steps and trotting barefoot across the sidewalk, and she was dressed, if you could call it that, in little more than a wisp of white silk that was clinging to her breasts and hips, the hem at mid-thigh.

Her hair was messy, sticking up in a million directions and that, almost as much as the silk nightie, turned me on so hard the frantic pace of my heartbeat worried me.

I made sure my doors were unlocked, and then she was in the cab with me, and her scent filled the truck and made me dizzy with its heady femininity. No perfume or lotions, just the natural scent of a woman.

She slid onto the seat, closed the door, and sat utterly still, staring at me. "Hi."

I let my gaze rake over her—the nightie was thin, the silk pressing against her skin—her nipples poked against the shimmery white material and fabric gathered at the apex of her thighs, which were bare to a point of mouthwatering tease, and only the fact that she had them pressed together prevented me from seeing anything.

"Good god*damn*, Olivia," I breathed. "I didn't think it was possible for me to want you any more than I already did, but now..." I had to swallow hard past the lump in my throat. "You're so fuckin' beautiful you make it hard to breathe."

Her inky black hair slipped in front of her eyes, but she didn't seem to notice—her eyes were glued to my torso, which was when I realized I'd forgotten a shirt. I'd lost quite a lot of fat in the last few months, so my chest and upper abdomen were taut and well-defined, and pretty muscular. My gut, just above my natural beltline, however, still needed some work but, according to Baxter, that was the most difficult place to lose fat, because it was the natural depository location for visceral fat and the stuff would hang on as long as possible, no matter what I did. Only lots of hard, consistent work, clean eating, and fasting would ever get rid of it, and only then well after the rest of me was taut and defined. I was proud of my work, though—proud of the body I'd carved out of the blubbery mess I'd been.

Her gaze raking eagerly and hungrily over me in that moment made every skipped meal and every bland salad, every barbell clean, deadlift, kettlebell snatch, every mile run, every wind sprint, barbell squat, burpee, and Turkish getup worth it.

"You have really worked hard, haven't you?" she breathed. "You look *amazing.*"

"Considering where I came from, physically speaking, I'd say I've made decent progress," I said.

Her hand lifted, reached across the console, traced the tribal design on my bicep, and then her fingertips skated down to my forearm, to the first tattoo Rem had done.

"What's this?" she asked.

"Sobriety celebration, and a reminder to never

forget why I stay sober and healthy—my three boys. Remington did it for me. It was the start of us repairing our relationship."

Her smile was small and tender. "So the work hasn't just been physical."

"Hell, no." I had no qualms discussing the rest of what I'd been up to with her—not now, not anymore. "I actually started seeing a therapist three months ago—before you left. Started seeing him three days a week, and now I'm seeing him twice a month. Roman and I are...I don't want to quite say we're *good*, but we're better than we've ever been. Ramsey and I are honestly great—I love working with him. He gets me in a way Rem and Rome don't." I paused, sighing. "Rem is the hardest nut to crack. His waters run real fuckin' deep, and his resentment for who and what I was when they was kids is a bitter fuckin' pill. We're gettin' there, though." I indicated my tattoos. "These are the way we connect. He'll talk to me while I'm under the needle in a way he won't otherwise, so I keep letting him ink me."

She was quiet a while. "Lucas...I don't even know where to start."

"The beginning?"

She rolled her eyes at me. "Ha, ha," she said dryly. "Truly, Lucas, what you've accomplished in a couple short months is remarkable."

My throat was tight. "You made me realize I wanted to be someone I could be proud of—someone my boys could be proud of." It was hard to get the next words out past the lump. "Someone *you* could be proud of."

She inhaled slowly through her nose. "Lucas." Her hand covered mine, resting on the console between us. "You didn't have to do any of this for that to be true."

I shook my head stubbornly. "Bullshit." I met her eyes. "Do *not* bullshit me, Olivia. I was a mess. I wasn't the kind of man you deserved. Don't blow sugar and sunshine up my ass."

She laughed gently. "Okay, you're right—you weren't. You *were* a mess, but I saw the man you were."

"The man I could be."

"The man you *are*," she said. "All you've done is reveal him. He was always there."

"Then you could see better than me. Took a lot of fuckin' work before I could see that."

Her hand rotated, slipped under mine—our fingers tangled, intertwining so naturally it felt like we'd been holding hands like this forever. "Drive us somewhere, Lucas," she whispered.

"Where?"

"Anywhere. It doesn't matter."

I turned on the motor and pulled out, heading out of town. Away from the lights, away from the buildings, along a narrow, winding dirt road uphill through the forest . Her hand stayed in mine the whole time, the radio was off and I had the windows cracked open to let the cool night air blow past us. My headlights illuminated a wedge of the road ahead, but all else around us was dark, and wild.

After twenty, maybe thirty, minutes of driving, the road curved to the edge of a precipice, with a wide shoulder edged by trees, overlooking Ketchikan and the bay, before meandering into the forest again. I pulled off the road and onto the dirt shoulder, shut off the engine and the headlights. I smiled at her, held up a finger in a "wait a minute" gesture, and reached into the back seat. I kept a blanket back there for emergencies, along with a few tools, some water and food, and a few other emergency supplies. I grabbed the blanket and hopped out, lowered the tailgate and spread out the blanket on the truck bed, then went around and opened Liv's door. She tiptoed across the dirt, her hand in mine, and then hopped up onto the tailgate to sit on the blanket.

I stood there for a moment, letting the cool air blow over my bare torso, just looking at her. "No wonder you wanted to get changed. Not sure I've ever seen anything as sexy as that nightie in my life."

She ducked her head, and when she spoke, her voice was thick and hard to read. "I, um…this isn't what I was wearing."

I blinked, sidling over to sit beside her. My bulk lowered the tail end of the truck several inches; my thigh brushed hers, and I felt her shivering in the cool. "No?"

She slowly shook her head. "I just threw it on as I came out—it was the first thing in my pajama drawer. I haven't worn it in…years."

"What *were* you wearing, then?"

She ran her palm over her thigh in a nervous gesture. She swallowed hard, glanced at me surreptitiously, and even in the darkness I could tell she was blushing furiously. "Just underwear."

I blew out a breath, and my eyes went to hers, and then slid down her torso—the wind blew the silk against her, flattening it over her curves, rendering her all but naked in outline. I could see every curve of her, the round swell of each breast, the hard points of her nipples, her diaphragm, her ribs, the ridges of her abs.

"So when you said you wanted to change into something appropriate…"

"I meant put *something* on."

I had to swallow hard, breathing slowly past the urge to gather her into my arms. "Jesus, Liv."

She licked her lips and lifted her eyes to me. "What?"

I shook my head. "Just...you. The thought of you wearing nothin' at all except a little pair of panties? I don't know how to handle that."

"Don't say panties," she muttered. "I hate that word."

I laughed. "Okay."

Her eyes were fixed on me, unblinking, seeing into me, reading my thoughts and giving away little of her own. "Tell me what you're thinking, Lucas."

"I just did."

"Tell me more."

I snorted. "I will if you will."

"Deal." She shifted on the tailgate, inching closer to me. "You go first—first thought, no filter."

I gazed at her, at those green-brown eyes, so wide, usually expressive but now reserved and opaque. "I'm thinking I want to kiss you more than I've ever wanted anything in my whole damn life." I let out my pent-up breath, now that I'd admitted that. "Your turn."

She hesitated a heartbeat...two...three. "I'm thinking I'd like that very much."

I couldn't believe what I was hearing, but I didn't second-guess it. I didn't dare wait, didn't dare hesitate, half worried she'd change her mind. I turned toward her, cupping her delicate jaw with my big paw;

she tilted her head up, twisting to face me, and our mouths met. Good god, her lips were soft. So warm. Pliant, welcoming. Damp. Eager. I couldn't breathe and didn't want to, I only wanted to dissolve into this feeling, into this moment. Into this kiss.

For a few moments, it was just our lips touching, but then the spark of lips on lips turned into a growing fire. Her lips moved on mine, seeking more and more. I slid my fingers past her jaw and around the back of her neck, pulling her closer, and she came willingly. Whose tongue moved first? Mine? Hers? I don't know. It didn't matter—our tongues found each other's, and danced like flames, tangling in a tang of familiar perfection.

Her lips pulled away, but her hands slid up my arms and curled around my shoulders, clinging to me rather than pushing me away. "Lucas…"

"I feel like…" I shook my head slightly. "I don't know how to put it." I fought for the words. "Like we've always kissed each other. Like this ain't the first time, even though it is. Like…like there's a whole lifetime of kissing behind this moment that we're somehow just now discovering."

Her laugh was one of amazement and agreement rather than scoffing or ridicule. "That's it exactly." Her palm brushed my cheek, her thumb moving over my goatee, rubbing my upper lip. "A whole lifetime of kissing behind this moment that we're just now discovering. I couldn't put it better, Lucas."

She kissed me, then, lifting her lips to mine, pulling me down to her with her other hand—a palm at the back of my head, the fingers of her other hand on my jaw, thumb on my cheek as our lips met and her tongue sought mine. She whimpered, gasped, and my heart stopped entirely, my stomach flipping.

Our mouths moved in synch, seeking each other, seeking more. Breath came in gasps, fingers slid on skin, tracing earlobes, jawlines, chins. My arm found her waist, wrapping around the slimness of it and drawing her closer. Her hands clawed into my shoulder, and she leaned into me. I leaned back against the side of the truck bed, pulling her with me, and now she was resting half on me.

Her palms flattened against my chest and her forehead pressed against mine, her lips parted from mine for a split second, just long enough for her to draw a deep breath, huffing it out, whimpering a sound that was all desire and confusion.

And then she buried her mouth on mine, and I fell backward to the bed of the truck, and she twisted in place. I was on my back, now, and she was on top of me, our lips locked together, her fingers digging into my chest. God, she was so soft, so warm, and so small. I barely felt her delicate weight, but her presence on top of me was my entire world—my whole universe.

Her thin, firm shoulders were under my palms, and then I traced the narrow S of her spine. The silk was cool and slippery, sliding under my hands as I ran my palms down her back. She arched against me, moaning into the kiss, pushing harder against me. And then, with a swelling soaring hammering heart, I felt the taut round bubble of her buttocks fill my hands, and I cupped her, caressed her, and she moaned, now pushing back into my hands.

I squeezed her ass, kneading it, memorizing the feel of it in my hands as if to make sure I could re-member the glory of the feel of her, should this be all of her I ever got...and I could die happy, if that was the case. As I caressed and cupped those perfect, taut, round globes, the silk of her nightie shimmied upward, and then I had her bare flesh in my hands, along with a tiny sliver of cotton wedged between the cheeks. I groaned in my chest as I held the bare wonder of her backside in my hands, and I knew, as a fact, that never in all my life had I known perfection like this.

Her lips broke away from mine, and she pulled back enough to look into my eyes—hers were wide and glittering and filled with an impossible amount of emotion, her hair falling in black drifts across her eyes. I petted her ass, and she grinned, biting her lower lip.

"God, Liv." I tried to find something else to say, but had nothing. "You—you're…"

She scooted higher up my body, burying herself against me, into me. Burrowing, nestling in my arms. Devouring my mouth, tangling her tongue against mine. She fit in my arms perfectly, fit against my body as if it was made to nestle there.

The wind blew cold, and she shivered.

"Liv—" I wrapped my arms around her to keep her warm. "Let's get back in the truck. It's cold out here."

She nodded, shivering. I sat up and slid off the bed, taking her with me, lifting her in my arms with the blanket wrapped around her. I settled her in the passenger seat, buckled her in, and got behind the wheel.

I drove back toward the city, my hand resting on the console, hoping for her touch.

She slipped her hand out from under the blanket to take mine, and didn't look away from me as I drove us back to town.

"Lucas…" she breathed.

I glanced at her, at the road. "Yeah, Liv?"

She swallowed hard. "I've never been kissed like that in my life."

I couldn't look at the enormous totality of that statement, let alone find the words to ask her if she meant it literally or figuratively. I just knew it made my chest swell, my heart ache, my head spin, and my cock throb.

I never even gave a thought to where we were going—I just drove. We ended up at my condo, and there was no hesitation in her as I lifted her out, carried her to my unit, and inside. The living room was dark, the only light coming from the microwave clock, and a sliver of moonlight coming in through the window.

I didn't stop in the living room. I took her to my bedroom. Settled her on my bed, still wrapped in the blanket. I closed my door then walked over and knelt on the bed beside her.

She reached for me, throwing open the blanket. Her hands clawed into the back of my shoulders and drew me to her—down to her, as she lay back. I braced myself over her, and she scratched my back in lazy circles and then smoothed her palms where she'd scratched.

I needed her. I had to have more of her—had to.

I leaned down, sliding my lips over hers, fitting them together like puzzle pieces. She breathed into my mouth, writhed her tongue on mine, palmed the back of my head and lowest part of my back. One hand braced on the bed, I cupped her cheek. Found the strap of her slip, drew it down over one shoulder, and then the other.

As I tugged the silk down, I kissed her while she gasped against my lips. Her breasts popped out over the top of the bodice, and I reared back to look at her. I gazed at her, in awe at the sight her bare skin— the pale tan of her areolae and the thick plumpness of her nipples and the round swell of her breasts swaying as she gasped.

She watched me, and my roving hand. I bit her lip as I ran my palm up her stomach. Her eyes slid closed for a moment, and then flew open as I caressed her breasts, first one and then the other.

She whimpered.

She gasped as I flicked her nipple, and rubbed it with my thumb. She became breathless as I lowered my mouth and kissed her chest, across her breast-bone and down the valley between her breasts and then across one, suckling her nipple into my mouth and tasting its sweetness…moving on to the other side, circling around the underside with kisses, running the flat of my tongue over the hard, erect nub of flesh that was her nipple. She sucked in a sharp breath and held it.

"Lucas…" she breathed. "Oh god…oh god."

I was hunger. I was need. It consumed me, then.

A fire I didn't know had been simmering inside me, a need I didn't know had been building in me swelled, took over.

I needed to see her—all of her. I needed to feel her flush against me. I needed...I needed things I'd not felt in so, so long. I needed them with *her*.

I shifted my balance so I was on my knees above her, her tiny delicate but strong and gorgeous body beneath me. I leaned down over her and kissed her lips. She carved her hands all over me, cupping my buttocks over the khaki of my shorts, and then sought the waistline, the button under my navel.

I let her.

She freed the button, tugged the shorts down, and I kicked them away, kneeling over her in nothing but a pair of black briefs. Her hands slid over my waist, to my ass, up my back to my shoulders, all over. I couldn't get enough. Feel enough.

Need won, then.

Impatient, ruled by an all-consuming need to have this perfect, beautiful creature bare in my hands and under my lips, I gripped the neckline of her slip in both hands and ripped it open—halfway down at first, with a growl. Liv shrieked in breathless surprise, and then I yanked again and the nightie was open, and her glorious, mouth-watering, heart-stopping body was utterly bare.

"Holy *shit*, Lucas, you could've just taken it off," she gasped, laughing.

I ran my hands over her, belly to throat, breasts to hipbones. Her underwear was nothing but a tiny triangle of white, outlining her sex and leaving her hipbones bare.

"Sorry," I muttered. "Wasn't sentimental, was it?"

She laughed again, shaking her head even as her eyes betrayed a myriad of conflicting emotions. "No—I bought it a few months ago, thinking I'd do something indulgent for myself, but I just felt silly wearing it." Despite the steadiness of her voice, her eyes shimmered and her breaths came short and quick, her flat stomach flexing in and out, her lower lip trembling.

"You don't look silly in it, that's for goddamn sure," I growled. "You're fuckin' perfect, Olivia."

I palmed her stomach, flattening my hand over her navel—my hand was so big and she was so small my hand nearly spanned her entire torso.

"Lucas..." she breathed.

I bent, touching my lips to her stomach, her diaphragm. The tender flesh on the underside of her breast. She gasped wordlessly, cupping the back of my head, one arm wrapped around my shoulders. I flicked my tongue over her nipple, and she whimpered, her entire body shaking.

I kissed her gently, breast and nipple, throat and belly, and my fingers stole down to the waist of her underwear. This time, I restrained the urge to rip them off. I slid them downward, and her thighs pressed together.

Her breath caught. "Lucas—" She slithered away, thighs trembling, pressed tight. "I—wait. Wait." She swallowed hard, tangling her fingers in mine. "It's too much, too fast." Stung, feeling rejected, I pulled away, but she kept hold of me through our intertwined hands. "Lucas, I'm sorry. It's not that I don't want... you, I just..."

I let out a slow breath to steady myself, and then tugged the blanket over so she could cover herself; she let out a grateful sigh as she pressed the comforter to her chest.

"It picked up heat pretty quick, I guess," I said, sinking back to sit on the bed next to her. "I'm sorry, I didn't mean to push you into anything you ain't ready for."

She slid her palm against mine, tucked her fingers between mine. "I came down dressed in a negligee, Lucas. I came down wanting to...explore things with you." She hesitated. "I don't know how to...how to navigate this. My feelings are so complicated, and—" Her eyes watered. "I don't want you to think I'm rejecting you, that I don't want to kiss you, that I didn't enjoy…" she fluttered a hand at me, the bed, "…all that. I did. But I'm just—I'm confused. So confused."

I hopped off the bed, went to my dresser and got a T-shirt out of the top drawer, which I gave to Liv. She shrugged into it, laughing quietly as the garment hung on her like a dress ten sizes too big—it covered her, though, and she rolled up the sleeves past her elbows.

"Talk to me, Liv."

She shook her head, swallowing hard. "I don't know how."

I cradled her close. "Liv, if you want to just kiss, we just kiss. You want to sit here and talk about nothin', we sit here and talk about nothin'. You want to try to tell me what's on your mind, I'll listen with an open mind. You want me to just take you home, I'll take you home. This is whatever you need, sweetheart." This time, it wasn't just an idle word, that *sweetheart*—I meant it, deeply. "I just wanna understand."

She rubbed her face with both hands, and then rejoined our hands. "I'll try."

FOURTEEN

Liv

GOD, WHERE TO START? I didn't know what I was feeling myself, much less how to articulate it in a way that Lucas would understand. Why had I stopped? I'd been enjoying his touch, his kisses—quite possibly more than I'd ever enjoyed anything like this…ever.

Ah, and there it is.

That's the reason behind my full-on anxiety attack. I was masking it, hiding it, but I was in a full anxiety attack at the moment, unable to breathe, trembling, head spinning and racing.

I didn't know how to calm down. I couldn't catch my breath.

I exhaled long and hard, and then breathed in for a slow count of four, held it for a slow four count, and then let it out for another slow four count. I repeated this…twice, three times, four, and it was helping, but I still couldn't quite get a grip on myself.

Lucas slid over to me, wrapped a thick, burly, strong arm around my shoulders, and tucked me against his massive chest. His bare skin was warm and soft, the muscle hard yet pliant. I could hear his heartbeat—*whum-WHUMP-whum-WHUMP-whum-WHUMP*. His embrace enveloped me; his scent subsumed me—the male woodsy scent that defined him.

"Breathe, Liv. It's okay." His rough, rumbling voice hummed through me.

I nodded, and after a few minutes of breathing and focusing on nothing but my breath and Lucas's calming presence all around me, I was able to begin some kind of a start to the explanation Lucas deserved.

"I was with Darren for thirty years—we met in middle school, started dating when I was sixteen, married when I was twenty-one." I paused a moment, closed my eyes and continued; Lucas's heartbeat thumped quietly and reassuringly under my ear. "He was my first—my everything. First hand I ever held, first kiss, first sexual experience—and I was his, too. My entire life, there had only been Darren.

Until just now, I've never…felt anything with anyone but Darren. Never kissed another man, never held another man's hand, never snuggled in bed…nothing." I felt myself getting emotional, but I knew there was no way to get through this without crying, and I didn't try to hold it back; my eyes misted, my throat closed around a hot lump, but I kept going.

"When he died, I… I can't begin to explain how devastated I was. I didn't get out of bed for a week. Cried nearly the entire time, barely ate or drank—I lost fifteen pounds, and had to be hospitalized for dehydration."

"Jesus, Liv."

"He was my whole world, my entire life. I'd not really even liked another boy, except for those stupid crushes you get in middle school. He was my first love."

"And then you lost him."

I nodded. "I had to learn how to live—and I had to learn things all over again. He paid the bills, got the oil changed, put gas in the cars, did most of the driving, except for when I was working. He even did a lot of the cooking, because he was such a foodie. I had to learn how to do everything all on my own. My girls helped, but I couldn't lean on them too much, you know? They'd just lost their dad." I sucked in a breath; held it, let it out slowly. "The point to all this is that

I never dated. I couldn't. I couldn't bear to…to even think about another man the way I—the way Darren had been for me. Where was I supposed to even start? He knew every single thing about me. Everything. He knew when my cycle was coming before I did, he knew my most obscure dislikes, and he knew my past, because he *was* my past. How I could even begin to let anyone else into my life?"

Lucas was quiet, not breaking the silence that now fell over the room.

But I'd started the flood, and now it all poured out. "I don't have anything to compare it to, obviously, but I thought my sex life with Darren was… fulfilling. I don't know if you want to hear about this, especially after you and I just—"

"I want to understand, Liv," Lucas said. "There's nothing I don't want to hear. Sure, hearing about your sex life with your husband may be a little uncomfortable, but I can't understand you without understanding that."

"I don't really want to talk about it too much either, because it's…I don't want to say private, or sacred, but…it was *ours*, Darren's and mine."

"I understand completely, Liv. Like I said, I just want to…" he sighed. "I want to know you. I want to understand you."

I nodded. "When you have a relationship with

the same person for thirty years, there are a lot of lay-
ers and levels and nuances to it. It shifts and changes
with time. At first, being just kids, it was clumsy
and crazy and spontaneous, and…reckless, at times.
Then as we grew closer and more comfortable with
each other, it sort of evened out. We discovered what
worked for us, and what didn't. Then, as we started to
age a little, post-forty and such, things…I don't want
to say cooled off, but slowed down some. It wasn't as
much of a priority for either of us." I sighed. "I suppose to really make this worth the telling, I have to be
truthful with myself, huh?"

"Probably."

I wiped tears away. "The truth, then, is that the
cooling off came more from Darren. I guess it was a
symptom of his declining health. I thought it was a
normal middle-aged male…thing, but I don't know
for sure. I just knew that he still loved me as much as
ever, and was as attracted to me as ever, but the ini-
tiation of sex came more and more from me instead
of him, and with teenaged girls to raise, and an exploding career as an interior designer to balance, my
energy and time were…not always there. And then,
about six months before he died, he threw out his
back, and all sex stopped completely."

"Jeez. That's rough."

I shifted and ran my hand over his chest, his

shoulder, finding comfort in simply touching his skin. "I...I don't know how to—how to encapsulate it all." I blinked hard. "I loved Darren, and he loved me."

"I don't doubt that."

"But in the years since his death, and since meeting you, and now with what you and I just shared, I guess I'm realizing some things about my sexual relationship with Darren that I never knew before."

"Like?" Lucas prompted.

"Like the fact that I was pretty unsatisfied, sexually, for the last...three, maybe even four years of my marriage with Darren. When we did have sex, it was...not perfunctory, but just..." I shook my head, dislodging tears that I didn't wipe away. "I don't know. I was left feeling like there was something I wanted, something I needed that I wasn't getting. I used to get it from our relationship, but that wasn't happening anymore. What that is, I'm still not sure. I don't know. I just know it was...something."

"Passion?"

I shook my head. "No...well, maybe. I mean, after thirty years, passion becomes something else I don't know we have a word for. It's not always... high-octane fire, you know?"

He shook his head. "No, I don't. I was never with anyone long enough to know about that. But if you're passionate about someone, I guess I'd personally find it hard to believe that just goes away. But what do I know?"

I blinked, tried to breathe normally—but couldn't. "I don't want to disrespect my memory of Darren. I loved our life together. I wasn't unhappy."

"I don't want to put anything negative on it either, Liv. You used the word sacred earlier, and I guess I think that would apply, you know?"

I nodded. "Yeah, but my point is that I have to be honest with myself, because I'm dealing with these feelings inside myself that I don't know how to navigate."

"Like what?"

"Like the fact that with you just now, I felt more alive, and more…*desired*, than…than I have in a long, long, long time. That kind of hurts, because it means I wasn't feeling that from the man I spent my entire life with, and I don't know what to do with that fact. I can't deny what I had with Darren, but I also can't ignore what I feel with you."

"Which is what?"

"Amazing. Passionate. Womanly. " I swallowed hard, twisting my head to meet his eyes. "Desired… needy."

"Needy, huh?"

I nodded. "I feel out of control. Since we met I felt like if I didn't push down and hold back my attraction to you, I would just…lose all control over it, and I'm scared to do that."

"Why?"

"Because healing and learning to move on has been an exercise in learning to control my feelings. Learning to live through the grief, to let it just be there without letting it take over and stop me from living my life. I've had anxiety attacks pretty regularly, too, and I've had to learn to deal with those—life just overwhelms me sometimes and sometimes I feel like I'll never be able to start again. It's been about control." I had to pause for a long time to figure out how to say the next part. "Since Darren died, I've been shut down, sexually. I just couldn't think about myself as a sexual being anymore, because my identity as a woman, as a sexual being, had been so completely tied up in him, in us."

"And then suddenly you have these desires for someone else," he guessed.

I nodded. "Very, very powerful feelings," I said, looking up at him. "Very, very, *very* powerful desires. It's confusing and, as you can tell, it's messing with my mind."

"I can't imagine."

"Being around you is confusing. It's hard. And now that we've crossed over into a physical relationship, I'm even more confused. Because I…I want you.

I *need*…what you were making me feel. It's been so long since I've felt any kind of physical pleasure at all, and now that I've had a taste of it, I need more."

"So, a question."

I glanced at him. "Yes?"

"You said any kind of physical pleasure." He hesitated. "Does that mean even on your own?"

I blushed, ducked my head, nodding. "Yeah."

"Damn."

"Well, you have to understand, that was never something I…did." I swallowed hard. "I, um. From the very start of my body changing and discovering sexual feelings as a young girl, it was tied up completely in my relationship with Darren. I didn't… um…I never masturbated—ever. I didn't *need* to, or want to—I had Darren. Sex meant Darren. Need, desire, release, all that, it was all about him."

He mused silently. "Literally, everything was wrapped up in your husband."

I nodded. "Yes. Entirely."

"And when he died, you lost…" he trailed off, unsure how to put it.

"I lost sex as an aspect of my life. I don't know how to…do that. How to go there, on my own. How to let myself feel things, want things, have things… that aren't *him*. It's not just habit, at this point, it's the instincts developed as a part of my personality. And now there's you, and my sexuality is…it's…" I shook my head, trying to find the words and failing. "I feel like I'm coming apart at the seams, exploding from the inside out, like everything I know about myself is in question. I learned how to get my oil changed and how to pay bills and fill up the gas tank and live alone, how to take care of myself without needing anyone. But I don't know how to relearn my sexuality. I don't even know where to start."

Lucas was quiet for a long time, and I knew I had to give him the space to work through what I was saying. Shoot, I needed time myself, because I'd never put any of this in so many words, even with my therapists—this was a topic too deep and dark and difficult even for therapy.

Yet somehow, I could talk about it with Lucas?

"I think there's a question in there somewhere, but I don't know how to ask it." He paused, scratched his goatee. "I ain't gonna lie, I like you and want you in a way I didn't know was possible. For the first time in forty years, I can heal from what happened with Lena. And that *is* you. Getting healthy, fixing myself and my relationship with the boys, that's me, for myself. But getting over Lena? That's you. She's gone, Liam's gone, it's all years past, now. But for me, she was always present, because I didn't know how to let her go. Then I met you, and I realized I was just fixed on her because no one could compare in my mind." He looked down at me. "You put her to shame. You eclipse her, in every possible way. My feelings for you make what I felt for her, what I may or may not have had with her—what I *thought* I had with her—seem like a fart in a hurricane." He laughed. "Sorry, that's vulgar and gross. Point is, I can't deny it, can't pretend it isn't as huge as it is. But I can say I'm willing to wait, willing to take this as slow as you need, and I'm sorry if I rushed you into things you weren't ready for."

I twisted toward him, looking up at him. "You didn't rush me, Lucas. I got…carried away. Lost, I guess, in feeling things I haven't felt in years. But then it started to get a little bit…more…than I guess I was ready for, and I freaked out. I'm sorry for that, Lucas. I really, really don't want you to feel…" I rolled a shoulder. "Rejected. Or…not wanted. I'm just—"

"How about neither of us apologize, then?" He slid down to lay on the bed, taking me with him, so I was curled in the protective shelter of his arms. "I did feel kinda stung at first, but then I saw that you were upset, and I got kinda scared I'd let myself get carried away, like I pushed you for too much, too fast. I…it's been a long time for me, too. A real, real long time. And what I did have was…not very personal, I guess, and it didn't last long. The boys' mother was never meant to be part of a family, and we just sort of made things work until she left. After that, I...I had a few flings, but I couldn't ever really...connect. Even physically. I mean, for one thing, I was a raging alcoholic, and in godawful shape, so there weren't exactly ladies lined up to shack up with me." He blinked a few times, cleared his throat. "I guess I been lonely a long time. Felt...undesirable. Like, why would anyone ever want to be with me? I think deep down, that's a lot of why I—" He stopped, breathing slowly. "Why I was so motivated to make real, drastic, lasting changes."

"You didn't think I could accept you, the way you were?"

He shook his head. "I didn't think I deserved to be. I guess I've sort of come to learn through therapy and long talks with the boys, and Bax—who, by the way, is a lot wiser and smarter than you'd think from first meeting him—that I have to accept myself and believe I deserve good things. Sounded like a lot of frou-frou self-help bullshit at first, but...you gotta know you're worth it, for anyone else to know you're worth it."

I blinked back tears yet again. "Lucas, I..." I sighed, sniffled. "I was falling for you, Lucas. It scared me. I sort of, maybe...um, used my own insecurities as a way to push you away because I was scared of how I was feeling for you." I touched his cheek with my palm. "As you were, *then*. For who you are." I rubbed his chest with my other hand, his abdomen, and the hard plane of muscle that was slowly beginning to reveal itself through his hard work. "How you look now is…" I smiled, sniffed a laugh. "Icing on the cake, I guess."

"Falling for me?" he asked, eyebrows lifted.

I nodded. "Falling for you. Have fallen? Am falling? I don't know."

"I'm gone, baby. I've totally fallen for you, and it's been that way since I first laid eyes on you."

I yawned. "Can I just…can I stay here with you?"

He tightened his hold on me. "I'd love that."

He adjusted the blanket, tugging it out from under us and draping it over us. I nuzzled into his shoulder, letting myself feel him, letting my feelings for him well up and take shape—examining them, trying to fathom them, and know them.

They were complex, and deep. I would always love Darren, he would always define me, as a person, but I also had this new life, this new me—informed by who I had been, the Olivia Goode who had grown up and spent her life with Darren Goode, the Olivia who had created a life, had five children and raised them to adulthood. That Olivia was still me, but now I was beginning to understand that I had to leave that part of my life in the past—but it would always be there, always be real, always be important. I wasn't leaving that Olivia behind, but I was moving on, and I was including her in the woman I was becoming:

A woman with a heart full of love that I needed to give away; a woman with a need to be known, to be held, to be touched, to be loved. I couldn't replace Darren, and I wasn't trying to. Lucas wasn't trying to replace him. He couldn't, and he didn't want to. But he did want to be a part of my life, and I wanted him there.

I heard his heartbeat under my ear, felt his arm around me, felt him breathing and heard his breath.

I was falling asleep, but my memories of what had just happened with him tonight were all I could think of.

I felt Lucas all around me. His skin was warm under me, his arm strong around me. I remembered the taste of his kiss, the tender, passionate, hungry way his lips had devoured mine. The way he'd ripped my nightie apart to get at my naked body—that had been exhilarating and scary. I'd never felt so *needed* in my life. I still felt a twinge of guilt and worry and anxiety, but I let the memory of the thrilling wild fury of his passion pulse through me—his mouth on my skin, on my breasts. His hands greedily clutching my flesh as if he couldn't get enough of me.

I felt sleep tugging me under, and I gave into it, but the ocean of need so long buried and ignored was coming to a boil inside me.

If I could feel safe enough to tell Lucas the deepest, darkest secret inside me—that I'd felt unfulfilled for the last several years of my marriage—surely I was safe enough with Lucas to give into that boiling ocean of need. Surely I could let it boil over, let myself go. Give up control. Let need reign, let desire rule.

I fell asleep wondering and trying to picture what that would look like.

When I awoke, I was on my side, being spooned by Lucas's huge hot hard bulk. His arm was slung low over my waist, his chest expanding against my back with a soft, growling snore. Sunlight poured in through his open window.

I felt so safe, so secure. I never wanted to move, or to leave this moment. I wanted to bask in the warmth and safety of Lucas's arms. I let myself drift, but never quite fell back asleep. Instead, I was focused on the feel of him behind me.

He stirred, murmured something unintelligible. Shifted. I twisted to face him, his hand now resting on my hip. I was naked, but for my underwear—I saw my nightie on the floor, ripped open, and shivered at the memory of Lucas tearing it apart like paper. My skin pebbled, and my nipples hardened.

I thought of the way he'd kissed me, his mouth on mine, his hands wandering, possessing. That ocean of need was boiling, sudden and furious. My skin tightened, heating. My breath was shallow. His bulk was slack, the huge muscles at rest. I ran my hand over his shoulder, down one thick arm and his hand tightened on my hip.

I bit my lip, not knowing what to do, or how to handle this. How to take what I wanted. I didn't want to wake him up, but I...god, need and desire were pounding through me.

Lucas stirred again, snorted, sniffed, growled in his chest. His eyes fluttered. Opened. Deep liquid brown focused on mine.

"Mornin', beautiful," he murmured.

"Good morning, handsome."

His smile was breathtaking, the tenderness in his eyes as he gazed at me left me gasping for breath, left my stomach churning and my blood pounding and my thighs pressing together to quench the growing ache between them.

"I slept better than I have in...god, ever," he said.

"Me, too."

"Thanks for bein' willing to tell me all that, last night. Means a lot that you trusted me with it."

"Thank *you* for listening with an open mind."

"I just want you to know I'm here. That I...I care

about you. That I'm all in, and that whatever we've got going on can happen at your pace. I want…everything, but I can be patient."

I shifted toward him, realizing that I'd been covering my chest with my arm out of some instinctual habit of modesty. Now, I moved my arm, letting my breasts drape free, nestling against his chest. I ran my hand over his side, to his waist.

I swallowed hard. "I…don't know how this will go. I may freak out again, I don't know. But I…" I searched his eyes, bit my lip, exhaled a nervous, shaky breath. "But I would really like it if you kissed me again."

He smiled at me. "I think I could do that."

He gathered me in his arms and drew me closer, and suddenly he was all around me again, his breath on my lips, his eyes on mine, his arms protective iron bands around my shoulders and waist, his hands splayed against my spine and shoulder blades. I nuzzled closer, short of breath as his lips touched mine in a soft questing exploration.

I was dizzy at the first press of his kiss. Hungry as the questing kiss became more. Desperate as his tongue found mine. Something beyond desperate— wild, an inferno of sudden unquenchable need as I lost myself in his kiss.

I arched my back and pressed against him, moaning as he kissed me to breathlessness.

I couldn't breathe, and I didn't want to, but I felt myself pulling away to suck in a delicious breath of his nearness.

"Okay?" he muttered.

"More than okay," I breathed. "Keep going." I palmed his chest, ran my fingers down his belly. "I need more."

"If you need to stop—"

I touched his lips. "I don't want to. I want this. I *need* this."

His smile was a blaze of delight and ravenous rapture as he twisted into me, pressing me to my back. He levered himself over me, and reveled in the feeling of my own smallness and delicacy beneath his powerful form. He rested on an elbow and bent over me, kissing my lips. I clutched at his shoulders, and then let my hands wander. To his waist. To his hips. Clutched the hard, firm, flexing mounds of his buttocks over his shorts. Ran my hands over the back of his head as he moved down from my mouth, tipping my head back so he could kiss my throat. My chest.

My breasts—and oh, oh, oh god, that was glorious. The aching tug in me traveled from my nipples to my core, and I was on fire, heat blasting inside me, throbbing at my core. Each breast in turn, he licked and lapped and suckled, and shifted so he could massage and squeeze and caress one while plying the other with his mouth.

I whimpered, moaned, and clawed my fingers down his spine. Ached to feel more, to lose myself more fully in this. Fear snuck through me, but I didn't let it take over.

I was safe.

I wanted this.

I could have this.

It wasn't going to change what I'd had—but I was adding it to the new life I was creating for myself, a life I was allowed to have.

Lucas kissed my belly, and his fingers curled into the elastic of my underwear at each hip—he paused, watching me, meeting my eyes.

I bit my lip and lifted my butt off the mattress, an invitation. I kept my eyes on his, nervous and afraid and exhilarated.

He tugged my last scrap of clothing down my thighs, and off. And then I was fully bared, naked for him, and his eyes raked over me, from my eyes to my breasts to my sex, and his chest swelled and his shoulders lifted and tensed.

"Jesus, Liv. So fuckin' gorgeous." He knelt over me, hands running across my stomach, over my hips. He licked his lips and hesitated, hands gripping my hipbones. "I want to touch you."

My heart hammered in my chest, my pulse loud in my ears. I wanted his touch. I couldn't say it, couldn't find the words, so I grabbed his wrist and brought his hand to my lips and kissed his palm. My eyes never left his, and I knew he saw that I was scared; I guided his hand back down my body, my fingers over his as his palm skated down over my breasts and belly to my sex.

I left his hand there, ran my palms over his arm, clutching his bicep, breathless as he touched me intimately for the first time. I gasped, a shrill soft sound, as his finger trailed over my seam. Whimpered as he slid his fingertip inside me. I lifted my hips and whined in my throat when his fingers found my clitoris. I watched my hips flex under his touch, let my voice rise. He kissed my breast, suckled my nipples, one and the other in turn, as his fingers circled me.

I cried out—or, very simply, just cried as he touched me with tender and loving perfection, as if he knew me intimately already, touched me as if he knew exactly how to bring the most pleasure.

My stomach curved in, my hips pushed up, my back arched, my eyes closed involuntarily, and I clutched at Lucas, wherever my hands could find his skin. Heat billowed inside me, a pressure building madly in my core, expanding through me until I felt like even the tips of my fingers and toes were near detonation.

And then his finger slid deeper into me, and another when I accepted the first with a gasp and flex of my hips. In and out. Then a thumb or his palm or something was grinding against my sensitive, throbbing clit.

"Oh god, Lucas—oh god!" I heard my voice crying in a loud, breathless shriek. "Yes, god yes!"

His mouth moved from breast to breast, back and forth, keeping my nipples wet and hard, his tongue flicking. I grabbed at him—where? Hips, shoulders, buttocks.

I needed his flesh. Needed him with my whole being.

I felt the madness in myself, the wild need for all I could get, all I could feel and hold and touch and taste as he brought me to a screaming climax.

I forgot about touching him for a split second— the exploding scream inside me took over everything, a blast of wild ecstasy shredding me apart under his fingers and mouth.

When the crashing waves of climax subsided, I was sweating and shaking and smiling and laughing. "Oh god, Lucas," I breathed. "God, thank you."

He kissed my lips gently. "You're even more gorgeous when you're coming, Liv. Didn't know that was even possible."

"I don't know that I've ever felt anything like that

in my life." The stab of emotion came and went, and I let it go.

"You okay?"

"More than okay." I grinned up at him, eager and desperate for what was next, for more. "So much more than just okay."

I rolled into him, nuzzled against him. Whispered in his ear. "My turn."

FIFTEEN

Lucas

I FOUND MYSELF ON MY BACK, AN ERECTION THROBBING SO hard underneath my underwear that it hurt like hell. Liv was rolling toward me, moving to her hands and knees, and then kneeling beside me. Leaning over me, small, firm, soft breasts sliding against my chest, peaked nipples brushing my skin. Naked body curved like a goddess, eyes shining, sweat dotted here and there, a need in her eyes and a wildness in her that made me crazy, made me understand that I hadn't just fallen for her, that I didn't just care about her—I fucking loved her.

"Liv," I whispered.

She touched my lips. "Just…sssshhhh. I know—I know."

She saw it.

I saw it in her, and I knew that we weren't ready to exchange those words, but each of us knowing they existed was enough, for the moment.

She bit her lower lip and raked her gaze over my prone body, tracing her fingers down my chest and over my ribs, over my stomach to the waistband of my underwear. She curled her fingers in the elastic, hooking the underwear...tugging them down.

She pulled them away from my erection and brought them down and over my knees, letting me kick them away, and her eyes were taking me in, the thick, fat-headed, purple-veined shaft of my cock, bobbing at my navel. Straining.

Her eyes widened, and she flattened her palm on my stomach just above it. She devoured me, my cock. Bigger than she was expecting, maybe, I don't know. Didn't matter. All that mattered was that she was touching me—wrapping her tiny hand around me, sliding her fingers down, then back up. I swallowed hard and felt myself reacting immediately.

"It's been so long, Liv—"

She bent over and kissed me. "Hush. Just let me touch you."

"But I—"

"I don't care if takes ten seconds or an hour.

I just want to—feel this. Feel *you*. We have all the time in the world."

I gasped as she slowly, gently stroked me. "Jesus, Liv. The way you're touching me—"

She brushed her breasts against my chest as she kissed my lips. "What about it?"

"So fuckin' good."

Her smile curved against my lips. "Yeah? How fucking good?"

I rumbled a laugh, turned on even more by the curse falling so unexpectedly from her lips. "Better than anything in my entire fuckin' life. God, please—don't stop."

Her mouth demanded a kiss, and I gave it to her, dizzy from the furious passion with which her lips and tongue tangled with mine, even as her fist oh so slowly and tenderly caressed my length.

"I won't." Her voice was so quiet, so small.

I watched, barely able to draw a breath, as her hand slid teasingly over my cock, twisting and rubbing the tip with her thumb until I was groaning and growling and tilting my hips up to get more of her touch. I reached the edge within minutes, perhaps even less—there was no concept of time, no way to measure how much time passed while she explored me.

I didn't want it to end; not at all, and not like this,

not so soon, not without feeling more of her. Hearing more of those sweet, wild sounds of her release.

I grabbed her wrists in both of my hands, pulling them away from me. "Wait, Liv—wait."

She stared at me, confused. "I thought you said you didn't want me to stop?"

"I don't." I hauled her up my body, over on top of me until she was astride me, sitting on my belly. "I need you. I don't want to come from your hand, sweetheart—I want to come inside you. I want to make love to you. I *need* to make love to you."

She sniffed a laugh. "Make love to me?"

I palmed her cheek, dragged my thumb across her lips. "What? Somethin' wrong with that?"

She laughed aloud, then leaned down to kiss me—and I could've come just from that, from the view of her on top of me, her breasts hanging to trace over my chest. "No, Lucas. I just expected you to say something else…" She shrugged.

"Something vulgar?" I suggested.

"Yeah."

"You sounded almost disappointed," I said between kisses as my hands roamed her body, arcing over her shoulders, down her back, cupping her beautiful taut ass, and caressing and patting and kneading, then back up her spine. Liv was straddling me, just above my cock, her core slick and grinding on my stomach, her hands in my hair and scraping down my cheeks as she devoured my mouth, greedily taking my kisses and demanding more with her tongue and quiet breathless moans.

"I've come to like the way you talk. It's refreshing and different. A little vulgar sometimes but, strangely, I like that too."

"So…" I reached between her thighs and found her wet and waiting, her pussy tight around my fingers and her moans eager as I explored her again. "If I told you instead that I wanna fuck you…"

She gasped, tightening around my fingers as I circled her clit and then delved inside her. "Yeah?"

"You'd like that?"

"Yes, Lucas." She reached back and grasped me, stroking me to the same rhythm that I circled her clit. "I want you to make love to me. I want you to fuck me. I want all of it. Right now. Please, right now."

"God, Liv—you got no fuckin' idea what it does to me when you swear."

She pressed her lips to my ear. "I don't think I've ever said anything like that before. I'm not someone who swears or talks dirty."

"I like it. A lot."

"You do, huh?" She bent over me, tilting her core away, lifting up, and slid down my body so my cock was nestled just inside her slit. "You like it when I swear?"

"A fuckin' lot."

"So if I told you I've had wet dreams, naughty dreams about this…about you fucking me…"

I groaned, flexing to get deeper. "Fuck, Liv. You're too much."

She writhed on me. "I almost don't recognize my-self right now."

"It's beautiful, Liv."

"Does it make me…tawdry?"

I laughed, cupping her breast with one hand and palming her ass with the other. "No clue what the fuck that means, babe."

"Cheap. Slutty."

I caressed her cheek, locking eyes with her, stop-ping everything. "Olivia—no. It makes you a woman who knows what she wants and ain't afraid to take it, to be bold about what she wants. That there is a hell of a beautiful thing."

Her eyes searched mine, wavering. "You really think so?"

"Down to the depths of my soul, babe. Don't hold back. Don't be shy. I wanna know what you want so I can do everything I can to give it to you." I kissed her. "This is you and me, Liv. Just us. We're creatin' something new between us, and there's no rules but what we make."

She blinked back tears, then let them fall, and I

reached up to wipe them away. "I really like that idea, Lucas." She moved, and I was still almost but not quite inside her. "I want…"

"Tell me."

She bit her lip, touched her forehead to mine, swallowing loudly, speaking in a hoarse whisper. "Make love to me. Fuck me. Show me how amazing it can be."

"I…" A realization shot through me. "We ain't wearing' no protection…or, I ain't. And I don't have any. I honestly wasn't sure this would ever happen, barely dared to dream of it. Goin' out and buyin' condoms seemed a bit presumptuous."

"Have you been with anyone recently?"

I shook my head. "Naw. Not in years. And I used protection then, and every time before that."

"I can't have any more children, Lucas. I can't get pregnant." She nuzzled her cheek against mine. "I… had a scare, about six years ago. I was turning forty, and got cramps that wouldn't go away, heavy bleeding… sorry, not exactly sexy talk. But the point is, I had to get a hysterectomy. So…we don't need protection, as long as you're clean."

"I am. Got checked actually, as part of a recent checkup at the doctor. I have the results somewhere, if you want to see them."

She shook her head. "No, I believe you." A brief pause. "I trust you."

"So we don't need nothin'?" I asked.

She shook her head. "No. Nothing between us."

I groaned. "I've never…done that. Bare, nothin'."

"No?"

I shook my head. "Nope. Never."

"There's nothing like it." Another hesitation, and I could see something in her eyes.

"There's somethin' else, ain't there?" I asked.

She nodded, suddenly shy. "I want…I want to be underneath you."

I rolled, and she went with me, twisting to her back and welcoming me on top of her, caressing my shoulders and spine with her hands, tracing down to my ass, and then between my thighs, clutching my cock in her small, eager hands. I slid my finger down her seam, found her clit, and she gasped, guiding me to her opening.

She hesitated, then. "Lucas?"

"Hmm?" I asked, touching her and kissing her at the same time, eager to taste her, more eager still to finally bury myself inside her.

"You don't need to say it, or say it back."

I knew exactly what she meant. But I wasn't accepting it. "Liv, honey. If I say it, it'll be because I mean it. And you best know this, too, babe—I ain't ever said those words to a woman. Barely even said 'em to my kids. But I'll say 'em to you, and I'll mean it more'n I ever meant anything in my entire fuckin' life."

"You've never told a woman you love her?"

I shook my head. "Nope. Never heard it back either."

She seemed on the verge of tears again, then sniffed, laughing. "I can't wait to say it to you, then."

I nuzzled her cheek, and then flexed my hips, aching to be inside her. "Liv…I need you. I can't wait any longer."

She bit her lip, stroking my cock in a way that seemed nervous. Her eyes watered. "I'm scared."

"We can wait."

She shook her head. "Not like you're thinking." She swallowed hard. "I'm not scared of you, of being with you. It's been so long—and I'm…I'm scared of disappointing you. Not being good enough. I'm scared there was something about me that made Darren not want me."

"Impossible." I bent and kissed her lips, and then her chest, and then her breasts. "There ain't a goddamn thing you could do to disappoint me, not even if you told me you need to wait."

"I don't want to wait. I'm dying to have you inside me. I'm going crazy for it. But I'm just so scared—that I've built it up in my mind, that I won't be good, that something will go wrong…"

I kissed her to shut her up, and then licked a nipple until she gasped. "You're overthinking it. You're getting stuck in your head."

"Yes."

I met her eyes. Flexed my hips. "Be with me, Liv. Be here with me, now. Don't think—feel. Just feel." I palmed her breast, caressed it. "How's that feel?"

"So good," she breathed, closing her eyes. "I love how rough and strong your hand is."

I took her breast in my mouth and traced her sex, circling her hardening clit with a fingertip. "How about that? How does that feel?"

"Ohhh, oh god, *so* good. Like lightning striking me, like…like I'm on fire, but it just makes me want more."

I slid my finger inside her. Curled, withdrew, added a second, teasing the motion of sex with my fingers—in and out, in and out, curling through her slick, dripping pussy until she was writhing, and then using her own essence to wet her clit and flick it and circle.

"How does that feel, Liv?"

She reached for me, found my cock and brought it to her slit, pushed my hand away and slipped me inside her. With a moan, she flicked open her eyes and fixed them on mine; her brown-green-hazel eyes were wide and shimmering, and she whimpered.

"It feels like I need *this*," she whispered.

SIXTEEN

Liv

LUCAS BADD WAS BURIED DEEP INSIDE ME, AND HE FIT AS if he was made to be there. Stretching me to a beautiful ache, making me dizzy with the rapturous perfection of being filled to bursting. I couldn't breathe for how incredible he felt, how wonderful his cock felt inside me, how much I loved being wrapped around him, being beneath him, letting myself get lost in him.

I cried out as he pushed deep, gasped as he pulled back; wrapping my legs around his buttocks, I clutched his neck with two trembling hands and bit his shoulder as he began to move. Sliding slowly, grinding, gliding, not rushed at all, unhurried—but I could see the desperation in his eyes, the wild frantic need in his gaze. I could feel how intense this was for him, and the way he shook all over as he drew out his movements into slow, deliberate gyrations made me quaver with excitement, with renewed furious passion. I clawed at him, flexed my hips, needing more of him, even though he was already fully seated in me and was making love to me with an aching rhythm, I needed more.

I felt his tears on my face, mixed with my own—and he was groaning, gasping breathlessly.

"Liv...god, Liv. Olivia..." he whispered, his lips on my cheek, his breath on my ear.

"Lucas," I groaned back, driving against him frantically.

I shook all over, trembling uncontrollably, panting in a breathless endless whine of ecstasy and wonder as we moved in perfect unison, meeting each other thrust for thrust, gasp for gasp. One of his fists was planted in the mattress beside my face, the other was clutching at my breasts and squeezing and caressing my face and tugging at my hip to bring me closer, getting himself deeper, joining us more tightly. My legs were around his waist, my ankles hooked together around his ass, my fingernails clawing roughly down his spine and grasping at his neck.

"Oh, god—Lucas!" I whimpered, my lungs

unable to draw breath, a climax searing through me, shaking me in the grip of a spasming, wrenching orgasm which I had no choice but to scream through, burying my face in his neck and screaming and screaming until I went hoarse as my entire body was consumed by fury and flames…

And then I felt Lucas's thrusts go wild, losing the rhythm, the studied pace. His groans became gasped grunts and mad curses. The feeling of Lucas reaching climax was almost as potent as my own orgasm—my core was clamping and pulsating around him as he powered into me again and again, harder and harder, faster and faster.

"Liv, oh fuck, Olivia, god you feel…ohhh fuck—you feel perfect, you feel like fuckin' heaven—you feel like home, baby, oh god…"

"I love this, Lucas, I love the way you feel inside me," I whispered into his ear, my voice a hoarse rasp from my screams. "I love this, I love this—"

He was thrusting with total abandon, and I felt each one in every molecule of my body, and I pulsed around his cock, squeezing the muscles of my sex as hard as I could and writhing with him as he gave into his release.

In the moment of his orgasm, he rested his forehead against mine, his lips quaking against my mouth, and I felt him let loose, coming inside me with a shout, and then he whispered, "Olivia, holy fuck, Olivia—I love you…"

Tears trickled down my face as I saw in his eyes and on his face and in the crazed shaking vulnerability in every line of his body how deeply he meant those words—and they meant all the more to me knowing that he'd never spoken them to a woman before, and that he didn't just say so in the heat of orgasm.

I cupped his stubble-roughened cheek and pressed a thousand tiny kisses to his lips, my other hand clawed into the meat of his tensed buttocks, pulling him against me with each of his stuttering thrusts. "Lucas, ohh…my…*Lucas*…"

I wasn't sure if I meant that as *oh my, Lucas* or *ohhh, my Lucas*; both perhaps.

He filled me, wet warmth spreading into me and leaking out as he continued to release, groaning my name in a chant, now—*Liv, Liv, Liv, god, Liv.*

"Yes, Lucas—don't stop, don't stop," I whispered, shaking all over anew, his wild thrusts reaching a place inside me I didn't know existed, his angle rubbing against my hypersensitive clit, bringing me to climax with him, a second one hard on the heels of the first, synched with his seemingly endless orgasm—a second climax for me, something I'd never felt in my life.

And this one was…shattering.

I couldn't even scream at first, was too hoarse from the first, and then I was panting in his ear and chanting something—what was I saying? I wasn't in control of my voice, or body or anything. I'd totally surrendered to this, to him, to what I was feeling with him.

"I love you, I love you, I love you," I heard myself gasping. "Lucas, Lucas—ohhh, I love this and I love you, don't stop—don't stop, oh god, you feel so fucking incredible!"

He groaned one last time, trembling spasmodically inside me, thrusting once more, and then collapsing partially on top of me, panting breathlessly.

For several long minutes, he rested his heavy head on my breasts, our ragged breathing synched, my fingers tracing lazy circles over his shoulders, scalp, neck, spine, and butt.

"I meant it, Olivia," he rumbled, his voice rough and deep. "Wasn't just…something I said in the moment. I meant it. I love you."

I circled my arms around him, held him tight. "I meant it too, Lucas." I touched my lips to his ear. "I love you—I'm in love with you. It scares me, but it's real. It's true."

He lifted up to gaze down at me, then rolled onto his back and cradled my head against his chest, his arms around me, breathing deeply, raggedly. "Most amazing thing I've ever heard in my life, Liv." He laughed quietly. "Except maybe the way you sound when you come."

I buried my face in his chest to hide my blush. "Lucas..."

He touched my chin, lifted my face to look at him. "Don't hide it, Liv. It's beautiful. You're beautiful. What we did together was beautiful. Nothing to be shy about."

"I've never...screamed like that, or sounded like that. Said those things." I inhaled sharply. "I never thought I'd love again."

"God, me either, honey." He sighed. "Except, now that I know what it's like to love you and be loved back, I don't think what Lena and I had was love. Not even close. This—" he squeezed me close, and I gasped a laugh at the sudden fierce strength of his embrace, "this is *real*. You're real."

"I am real, Lucas." I gazed up at him. "I'm here, and I'm real." I giggled. "And really, really messy."

Lucas rumbled a laugh and scooted out of his bed, went to the bathroom and returned with a wash-cloth. He cleaned me so gently it was almost ineffective, but it was done with such love and tenderness that I let him, and then I took the washcloth from him and made sure I was cleaned more thoroughly.

Naked and sated—for the moment, at least—I rested in his arms and luxuriated in the silence and warmth of his embrace, in the basking perfection of afterglow.

I felt a peace and a happiness so deep and so thorough, I knew I'd never want to leave, and that I would be here—in Lucas's strong arms, naked and gloriously well loved, breathing his scent and feeling him all around me, and happier than I had ever imagined possible—every day for the rest of my life.

THE END

EPILOGUE

Cassie

WHEN I WOKE UP THE NEXT MORNING, MOM WAS gone. Not in her bed, phone on the charger, purse on the kitchen counter. I had a feeling I knew where she was, and I honestly felt happy for her. Lucas seemed like a genuinely nice guy, albeit a little rough around the edges. But I could tell he cared for Mom, and that she felt the same way about him; and that was all that mattered. Mom had been through a lot, and had been alone for a long time, and she deserved some happiness.

God knows things with Dad had been a little…off, the last few years of his life, and the last few months especially. It stung me to admit it, but Dad had kind of…stopped trying. With us girls, and with Mom, especially. He worked a lot, leaving early and coming home late, and when he was around, he seemed…apathetic. Mom had pretended to be fine, but I'd seen the reality under the surface; she had been unhappy. She loved Dad, and would never have admitted anything different, and obviously would never have left him or anything. But she'd just been unhappy. When he died, I think there had been a sense of relief buried way down deep under the grief, and Mom had felt guilty about that, deeply, horribly guilty. I honestly don't think even now, with this Lucas Badd in the picture, that she'd ever admit to feeling relieved Dad had died.

God knows she missed him, we all did, and we would never have wanted him to die, but he'd stopped trying. It was as if he didn't care about anything anymore, especially himself. And it had taken a toll on all of us.

I know Dad's behavior had led Charlie to move out, and to quickly develop a relationship with the smarmy lawyer-politician or whatever he was, whom I'd never liked. To me, it seemed like she had rebounded from Dad to the first available guy.

Dad made things difficult at home and it led me to come up with ever-increasing excuses to stay on overseas tours—to stay away, because I couldn't handle the way things had become at home.

Dad's apathy had certainly lit the fire of vehe-
ment liberal feminism and social justice crusading inside of Lexie—along with, weirdly, an absurdly high-
rev sex drive, which she sated with a revolving door
of loser guys…reversing the role of the player where
she was the player, the sexually liberated female who
just used guys for what they could give her in bed.

Torie…was Torie. But if Dad's gradual slide into
not seeming to care about us girls, or his wife, had
done anything to Torie, it was to make her use pot
to escape—which had, in turn, made her content to
just drift through life without a passion. This worried
me—it worried all of us—because she really did have
a lot of talents, things she could do and do amazingly
well if she were to care enough to try.

Poppy seemed the least affected of all of us, somehow. Perhaps because she'd lived most of her life with
Dad when he was on the downward slide of ill health
and lackluster fatherhood, so she had just accepted
it as a way of life. But, according to Mom, right now
Poppy was in a crisis over quitting school—which was
crazy to me, seeing as she'd gotten such a huge ride
to a prestigious university. She was insanely talented,
but you couldn't always bank on talent alone.

As I was learning myself, the very, very hard way.
I was a seriously talented and skilled dancer…with a
shattered leg, three sets of plates and screws, and a

long road of physical therapy and exercise ahead of me before I could even walk without a limp. So all that talent, all that skill, all those years of hard work… were useless to me. I'd danced until my feet had literally bled, until I couldn't walk because my legs were jelly and my feet hurt so bad…and I'd toughed it out and had kept dancing. I'd been the lead dancer in the troupe, a position I'd fought for with all the tenacity and ruthlessness I possessed.

And it had been taken away from me in a split second.

Everything had been taken away.

Including Rick.

I couldn't sit here and think about Rick, or Dad anymore, so I threw my sling bag on, locked the door to Mom's condo, and set out to walk to the nearest place I could find food and a strong drink—damn the fact that it was only eleven in the morning, I needed a drink. Mom had been watching me like a hawk, refusing to let me drink my stress and bitterness away.

I hobbled in the direction I remembered seeing something like civilization last night when we were driving to Mom's condo, and I grimly let my mind wander to the blow up with Rick.

He'd been in a medically induced coma for three weeks, and when they brought him out, he wasn't himself. I'd hoped it would be a temporary thing, but…it didn't seem that way. He was angry, bitter, re-sentful, morose. The diametric opposite to the Rick I'd fallen in love with. He had no other injuries except to his head, so once he recovered from that, he would hopefully be back to his normal life. It would take six months to a year, his doctors had said. I had sat with him, reassured him that I loved him. I'd been at his side the entire time he was in a coma, even when I was in a wheelchair myself after my own surgery, dizzy from pain meds that had only partially dulled the ache in my leg, and had done nothing whatsoever to dull the rage and agony in my head over losing my career.

He'd barely spoken to me after waking up, re-sponding in grunts and monosyllables at most. I'd tried cajoling, sneaking into his bed with him, even trying to get sexy with him—but he wasn't having it. There was no memory loss, meaning, he knew who I was and who he was, he remembered his family who had come to Paris to be with him, he remembered the various members of our troupe who came to visit and support us both every chance they got—he re-membered the accident, he knew all about our rela-tionship and the fact that he'd proposed just a month before the accident, and that we were planning a Paris wedding…

He just didn't want me. He didn't love me anymore.

And he told me so.

The doctors told me brain injuries were strange, unpredictable things that no one totally understood, and they did things to the victims that couldn't always be explained.

Such was the case with Rick, my boyfriend of four years, my fiancé. He fell out of love with me upon waking up from the coma.

I'd stuck by him despite the heartbreak, insisting it was a phase, refusing to believe he meant it. Hoping he would snap out of it, that he'd remember that he loved me, that we were going to get married under the Arc de Triomphe, live near the Eiffel Tower, and have three babies. We would open our own dance studio and I would be Madame Goode, because we were modern and sophisticated and I'd be keeping my own name.

But, no. All those plans had faded into the ether.

He told me he was sorry, but things had changed. For him. He felt lost and needed to be alone to figure things out. I wanted to stay with him, help him figure things out.

No.

He wanted to be alone.

It wasn't fair to me for him to ask me to stay with him when his feelings had changed. He no longer loved me, and didn't see that changing any time soon.

Was this all because I couldn't dance anymore?

He couldn't explain it.

He had just …changed.

It was best I leave.

I sobbed, wept, pleaded...but in the end, I'd given him his ring back and walked out—limped out. Alone.

When I was physically able, I came to Ketchikan with Mom, to a city I'd never been to before. My childhood home in Connecticut was gone. My home and family with the troupe was gone. Oh, the director had assured me I would always have a place, that I could choreograph and help direct and work with the dancers, but I knew myself—that would be torture. I had fought my way to the top, and then to watch Ariadne du Champs take over? No. No way I could do that, not in a million fucking years.

So, here I was, in Ketchikan, without a career, without a future, without a single thought of what to do with my life. No boyfriend, no fiancé, just heart-break on all fronts.

As I was walking I wasn't paying attention at all, I admit that fully—and what happened next was entirely my fault.

I was in a rage, a bitter diatribe against life and fate and Rick and love and everything else. An endless loop of pain and misery was playing full blast inside my head. I was not looking where I was going, I was unaware of, well…anything. I had no idea how long I'd been walking, or where I was walking, or what was in front of me. My head was down, just watching my feet, watching my own limp and hating it, too.

Suddenly, I was in the air, salt water splashing in droplets against my face; something had hold of the hood of my sweatshirt and was holding me up by it—I was dangling nearly horizontal over the water, over the edge of a dock or wharf, the green water and sunlight splashing six feet below me.

The thing which had hold of my hood gently tugged me backward, and a hand—at least, it felt like a hand, wrapped around my waist and pulled me upright.

Before I describe the owner of the hand, I should be clear about my own appearance: five-three, weighing just over a hundred pounds, slender at the hips and bust—I was insanely fit, with minimal body fat, and high muscle mass for my size and build. I had platinum blonde hair, the only one of my siblings that wasn't dark-haired like Mom and Dad had both been—Dad, according to stories and old photos, had been a towhead as a kid, only darkening as he got older, and his uncle and mother had both been platinum blonde like me, which was where I got it. I had Mom's eyes: gray-brown-green, a changeable hazel.

The owner of the hand was a bear.

Andre the giant.

Goliath.

Towering well over a foot above me, if not more, he was built like that bear from *Brave*, the evil one. Massively broad shoulders, arms the size of my waist, thighs thicker than any part of me. Dark skin, caramel and mahogany skin bare from the waist up, wearing only shorts, no shoes, no shirt. His hair was black as a raven's wing, and he had a thick shaggy beard hanging over his chest. Every inch of his skin was covered in tattoos, the kind that looked to my very ignorant eyes to be ritual native tattoos. Blue ink or black or purple, lines and dots, animal forms like you'd see on a totem pole. I stared up at him, trying to take in his size and gargantuan build and the dizzying, myriad array of tattoos all at once.

"Water's mighty cold," he murmured in a rumble so deep I felt it. "Not sure where you were going."

"Me...me either." I blinked, swallowed. I'd never seen anyone like this man. "I...thank you."

He just stared down at me. "Damn, but if you ain't a tiny little thing."

I frowned up at him. "Yeah, well, you're a goddamn giant."

He shrugged, nodded. "Yeah." He glanced around us—a dock running in both directions, and a road lined with shops a thousand feet behind me. "Where *were* you going?"

I shrugged. "I…I really don't know. I was…um. Lost. In thought."

"You were walking like a woman on a mission."

I nodded, licked my lips. "You've never gone for a walk so pissed off you weren't looking where you were going?"

He dragged thick fingers through his beard— even the backs of his hand, his palm, and his fingers were tattooed. "I don't give things that kind of power over me."

"Yeah, well, good for you. You're not the one whose entire life is fucked up." I felt my throat closing, turned away, embarrassed to be falling apart in front of a total stranger.

"My cousins-in-law own that bar over there," he said, and I turned to see where he was pointing. "I think you need a drink." That was a statement, not a question. "You can tell me about it."

"You don't want to hear my stupid story." I turned back to the water, staring out at the amazing, breathtaking view of the channel and the islands opposite.

That huge, tattooed paw of his spun me around as easily as if I were a toy, and his finger touched my chin. "Eyes." It was a command, and for some reason, I found myself turning my gaze to his own.

Warm, deep dark brown eyes gazed at me, the eyes of a bear, overflowing with bottomless wells of wisdom and kindness. I drowned in them, got lost in them. They were eyes that *cared*.

He didn't need to say anything; everything he wanted to communicate was in his gaze.

"Name?" Another rumble so deep my chest buzzed with it.

"Cassandra Goode. Cassie."

"Which?"

"Cassie."

His hand closed around mine, engulfing it, shaking it gently and firmly. "Ink Isaac."

"Ink?"

He nodded. "Ink. It's on the birth certificate."

"Fitting, huh?"

He smiled, a small curve on one side of his mouth. "Yeah." He gestured with a jerk of his head. "C'mon. They got good food, too. You're hungry, I think."

The one nice thing about having my career as a dancer taken away from me was that I didn't have to stay fit anymore. I could eat whatever I wanted, now.

"Do they have greasy, delicious comfort food?" I asked.

"Best in town."

It was crazy, but my life made no sense anymore, and I may as well go with it. "Let's go," I said. "I'm hungry, and I want to get blackout drunk."

He didn't answer that, but he didn't have to. I glanced up at the giant walking beside me, a giant with miles of incredible tattoos, acres of massive muscle, eyes that drowned me in wisdom and warmth, hands so big he could wrap one around my entire waist, and a voice so deep it came from the center of the earth.

It was crazy to go anywhere with him, but I went anyway.

Consequences be damned. What did I have to lose?

Jasinda Wilder

Visit me at my website: **www.jasindawilder.com**
Email me: **jasindawilder@gmail.com**

If you enjoyed this book, you can help others enjoy it as well by recommending it to friends and family, or by mentioning it in reading and discussion groups and online forums. You can also review it on the site from which you purchased it. But, whether you recommend it to anyone else or not, thank you *so much* for taking the time to read my book! Your support means the world to me!

My other titles:

The Preacher's Son:
Unbound
Unleashed
Unbroken

Biker Billionaire:
Wild Ride

Big Girls Do It:
Better (#1), Wetter (#2), Wilder (#3), On Top (#4)
Married (#5)
On Christmas (#5.5)
Pregnant (#6)
Boxed Set

Rock Stars Do It:
Harder
Dirty
Forever
Boxed Set

From the world of Big Girls and Rock Stars:
Big Love Abroad

Delilah's Diary:
A Sexy Journey
La Vita Sexy
A Sexy Surrender

The Falling Series:
Falling Into You
Falling Into Us
Falling Under
Falling Away
Falling for Colton

The Ever Trilogy:
Forever & Always
After Forever
Saving Forever

The world of *Alpha*:
Alpha
Beta
Omega
Harris: Alpha One Security Book 1
Thresh: Alpha One Security Book 2
Duke: Alpha One Security Book 3
Puck: Alpha One Security Book 4

The world of Stripped:
Stripped
Trashed

The world of *Wounded*:
Wounded
Captured

The Houri Legends:
Jack and Djinn
Djinn and Tonic

The Madame X Series:

Madame X

Exposed

Exiled

**The Black Room
(With Jade London):**

Door One

Door Two

Door Three

Door Four

Door Five

Door Six

Door Seven

Door Eight

Deleted Door

The One Series

The Long Way Home

Where the Heart Is

There's No Place Like Home

Badd Brothers:

Badd Motherf*cker

Badd Ass

Badd to the Bone

Good Girl Gone Badd

Badd Luck

Badd Mojo

Big Badd Wolf

Badd Boy

Badd Kitty

Badd Business

Badd Medicine

Dad Bod Contracting:

Hammered

Drilled

Nailed

Screwed

Standalone titles:

Yours

Non-Fiction titles:

You Can Do It

You Can Do It: Strength

You Can Do It: Fasting

Jack Wilder Titles:

The Missionary

JJ Wilder Titles:

Ark

To be informed of new releases, special offers, and other Jasinda news, sign up for Jasinda's email newsletter.

Made in the USA
Monee, IL
22 June 2020